C090015698

Reviews of Julian Ruck's Novels

'A fascinating read.' – *Steve Allen, LBC*

'The meteoric rise of "Britain's Greatest Boy Soprano" back in the mid 1930's rivalled that of any X Factor overnight sensation.' – *Daily Express*

'A gripping if somewhat harrowing read.' – *The Bookbag*

'Julian Ruck's style is distinctive and vigorous, in tune with the attitudes and of the time he recreates and the growing sensibilities of his central characters.' – *Caroline Clarke, Welsh Books Council*

'Love, action, suspense, and a rivetting trial. It's all here. The author's legal background makes *The Bent Brief* a truly realistic read.' – *Daily Post*

'There's an interesting symmetry in the boys' pasts that only becomes clear toward the end of the book. The undertone of innocence soon to be lost is cleverly weaved through the historical setting and the characters' maturation . . . there's enough to keep readers involved!' – *Buzz Magazine*

'Like all good books, *The Bent Brief* has brilliant observations on life and some good literary quotes. The book draws you in and shows both sides of infidelity. It has very good twists which I didn't see coming . . . Readers will be on the edge of their seats until the very end to find out the truth.' – *Frost Magazine, A Thinker's Lifestyle Magazine*

'Julian Ruck has done it again. Ripe language and explicit sex is combined with a tinge of pathos throughout the novel. Ruck is an ebullient and talented raconteur, who obviously thrives on controversy.' – *Norma Penfold*

'A very enjoyable read, once you pick it up you can't put it down. I was hooked.' – South Wales Evening Post

'A gripping read, impossible to put down. An intriguing story, sharply told.' – *Western Telegraph*

'More twists and turns than a country lane . . . a cracking read.'
– *Western Mail*

'What an emotional roller coaster of a novel! One certainly needs concentration as the highly colourful and incorrigible characters race across the page. There is never a dull moment. There is an engaging humour, together with a controversial, if not politically incorrect, dialogue. Ruck is a masterful and perceptive storyteller; he would have to be with such an abundance of characters in his narrative. This is the first of Julian Ruck's novels that I have read. I shall now be scouring the bookshelves for his name.' – *David Blatchford, Literary Critic*

'A captivating read in a beautiful setting . . . with an incredible twist in this pacey tale' – *Western Mail*

A Judge And Nothing But

Julian Ruck

DINEFWR
PUBLISHERS

Copyright © Julian Ruck, 2015

Published in 2015
in the United Kingdom by
Dinefwr Publishers
Rawlings Road, Llandybie
Carmarthenshire, SA18 3YD

The right of Julian Ruck to be identified as the author
of this work has been asserted in accordance with the
Copyright, Designs and Patents Act 1988

All rights reserved. No part of this book may be reproduced,
stored in a retrieval system, or transmitted, in any form or by any
means, electronic, mechanical, photocopying, recording or otherwise,
without the prior permission of the copyright owner.

The author would like to stress that
this is a work of fiction and no resemblance
to any actual individual or institution
is intended or implied.

A catalogue record for this book
is available from The British Library.

ISBN 978-1-904323-32-7

Cover Artwork: Jeff Kirkhouse

Printed in the UK

For my darling wife Lynney,
who will always be more
equal than my humble,
but good self!

CHAPTER 1

London

Lady Charlotte Treharne had not reached the top of her profession to be an apologist for the criminal antics of every Tom, Dick and terrorist Harry. As far as she was concerned the Human Rights Act could go and sing, albeit that some of her more liberal (and in her view misguided), legal brethren believed otherwise.

She was a maverick.

Always had been, always would be.

She was the Home Secretary's friend, a champion of the popular press and the peoples' guardian of common sense law.

She sat at the top table of legal deliverance, one of only two women who had ever been afforded such an honour: The Supreme Court.

The journey had been tough and demanding, but she had got there. Some judges who sat with her, hated the new TV world of open justice but Lady Charlotte Treharne, or Lottie as she was called by family and friends, loved it.

Performing was her style.

Age had been kind to her. Her skin had managed to delay the inevitable wear and tear of years gone by without the need for a surgeon's knife or lashings of make-up – using a shovel to cake up her face had always been avoided at all costs and as for cosmetic surgery, this was for desperate 'celebrity' delusion, fatuous tv interviewed ego trip and air-brushed fakery.

She treated all with a most wonderful contempt.

Her wild auburn curls and mature beauty also brought a learned, if not compelling and genuine glamour, to a world that had always been so out of reach for the average man in the street.

A bundle of papers sat on her desk willing her to take another look.

It was late evening and she was tired. This time they could wait. Whether or not the indefinite holding of finger-prints and DNA evidence of convicted IRA terrorists was an interference of their human rights was not going to spoil her weekend; God knows, over the years the law had spoilt far too many of them already.

She put her Mont Blanc fountain pen down on the bundles and headed for a cupboard in the corner of her office. Her petite frame moved with the grace that her position demanded and even at this hour, a hidden energy that could almost be touched.

She poured herself a large vodka and tonic and lit a cigarette. Two habits that even the Supreme Court hadn't been able to make her give up. This first sip of vodka and the sleazy grip of her tonsils by tobacco always made her feel so ridiculously rebellious. She smiled to herself as she stuck one firm middle finger in the air; extremely childish for a woman of her age and status she knew, but hell it made her feel good!

Maverick time again.

Knowledge of the law was power and by God did Charlotte Treharne know her law. She looked at the rows of All England Law Reports that stretched across her office walls. Unlike the tomes of case reporting past and present, the law never stood still. It was always changing, always adjusting.

She knew only too well, how one stroke of her pen could make or break the lives of the people she served, and she was their servant of this she had no doubt. Formidable and uncompromising, from her earliest days as a passionate law student she had resolved to serve and fight for those unable to fend for themselves. She was no easy touch and would never make excuses for indolent weakness but she did feel, she was compassionate and she always recognised that some people just couldn't help themselves.

For her, weakness had to be tested and analysed. If there was reason, good reason for it, she would bend and accommodate.

Charlotte had never forgotten who she was or where she had come from. Her mother had been a refugee from Denmark during the Second World War. Having suffered terrible violence at the hands of her own people, Lise Traharne had arrived in Wales penniless and broken, but she had fought back and eventually fallen in love with a self-made industrialist, Charlotte's father. The two had loved each other to the grave and beyond, their love never flinching, never failing.

Her beginnings had been humble and fraught with tragedy, both had taught her to use the law as a force for good, not tyranny. She held the government to account without fear or favour, she tamed corporate greed with a determined ruthlessness and she ruined criminal intent regardless of who got in the way.

Half an hour later and having enjoyed her early evening smoke and drink, Charlotte was standing in the foyer of her City of Westminster London office. It had all the usual trappings of a modern obscenity: open space with nothing but the odd deadpan plant to liven up the cringing monotony, not to mention a couple of receptionists looking bored out of their wits and waiting for that simple Facebook message that would bring some tantalising excitement to their uneventful lives.

'Hello darling.' Joel smiled as he arrived bang on time. Short-cropped grey haired and tall, he was never a minute late or a minute early. Her husband had been out of the military for some years now but he still wore a uniform of sorts. He was wearing a brown felt hat, wide brim, hand-made polished brogues and a long brown and green tweed coat. Underneath the coat, a bespoke three-piece suit cut from the finest Scottish tweeds, gripped a body that could react with the speed of a much younger man.

A quintessential country squire with hands that had killed, his dress rarely changed. The clothes like Joel himself, were practical and hard wearing.

As always Charlotte went to him and kissed his cheek. Ten years of marriage and still she wanted to kiss no holds barred.

An hour later they were driving along a country road on their way to some peace and quiet. The house they had bought five years ago was their retreat. It was a battered old Georgian property in West Sussex, still in need of some renovation but loved by them both.

There were no other vehicles on the road apart from a motorcyclist following them at a distance.

Charlotte dozed. She hated this surrender to age but couldn't help it.

Suddenly, the car's windows exploded and all she could hear was, 'Get down! Get down!'

There was a brief exchange of small arms fire and then silence.

CHAPTER 2

'Well Lady Treharne, everything seems to be fine. No problems with the X-Rays. How do you feel?'

'Doctor that is a profoundly stupid question. Someone has just tried to kill me, how do you think I feel? And it's not the first . . .' Charlotte quickly stopped herself, she had learnt a long time ago that where the medical profession was concerned the less information the better. These days you could be bundled into a nursing home just for forgetting your wedding anniversary – which she tended to do on a regular basis.

'Very well,' the doctor said without any hint of offense, 'you can go home then. Your husband is with you?' And thank God for that, he nearly added. Lady Treharne had a reputation, one that was best steered clear of.

'Yes, he's outside. Right doctor, thank you for your time and my apologies for wasting so much of it. Good day.'

With a single determined nod, Charlotte swept out of the consulting room.

Joel was waiting for her along with two other men in plain clothes. The Security Services. No matter how hard these characters tried to look plain, as far as Charlotte was concerned they stood out like a straight man in a gay bar.

'Gentleman,' Charlotte said with an edge that would have no truck with argument, 'you will no doubt have already ensured that none of this leaks out to the press. We simply cannot have assassins running around the place trying to kill Supreme Court judges. Bad for national security. Now, I can add little to what my husband must have already told you. I saw nothing and felt only my husband pushing me down into the well of the car.

11

'What have you got?'

'At the moment not much, Lady Treharne. Whoever it was, was a pro. Probably long gone but we're onto it.'

'Joel?' Charlotte's tone immediately changed as she looked at her husband, it was softer and there was a vulnerability in her eyes that only he could see. A couple of plasters covered his face where some shattered glass had managed to make their mark.

'Later Lottie. Not now. Let's get you home.'

'Yes Joel. Home.' Charlotte agreed. She was tired, so very tired.

'Lady Treharne, please,' one of the Security Services men tried to stop her in her tracks. 'You cannot go home until the proper security is in place. We cannot allow it. You are in serious danger. There may be another attempt.'

'I have all the security I need right next to me, officer. It is my desire to go home and this is precisely what I will do. By all means have your people wander around the grounds, but on no account will I allow anyone into the house, do I make myself clear? I assure you that my husband is more than capable of dealing with any threat that may presume to get that close to me.

'Now goodnight. We can talk again in the morning.'

The officer was about to say something but knew when he was beaten; he also knew that any argument was pointless. He had seen this woman in action years before at the trial of some bastard up for people trafficking. She had been a Queen's Counsel then. Jesus, the villain hadn't stood a chance, she had torn him to pieces. Apart from anything else, he knew all about her husband, Joel Samson. Decorated ex-Special Forces, a tough nut and no mistake.

'Very well, Lady Treharne. An officer will drive you both home.'

He shook his head as he watched his charges go their own way. There was nothing he could do and he knew it. He could

12

however, make bloody certain that no-one would get any-where near their front door.

It was going to be a long night.

My Lady hadn't said much, shock no doubt. But he knew she would want the who and the why in quick order and no messing about. He also knew that if he didn't come up with the goods she would skin him alive.

To make matters worse Treharne had the ear of the Home Secretary, his direct boss. It had been her phone call that had brought him to the hospital with the authority to step on any coppers who got in his way.

Christ, women. And they still reckoned there were plenty of glass ceilings to be smashed!

CHAPTER 3

'Hold me, Joel.' Charlotte said quietly. 'Just hold me. I need to feel your strength, I really do.'

They were standing in their kitchen. A place full to the brim with burly oak cupboards, battered worktops and Welsh dressers. It hadn't changed much since its glory days and this was just the way Charlotte and Joel liked it.

Joel Samson went to his wife and held her tight. He felt her shivers and knew that shock had yet to fully announce itself.

'So, what really happened, Joel? No frills please.'

'Can't this wait, Lottie? You're in shock. Let's go into the drawing room where you can have a drink and a cigarette. Not ideal but if I know you . . .' He smiled at his wife as he stroked her unruly curls and kissed her cheek.

'No soft soaping Joel. I want to know.' She looked at the not so handsome face staring at her. The odd scar, the green eyes that had ruined her all those years ago. At sixty Joel could still maker her swoon with unkempt desire. He was and always would be her weak spot, but what a lovely weak spot to have.

Joel knew she wouldn't shut up until he gave her chapter and verse.

'Ok. Have it your way, Lottie. I noticed the lone motor cyclist tailing us at a distance on the motorway. As you know that's what I'm good at, noticing things. There was just something about the driving, the speed and distance. When he followed us on to the country road to the house then I really knew something was wrong. It was a powerful bike, not the sort you see around here.

'I'm not even sure it was a "he". Could have been a woman, I just don't know, what with the leathers and helmet. When the shooting started, somehow the movements weren't right for a man. Anyway, it's a good job I'm trained in evasive and tactical driving techniques. I was prepared. Come to think of it, it's a good job too that the Home Secretary is a pal of yours, she allows me to carry my Sig around bless her.

'I can tell you one thing Lottie, the attacker was a professional no doubt about it and you were the target. I managed to unseat him after he'd let loose with some automatic fire and even hit him in the upper torso with a couple of bullets. He still managed to recover the bike and drive off.'

'You're sure I was the one he was trying to kill?' Charlotte asked. 'You have quite a background yourself.'

'Oh I'm sure, the positioning of the motorbike, the line of fire.' Joel replied with a certainty that she knew better than to argue with.

'And you shot him?' Charlotte seemed to take all this in her stride. She knew her husband's background and he had saved her life once before. 'But . . .'

'Must have been wearing a vest.'

'Who, Joel? Who?'

'Come on Lottie. You're a Supreme Court judge, now not to mention all the low life's you must have put away in your time, what about all big boys you've upset? The government, the Unions, even the Police Federation. Anyone's guess if you ask me. And what about this recent deportation stuff with that extremist . . . what's his name . . . ?

'Abdul Mani Atallah.'

'Yes that's the guy. Could have something to do with him. Let's face it, you're not flavour of the month with our Muslim brothers at the moment are you?'

Charlotte couldn't help but smile, even though she was scared out of her wits.

'Joel, I just love the way you manage to turn an assassination attempt into some kind of everyday occurrence. Come on, I need a drink, a smoke and some big hugs when we go to bed, and I mean some big hugs Joel Samson.'

Joel sighed.

With this woman, he was never off duty.

Later that night as Charlotte slept, one arm across his chest and a leg stretched over his thigh, Joel considered the events of a few hours earlier. His wife, the woman he loved with everything that he was or could ever hope to be, was in danger and not for the first time. At the moment he didn't have any answers but he would find them, if it killed him he would find them and eliminate the threat to his wife no matter what it took.

Joel Samson had been the best of all combat soldiers.

A thinker, with a mind behind the trigger.

Highly educated and intelligent, he was the most deadly of foes in war but utterly useless in times of peace. His eyes had never killed with desire but they had killed all the same. Like his wife he had never suffered fools gladly and again like his wife, he had never been a people pleaser or someone who tended to appease and blindly follow orders.

He had fought across the globe in many wars, some small some big, but he had never lost sight of his humanity. Conditional it may have been and age certainly hadn't mellowed the ruthless streak that could be called upon when required.

Joel would kill anyone without a second thought if they harmed or even tried to, Charlotte or for that matter any of the Treharne's.

CHAPTER 4

'Frankly Lottie, it's not their style. Our Islamist friends prefer a maximum body count and as much infrastructure chaos as possible. Public outrage and division is everything. It's the terrorist's creed. A lone assassin in the tranquil Sussex countryside just doesn't fit their modus operandi. Furthermore, there have been no announcements on social media or otherwise, that they are the culprits.

'I must tell you that the Security Services have been remarkably successful in preventing another 7/7 outrage. They've made it extremely difficult for terrorist cells to operate in the UK. Granted abroad is another matter, before you bring up Tunisia. This of course doesn't mean to say that they can stop any nutcase, 'clean skin' to use the latest security parlance or lone wolf, doing his or indeed her, worst. As you know, we've already had a couple of public killings by individual Islamic extremists and this is my point:

'If terrorists were behind the attack on you, why haven't they come out of the woodwork? The whole point of such an attack is to scare the public and declare the Second Coming of an Islamic Caliphate.

'Terrorist plots are becoming more complex and ambitious, Lottie. We are fighting on two fronts: the more organised and planned Al-Qaida and Islamic State spectacular variety and the unpredictable home grown local lot; the latter being far more difficult to contain and in many respects far more dangerous, for instance they don't leave any electronic or social media footprint. Attacks are planned amongst their close fanatical friends, so they stay underneath the security radar.

'Where you are concerned, my people tell me that as far as they are aware, although of course I don't have to tell you that they are certainly not infallible, there is no evidence pointing to extremists. GCHQ (Government Communications Headquarters), the Security Services, haven't picked up anything, neither have the initial forensic reports.

'So far we're up against a dead end, but we're still working on it and thank God at least the press hasn't got wind of anything, although how long this will last for is debateable, so be prepared. I've taken personal control of the situation, if this is any consolation.

'Anyway, how are you Lottie? This isn't the first time someone has tried to kill you.'

Typical Tricia Mayhew, Charlotte thought. Business first then the niceties as an afterthought. It was 6.30 am and they were sitting in the Home Secretary's oak panelled private study in Whitehall. Charlotte looked at her friend of many years. They had been in school together; Roedean, where old school ties never faded and where the right to rule never diminished.

'I don't agree with you, Tricia.' Charlotte said firmly.

'Well, nothing new there then.' Mayhew replied with a sigh.

'And as my for my general well-being, I'm fine thank you. Now, you know full well that my stance on the Abdul Mani Atallah case has incited more hatred than usual amongst the extreme Islamist minority in this country. God knows the right wing press have been making hay out of it. He *will* be deported, be in no doubt about that. He's a dangerous bastard, a mass murderer and I'm damned if I will kow-tow to the European Court of Human Rights or for that matter the appeasing left wing liberal idiocy of my learned colleagues.

'Trust me. I'll keep being an extremely sharp thorn in their self-righteous backsides until I get my way.'

'Oh I don't doubt that, Lottie. At least for once we have a senior judge on our side. That's off the record of course, can't have Executive interference in the sacred independence of the judiciary now, can we?' Mayhew smiled. Her friend could be a determined, recalcitrant bitch when she wanted to be. No wonder they had been close friends for so long!

'My point is this.' Charlotte continued. Here we go Mayhew thought. 'How do you know this character hasn't changed tactics? He's smart. The one thing that would put the Security Services off his scent is to do something totally out of character. He might be under house arrest but how do you know that the attack on me wasn't planned a couple of years ago, when he had the resources to execute such an outrage? You're assessments lack imagination Tricia, they also lack insight and a perception of the criminal mind, and Atallah is a criminal, nothing more nothing less.

'One man's terrorist being another man's freedom fighter is for the birds and academics. And while I'm at it, your own government has hardly endeared itself to the extreme elements of Islam, has it?'

'What do mean, Lottie?'

'Come on now, Tricia. Illegal rendition, getting into bed with your friends across the pond and not to mention all the Middle East blunders?'

'I don't know what you are talking about. Rendition? Perish the thought, Lottie.'

'Yes you do. All I can say is that you're fortunate your illegal rendering antics haven't come up before me.'

'Ummm . . . well . . . er they haven't, because the government has done nothing 'illegal' as you put it, overtly or covertly, so let's leave it at that.'

Lottie smiled at her friend as if to say,"You can fool some of the people some of the time . . ."

'Anyway where Atallah is concerned,' Mayhew continued, 'I agree you have a point and I will duly take it on board.

Even so, as you of all people well know, we can only act on the evidence before us and right now there is precious little of it. Fact.'

The same age as Charlotte, late fifties, Mayhew's physical features might have excluded her from a two page spread in *"Hello"* magazine, but what she lacked in good looks she made up for in determination and the will to succeed. As one of the most powerful people in the Government, she rarely took prisoners – literally. It was rumoured in the corridors of power that Mayhew could well be the next Prime Minister, albeit that she had never endeared herself to her parliamentary colleagues. She was a brave woman and always prepared to speak out.

Marks and Sparks had always been her outfitters of choice, and it showed. She wore little if any make-up, but even so when she walked into a room people knew about it. Patricia Mayhew enjoyed a natural charisma and genuine sincerity that few in Westminster were able to mimic.

Most importantly of all, the people trusted her.

'Well Tricia, I'll take your word for it.' Charlotte replied. 'If not Atallah, who then? Do you have anything at all?'

'Look Lottie, its early days. The attempt on your life only happened last night. I promise you we are doing everything we can to find out who this bastard is and who is behind him.'

'Joel thinks it may have been a woman.'

'Yes, I've read his statement. Quite possible but let's not jump to conclusions. I have my best people on it and this is all I can do for now. Lottie, I'm not going to give you the usual political garbage of "we will do everything in our power to bring these people to justice." I won't insult your intelligence.

'We don't have much to go on and whoever attacked you knew what they were doing. No motorbike has been found, not even a burnt up lump of metal. It's probably hidden away somewhere in some London lock-up. Impossible to find.'

Charlotte fixed Tricia with one of her uncompromising expressions as she said, 'Tricia, I'm not impressed. Like it or not I'm a Supreme Court judge and you know as well as I do, that if this gets out it's not going to do your career any good. You have huge resources at your disposal and I want some answers, without delay.

'I've survived one assassination attempt already, admittedly by a vengeful criminal, but this time it's different. That was ten years ago, the world has changed. Terrorism has changed. Islamist extremism makes the IRA bombing campaigns look like a day out at the park.

'How do I know if another attack isn't imminent? What about my son? Dear God if anything should happen to him. How safe is he? Is he in any danger? None of this is good enough Tricia, none of it!'

Patricia Mayhew understood her friend's anger. She had children too. Now was not the time to exchange harsh words though. She had to keep calm. Being a Home Secretary required toughness and resilience but it also demanded empathy and lots of it, even if such "empathy" was for public consumption only.

'Lottie, I do understand how you feel. I would want heads rolling too if I was in your position. Look, we've been friends for many years. On this you are just going to have to trust me. I've never let you down in the past and I won't do so now. Jolyan is already being watched, not that he is aware of it. I really am doing all I can Lottie, believe me.'

Charlotte hadn't realised that Jolyan was already being protected. Her anger began to subside.

'My gut feeling though Lottie, in spite of what you say, is that this is someone from your past. Maybe someone you've put away, maybe an organisation with an axe to grind because let's face it, you've upset an awful lot of people during your illustrious legal career. Powerful people from dare I say it, my own government, to your recent judgement against that

Holier Than Thou Lot at the Police Federation. Admittedly, the police have had it coming for a long time, shifty lot of bastards who spend most of their time sitting in swanky cars at roundabouts all night long scoffing jam donuts. Not to mention spending hours getting utterly confused by the *Sun* newspaper crossword. More to the point, no-one knows even now what they get up to with all the millions they have sitting in their Federation coffers, but . . .'

'Not quite your intellectual elite, I grant you.' Charlotte interrupted.

'Indeed they are not, Lottie,' the Home Secretary agreed, at least she and her friend could find some middle ground now and again, 'but like I say, this attempt on your life just doesn't have the right hall marks of a terrorist plot, an extremist free agent is possible but like I say, it just doesn't fit and my own people who really are the best, are of the same view.

'Now, your own personal security Lottie. Before you start objecting, I really must insist that one of my people sticks to you like glue, no arguments. For the time being anyway and until we know more. I appreciate that Joel is as good as it gets, but like it or not he's sixty. He may well keep himself fit but he's no Spring chicken, his reaction time is bound to be slower than a younger man's. This being the case, I have assigned one of my own, selected by me personally, to watch out for you. Some, shall we say 'value added' to your normal security arrangements. You'll meet him in a minute and don't be bloody rude to him Lottie, you know what you're like!'

Charlotte looked at her fingernails as a distraction from her boiling frustration. She knew that her friend was right but she didn't have to like it.

'Very well, Tricia.' Charlotte said without even a hint of grace. 'But note that I agree under protest.'

Mayhew smiled. 'I wouldn't have expected anything less from you, Lottie. Now, allow me to introduce your new baby sitter, oh and Joel can still be the senior partner as it were. Experience does count even in this age of teeny tyranny.'

The Home Secretary picked up a phone and said a few words.' Before you ask Lottie, here's his file. Official Secrets of course.'

'Of course,' Charlotte replied, she knew the form.

A few minutes later there was a knock at the door.

'Come!' Mayhew ordered.

A man of average height walked into the room, in fact he probably didn't even make "average". There was something of the Latin about him; olive skinned, black hair and extremely good looking.

Charlotte didn't look up from the file she was reading. Marc Rey was thirty two, of South American parentage. Coldstream Guards, SAS then special duties with the Home Office. Charlotte knew what "Special duties" meant: anything a bit messy and needed to be kept quiet.

'Home Secretary.' Rey nodded as he stood in front of her desk. 'Is this the subject?'

And Tricia had told Charlotte not to be rude!

'Young man, let me be clear." Charlotte seethed. "I am not your "subject" and how dare you address me as such. Until I *tell* you otherwise, I am Lady Treharne, do you understand?'

'Just about . . . Lady Treharne.' Rey replied absently.

Mayhew smiled behind her hand. She had chosen well, there two were going to get along like a house on fire!

Charlotte immediately took control of the situation. 'Young man, my husband is in the corridor, Joel Samson . . .'

'I noticed . . . um Lady Treharne,' Rey interrupted.

Dear God this man was beyond the pale! 'Do not interrupt when I am speaking er . . . Captain Rey. Now, my husband will lead and you will follow. You will exercise discretion at all times and this includes shadowing me. Yours is to do, not to question. Clear?'

Charlotte couldn't miss the slight smile that appeared across Rey's lips. The impertinence of the man!

'Now go and talk with my husband. He will tell you your duties.'

'Will do, Lady Treharne. Oh and a pleasure meeting you, your reputation precedes you.'

This time there was a charming sincerity in the man's words, they were almost irresistible. He was also extraordinarily handsome. This one had never experienced any problems attracting the opposite sex, Charlotte quickly concluded.

Mark Rey disappeared as quickly as he had arrived.

'Well Lottie, that went well.' Mayhew remarked with an edge of humour in her voice.

'Good God Tricia, sometimes these military types get above themselves and don't I just know it. I'm married to one!'

'Quite so, Lottie. Now I must get on. Keep in touch. You are in safe hands and so is Jolyan. If anything interesting crops up you will be the first to know.'

Charlotte stood up. There was a momentary pause as she looked at her old friend. For a few seconds they were school girls again.

'Thank you, Tricia. I know you're doing your best.'

The Home Secretary of Her Majesty's Government stood up and came around to Charlotte's side of the desk. She put her arms around her friend and said quietly, 'both of us have always had to be strong, Lottie. And we'll continue to be strong, at least until all those the sods out there wheel us away in a wooden box.

'Now away with you, I'm busy.'

Just as Charlotte turned to leave, the Home Secretary added, 'Oh and young Jolyan has been up to some high jinks again, I'm told. Drunk but not disorderly apparently, which is something I suppose. Trying to scale Nelson's Column in a state of inebriation is never a good idea . . . as we both well know! Do you want me to do anything?'

Charlotte thought for a moment. Nothing surprised her where her son was concerned. 'Certainly not, Tricia. The law must take its course. Let the little shit suffer, a good old fashioned dose of humiliation won't do him any harm.'

It was late. The ferocity of twenty four hour news meant that Whitehall rarely slept, but it did at least doze now and again.

It was time to go home, Patricia Mayhew thought as she scribbled one last note on a file. The prospect didn't inspire enthusiasm. There would be no husband to greet her or children to annoy and irritate. Her children were grown up and making their own mistakes and her husband led his own life and fucked his own women – with considerable discretion it should be added, this was part of the deal.

Her marriage, like so many other things in her life, had become an irrational necessity. A matrimonial hand was required from time to time, even a hasty kiss but only for the cameras and Breakfast Time television irrelevance.

Fifteen minutes later she was sitting in the back of a grey government issue Jaguar. She gave her driver one line of an address as she sat back in the luxurious leather and tried to enjoy some genuine reflection for a few moments. Her days were so full of noise, crises and dramas that she rarely had time to actually think.

It was the story of her life.

Ten minutes later the car pulled up outside a three storey house.

'Wait here, I'll be about an hour.' She told her driver, as she got out of the car and made her way to the basement flat of the house. The driver and back-up protection team knew the form. It was 10pm on a Thursday night. Always the same time, always the same place, at least when the Home Secretary wasn't out of the country on government business.

A few moments later, a tall muscular man opened the door to the flat. He smiled as he said, 'Hello, Home Secretary. For such a busy lady you are always so punctual!' His voice was smooth. Educated. He smiled again. 'Please come in. The usual? Oh and I've got a new device which I think you'll enjoy.'

The Home Secretary said nothing as she followed the man inside like a naughty schoolgirl being summoned to the Headmistress's study.

Irrational necessity time again.

CHAPTER 5

The expresso was strong, not that it made much difference to the person drinking it. She didn't need caffeine to keep her awake or for that matter give her a daytime buzz of energy. Reliance on anything was not her way. The back streets of the Gaza Strip had taught her that dependency on anything meant weakness, and this included food and drink.

She kept both to a minimum.

London had become a state within a state. A leviathan of unforgiving attitude and unkind self. The expresso drinker detested its bogus chaos and counterfeit multiculturalism. The latter had failed miserably, ruined by tribal segregation and the delusions of a most perfect society intent on the pitiful rejection of human nature.

The coffee drinker could have been anywhere between thirty five and forty five. It was impossible to tell. Her face was expressionless as she observed the unsavoury, self-contained worlds of the people passing by. For a moment she remembered other times, times when she had been part of the London intellectual elite. It had only been a hiatus, a brief fling, but that had been enough. The towering ignorance, belied by a university education that had nothing to do with life had sickened her. The bookish fantasy of how the real world worked had forced her down a path of self-determination which could bite back.

Then it happened.

Her family wiped out by some artificially intelligent bomb. She remembered the destruction of her home, the rubble coated with blood and body parts turned into unrecognisable lumps of demolished flesh. The white sheets filled with pieces of human beings put together quickly and buried, in order to bring some kind of ending to a horror that no-one understood.

There had been no looking back.

Trained in the deserts of the Middle East, she had become an expert in the art of death. She had given up asking herself why. She had given up any kind of allegiance to ideology or people. She had given up her own identity.

She had given up emotion.

She took another sip of her coffee. Her face was unremarkable in its lack of attention to detail. It was beyond plain, in that her features were easily forgotten, if even noticed in the first place. Her natural, unassuming brown hair had been cut short, but not so short that it attracted attention. She resisted anything of the feminine, or masculine for that matter. Her clothes were bi-sexual. Black baggy trousers, black waist length jacket.

Her whole life depended on invisibility and an adept talent for changing her appearance in seconds. Not that life meant much to her. Knowing that her own existence could be terminated at a moment's notice made little difference to her. Her life meant no more to her than the bundle of false passports lying in a drawer in another part of the world.

Fearless she may have been, but any inclination toward recklessness had been drilled out of her years ago. She lived to kill, her humanity bombed out of her the day her family had been wiped out. Her lack of passion for anything, be it religion, love, money or even something in between made her the perfect killing machine.

Revenge and motive were deadly incentives, both got you killed. She didn't care much about whose body passed through the cross hairs of her telescopic sights, as long as they were Westerners or Israeli.

She travelled the world, never remaining in one place long enough to become tied to it. Sometimes a piece of news would motivate her to call a cell number. She would text her availability and the rest was history.

Anonymity was always the name of the game. She never knew who her paymasters were, likewise they knew nothing about her, apart from her reputation that is.

For a moment, she considered her failure to kill the judge. It had been an aberration, a single second of doubt. She had pulled the trigger but something outside herself had forced her to alter her aim. She still couldn't explain why this had happened. Such a thing had never happened before. For the first time in her killing career, a seed of uncertainty had exploited her intention.

The driver of the car had been good, but even so it had been her sudden change of resolve that had saved the judge. Why? She was still pondering this question when her thoughts were interrupted.

'Do you mind if I take this seat?' A voice asked politely, 'there are no other seats free, I'm afraid.'

She looked up for a moment, her eyes saying nothing.

'Help yourself,' she replied in perfect English, her face revealing nothing.

The young man sat down. In an instant she concluded coldly, that he was well dressed, groomed and no doubt a member of the new, smart set London glitterati who believed they owned the world and knew it all. The media and British politics were full of them. Only just out of the playground and yet coated with an unpolished arrogance and slapstick savoir-faire, she loathed them and everything about them. Their pampered lives, their lack of brutal maturity.

An hour later she and the young man were lying naked in his bed. She masturbated herself and the young penis next to her to climax, then got dressed and left the flat without saying a word.

Like food and drink, sex was kept to a minimum.

CHAPTER 6

Jolyan Treharne opened his eyes slowly.

His arse ached, his stomach churned and his head felt as if it was about to explode.

He glanced around his surroundings. White walls and a metal door with a peep hole in it.

Where the hell was he?

His brain finally managed to compute: A cell for God's sake, it had to be. Next thought: His mother was going to go ape shit . . . again!

Jolyan sat up, his back ached too, hardly surprising, a thin length of bugger all had been his bed for the night.

Bit by bit things started to come back to him. A party in Knightsbridge, Nelson's Column, a girl with big tits and a bum to die for, a spliff or two and that was it. The rest? Well, here he was.

Before he was able to work out how exactly he had ended up in a police cell, the door opened, a policeman dumped some greasy eggs in front of him and said somewhat kindly which rather surprised Jolyan, 'eat up lad and then you can go home. You'll be in front of the Magistrates in a couple of weeks' time for being drunk. No aggravating circumstances as they say, so you'll probably get a small fine and a slap on the wrists. Don't reckon your mum is going to be too happy though. Good job you're not up before her!'

With that the policeman laughed and walked out, leaving the cell door open.

Slightly bemused Jolyan looked at the eggs, was nearly sick and decided for once to do as he was told.

Get out fast!

An hour later he was sitting in his mother's apartment in Chelsea. He'd lost his mobile phone the night before, which was a good excuse for not telephoning his mother and giving her the good news. He didn't know the Sussex house telephone number or where to find it, apart from anything else land lines just didn't bleep on his technological radar.

His mother would have to know, there was no getting away from it. Some thoughtful sod had no doubt already informed her of his drunken antics anyway, albeit that he wasn't too sure himself what the hell he had got up to. He doubted it was the girl with the big tits, in his state he wouldn't have been capable of getting a rise out of a can of Coke let alone anything else.

Come to think of it no wonder the police had nobbled him, the pair of them must have looked like a right couple of jellies wobbling around the West End!

Oh well, no-one could accuse him of not following in the Treharne tradition. His family was full, past and present, of boozed up womanising buggers and his mother was no angel either, according to her close relatives anyway.

He hadn't asked to have the Treharne blood in him, had he? Or the good looks and natural charm that always seemed to go with it. Thank God though, the reddish hair of boyhood had calmed down to a sort of auburnish, gold sovereign colour and the freckles had disappeared.

Imagine a life with that lot?! It didn't bear thinking about.

He'd face the music just as he always did, he wouldn't bother trying on the Treharne charm with his mum, waste of time. She'd just give him one of those stern looks of hers which could turn most people into quivering wrecks but where he was concerned bounced straight off him. He knew his mother, hard on the surface, soft as lights underneath. All the same, her temper wasn't to be trifled with and he knew there were limits.

After all, he hadn't hurt anyone had he? Just some pre-student exuberance getting on the wrong side of the law that's all.

He would just have to exploit the fact that in true Treharne tradition, he would be taking off to Oxford University to study Greats soon enough, after he had done a bit of travelling that is.

For a moment Jolyan thought about Oxford. Greek philosophy, politics and economics. A heady mix but one that should at least keep him out of mischief for a while.

On the other hand . . .

CHAPTER 7

Manhattan, New York

Dan Seloski looked out at the Manhattan skyline. It was always there, the power and the glory. Terrorists had tried to reshape it, but had got nowhere where the spirit of the place was concerned. He stood in his penthouse suite, daring the world below to get him out of it. Daring any sucker from the financial watchdogs to catch him out.

Seloski didn't give a flying fuck for income inequality. He had some vague idea that Manhattan enjoyed the biggest gap between those who have and those who haven't in America, but this was a far as it went. Life was a bitch and that's all there was to it. Survival of the fittest was his creed, not that he knew a damn thing about Darwin or much else for that matter, apart from making money that is.

He swallowed a mouthful of Scotch and took a deep pull on a Havana cigar. The skyline never failed to fascinate him. He could stare at it for a hundred years and never get tired of it. It was him. The terrible excitement, the ruthless intent and mockery of the moral bullshit that plagued the liberal bastards whose lives would always be doomed to mediocrity and failure.

Failure was a word for fools and Dan Seloski was no fool.

He had a made a fortune from nothing. He had lost the odd fortune too, but had started again, rebuilt and survived. He was always building, it never stopped. A billionaire but still he had to make money. It was all he cared about. He had tried loving something else, but money had always gotten in the way.

Money was his wife, mistress, whore and pretty gay boy.

Nothing else mattered.

He felt some hands untie his bath robe and move to his cock. He didn't move. The gentle massaging had the desired effect. At fifty years of age and in spite of all the booze and tobacco, Dan could still respond quickly and without any real effort to the right physical stimulus.

'I want you, Danny. Come back to bed.' The voice was masculine but with a woman's touch. Just like the fingers.

Seloski turned around and looked at the face staring at him. Seventeen years of pure sex, the boy knew how to please. The affair had lasted longer than usual, four weeks in fact, but the sex had been the best for a long time and hard to let go of, for now anyway.

Seloski over-indulged in most things and not just money. Sex, alcohol, tobacco, food and drink, it made no difference. He was overweight and just plain ugly, but looks didn't matter much to him either. When you had his kind of money, everyone and everything could be bought. Nothing was priceless and this included people.

He touched the boy's chin.

'You want more, do you?' Seloski asked.

'Oh yes,' the smooth face smiled, 'as much as you can take.' Money again.

The boy led his new client back to the bedroom. Man and boy were more alike than they realised.

They would both do anything for money.

The following morning it was business as usual.

'I don't care what you have to do. I want Treharne Holdings plc.' Seloski said in his usual harsh way.

'Look Dan, we've already bought some stock but we have to do things slowly, if we go in like a bunch of trigger happy Marines we'll spook the major shareholders. Our research tells us they are a tight family. They stick together. Any hint of a hostile takeover and they'll close ranks and we'll be fucked. We're dealing with some serious players here. One of them is a Supreme Court judge for Christ's sake, and the Chief Exec is a sharp cookie. He'll smell a rat at a hundred paces if we aren't careful.

'We must tread with caution this time, trust me Dan.'

'Caution sucks. It's never done anything for me.' Seloski sneered, as he looked at his second in command. Direct action had always been his way, although right now some things were best kept to himself.

They were sitting in an office that could easily have provided luxury accommodation for a good few of New York's homeless.

Fred Goodwinson looked at his boss. Jesus, his face really was enough to put you off breakfast. The piggy eyes that seemed unable to work out which way to focus, the jowls of fat that hung over his shirt collar like lumps of oiled up pasta and a nose that had just given up and retreated back into his skull for safety. It was no wonder his wife wouldn't go anywhere near Dan, he scared the shit out of her.

Goodwinson on the other hand was the opposite of his boss, albeit that they were roughly the same age: tailored, good-looking, handsome and oozing unnatural charm. He was also a ruthless son of a bitch who would sell his own children if he thought they could make him a quick profit.

The two men made quite a team. Beauty and the Beast they may have been, but their names were treated with respect on Wall Street, if not out and out fear.

'Carry on then, Fred.' Seloski finally agreed. 'But like I say, I want that company and as you know, I always get what I want. Their chain of hotels will fill a gap in our investment portfolio. I've been saying for a while that we need to put more money into leisure and tourism. Right now the market is down, so now is the time to buy.'

'Leave it with me, Dan. I'll see to it but it might take time.'

'Time is a robbing bitch, Fred. So don't hang around. Right? Goddamn Brits, they still think they're running an empire and yet when we say jump, they have to ask how high. Special relationship?! Obama got it right for once when he gave their Prime Minister twenty five DVD's of classic America films as a gift and removed the bust of that fat fuck Churchill out of the Oval Office. Brits, bunch of assholes!'

'Right,' Fred responded as he turned to leave, 'I'll see to it.' He didn't feel quite as anti-British as his boss, after all many Americans had Brit blood in them somewhere or other but saying anything would be a waste of time.

CHAPTER 8

Gower Peninsula, South Wales

Pills! Most of his generation would be six foot under, or cooked in the basement of some overcrowded crematorium if it wasn't for pills. And of course, the best bit about keeping everyone alive for as long as possible, was that the planet was suffering an over population crisis. Bloody crazy. But then as far as Paul Treharne was concerned the whole world was crazy and that's all there was to it.

Not being renowned for exploring the more subtle philosophical paradigms of life, Paul Treharne swallowed the pills. All sixteen of them. It was sixteen every day, day in day out and if he didn't take them then according to his doc, he was toast.

On the wrong side of sixty, he looked more like his father every day: bald, short, and tending to roll about the place. Too many fags, too many bottles of whisky and too many custard slices had nearly done for him a couple of times, but he was still here and always ready and willing to annoy the hell out of the rest of the Treharne clan – especially his aunty Lottie. Aunty? Well now that was a bit of a complicated one, like just about everything else where the Treharne's were concerned. Second marriages, bastard children (he had been one of them) and general unrestrained lust had resulted in a family closely related but nevertheless confusing.

Lottie's father, William Treharne and founder of everything that Paul had worked for all his life, was his grandfather. Lottie was his aunty albeit that they were not far off in age, in fact she was younger by about ten years.

Paul still couldn't work out why all these twats on the Idiot's Lantern (television) were always so hell bent on discovering how they had come from a line of brigands, thieves and criminals, but no accounting for taste or as far he was concerned, pathetic ego trip.

It was late. It had been a hard, trying day.

For all his faults, Paul Treharne was a grafter. He ran Treharne Holdings plc with a rod of iron discipline and uncompromising attention to profit.

Lottie's mother, the self-willed and gloriously stubborn Lise Treharne, had built the first internationally renowned hotel *Ragged Cliffs*, back in the 1960's.

Paul had developed the business into a £billion global chain of luxury hotels stretching from Dubai to New York, almost singlehandedly.

He was a down to earth man and always spoke as he found. Always. He had learnt his trade at the sharp end, from cleaning toilets right up to Chief Executive Officer and no public school in between. Paul had earned his right to rule and so, he grudgingly had to admit, had his aunty, they had just taken different roads to achieve it. Thus the mutual respect and affection they had always held for each other, in spite of the locking of horns from time to time.

They were both Treharne's to their core. Both wilful and highly intelligent. Both thrived on conflict and confrontation.

In spite of the international nature of the business, the Ragged Cliffs Hotel was home for Paul. The place where it had all began. He had never felt inclined to live anywhere else. There was just something about the place. The ghosts of his predecessors still seemed to wink at him from time to time or bring him down a peg or two if he started getting above himself.

It was 8pm in the evening.

Autumn was just around the corner but it was still quite warm. Paul rummaged around in one of his desk drawers and eventually found what he was looking for. A packet of cigarettes. To hell with the doctors and all those other bleeding heart, social justice fanatics who kept telling him how he should eat, drink and sleep.

The Guardian newspaper and the Islington smart set could go to hell in a handcart and bugger the planet too. He lived in the real world, with real people. Sod the lot of 'em.

A few minutes later he was sitting in his grandfather's rose garden, enjoying a death defying smoke. It was always quiet at this time, guests were either busy having dinner or getting dressed for it – jeans and trainers were banned from the hotel's dining room. The vulgarity of a sartorial free for all was forbidden in all Treharne hotel dining rooms. Standards were everything.

William Treharne had bought the old house in the 1950's as a home for his new wife, Lise Traharne. It was William who had created the rose garden but Lise who had turned the house into a hotel after his death. Paul looked across at the acres of landscaped sloping lawns and formal gardens. His grandfather had created a combination of the old Dutch and mid-Victorian fashion of carpet bedding. Nothing had changed. In spring, the gardens exploded into a fanfare of colour and delight. Each year the gardeners made sure the spectacle changed. Each year to Paul's eyes, they became more beautiful.

His grandfather had made sure that the fewer manufactured articles in the gardens the better. The only man-made objects in sight were a sundial and a stone seat, and not forgetting a tennis court and croquet lawn.

The interior of the hotel hadn't changed much either. It remained a hotchpot of art Deco, Victorian and Regency and yet the polished oak floors, soft lights and secret nooks and crannies still maintained the original Edwardian grandeur of the place.

Ragged Cliffs was a luxurious hotel and one that guests rarely forgot in a hurry. It was its contempt for the new and shiny that made it so different and in a class all of its own.

The Treharne's had known tragedy, they had also known joy and success. Ragged Cliffs had seen it all. The imposing house sat on the Gower Peninsula in South Wales, enclosed by the Atlantic Ocean and Bristol Channel, it overlooked seas that whispered memories and grasped the mind with a compulsion that could never quite be touched or explained.

Paul always came to the rose garden to think. As petals began to dry up and say goodbye, his mind as always, was forced to reflect. It was a place where nothing could ever be undone or changed. The only masters here were the skies above, and the seasons that kept on delivering. He looked out across the sea and wondered what was next. Life was so short, so impossible and yet he had grabbed it by the throat and tried to do the best he could.

There was something going on, a threat. He couldn't be sure yet, but he was troubled. His business acumen was beyond reproach, he usually noticed things that would pass other people by. There had been some unusual movement on the Stock Market with the shares in Treharne Holdings earlier in the day. Not much and it was probably nothing, but Paul noticed and for him this was enough.

He managed all the family's business interests, at least he sat on top of the pile and no major decisions were made without his say so. Touching seventy, he still had all his marbles and he wasn't about to give them up for anyone

The Treharne's together, were majority shareholders in their publicly quoted company, but only just. Together they held 51% of the shares, the rest were owned by private investors, financial institutions and pension funds.

Paul rarely saw his offspring. That was children for you. You give them all the love and care in the world, they bleed you dry and then they bugger off without as much as a by your leave.

He still had his wife Bethan though. She talked him into a coma, blasted him with female trivia but he loved her all the same. Fat as butter and still addicted to Walkers Crisps, he wouldn't be without her. She was the mother of his brood, and had always been there right behind him when the weather roughed up.

He finished the cigarette and threw the butt into a large, sand filled flower pot put there for this very reason. As he did so, he noticed there were about ten other butts ready and willing to meet his own. Well this wasn't on, he'd get on to the maintenance team in the morning. What the hell were they playing at? He enjoyed a cigarette himself but he wasn't about to condone the off-putting debris they left behind.

Bad for guests, bad for business.

He sat still for a few minutes more. There were other matters he needed to think about while he had some peace and quiet.

Only that morning a letter from the Welsh Language Commissioner (the uncompromising enforcer of the language) had arrived, telling him that his company's promotion material etc should be bilingual.

He had met this "Commissioner" one Meri Siencyn (take that for Mary Jenkins, many Welsh speakers changed their English birth certificate names into Welsh ones), at some dinner or other a while back. The bloody woman enjoyed the charisma of a used up toilet roll with the looks to match. No class, no style, no breeding and she quite obviously used a spatula to put on her makeup.

Anyway, this hatchet faced slapper was trying to tell him how to run his business, even a Supreme Court judge knew better than that!

Not a good idea.

Bending his knee was not one of Paul's strong points, so a letter had gone back telling the Commissioner that Treharne Holdings plc, as a company registered in London and not publicly funded or providing a public service, was outside the tyranny of Welsh language legislation, so would she kindly go and persecute someone else.

He hadn't heard anything since.

A few minutes later, he was sitting in his favourite reclining armchair, staring at an array of colourful United Nations flags draped across a clothes horse.

Beth's knickers.

Jesus he thought, his wife's arse would keep expanding even when she was six foot under. A threatening piece of kit by anyone's standards.

As always he wondered why on earth she kept on doing their laundry. She also insisted on cleaning the apartment herself and doing all the cooking.

They were rich and there was an army of cooks and cleaners a stone's throw away, but Beth wouldn't have any of it. The apartment was her turf, she liked doing things her way and apart from anything else, it was her job to make sure her husband was looked after properly. Not quite the modern way Paul had to admit but what the hell, who was he to complain?

Beth was old school and she sure as hell wasn't going to change, neither was her fat arse come to think of it. He remembered an occasion years ago when his darling Beth had tried to top herself. Hanging herself from the branch of an oak tree had apparently been the idea. Anyway, she jumped off the ladder with a rope around her neck but instead of a merciful end, the bloody branch had snapped due to her lard filled girth being too much for it.

There had also been the somewhat inconvenient fact that even if the branch hadn't snapped her feet were still too near the ground to have done any damage. A cry for help? Not quite, just Beth's way of saying to Paul, you're not taking enough notice of me so get a grip.

Bit dramatic admittedly, but he had got the point.

'Lamb chops and mint sauce alright, dear?' Beth's Welsh accent echoed from the kitchen, a science fiction affair where all one really needed to do was look at things and they would just get on with it. Not that this modern way had any effect on Beth, she still refused to use a dish washer or God forbid a microwave. Home cooking from scratch was her way, and she wasn't going to give in to anyone, and this included Paul.

Ready meals? Disgusting!

'Fine Beth.' Paul answered, knowing full well that he really wouldn't have had it any other way. His wife was a damned good cook, traditional maybe but all the best ingredients went into her grub, which was probably why he was still alive and able to eat it. A triple heart bypass had changed his life style but he knew one thing, his cholesterol levels had always been bang on and his condition had had nothing to do with Beth's food.

Fags, whisky and stress had been the sods that had put him in hospital, not Beth's grub.

Five minutes later they were eating their supper. Even now and in spite of all the lard, which in truth wasn't really that much, Beth was more a chubby than a fatty, he just enjoyed winding her up. He could still look at his wife and love. He still saw that prettiness and warmth in the smile that had nobbled him all those years ago.

'Abigail was on the phone earlier . . .' Here we go, Paul thought. Abigail was one of their offspring. Beth spent half her life talking on the phone to their children. Phonework, Paul called it.

'Oh yes. How is she?'

'Boyfriend trouble again, I'm afraid Paul.'

'Oh well, nothing new there then. The girl certainly picks them, I'll give her that. What have we had lately? One who can't make up his mind whether he likes girls or boys, one alki being brainwashed by AA, one sending photos of his pulsating knob, and according to Abi the last time we spoke, one chap who can't make up his mind whether he wants to have a 'virtual' fling or an actual meet where they can talk face to face. It's all bloody ridiculous if you ask me, all this internet dating crap. It's just a platform for inadequate imbeciles who wouldn't know what to do with love if it was shoved right up their arses. On second thoughts, I take that back. According to Abi, most young men these days are fudge packers. It's the 'in thing' she tells me. 'In' being the operative word. It's all very fashionable according to her and she should know, most of her bloody friends are gay!'

Beth was used to her husband's foul mouth, his crude observations on life had started to bounce off her years ago. It was just his way.

Paul dug his knife into a lamb chop. Young 'uns and the new modern day internet world got right on his tits. People were forgetting their humanity. Thank God he had been born in another time, a time when people didn't want so much, were more content with what they had and were just happy to get along with each other without being perfect human beings. He had known what it was like to go without. In his early days he had been skint too, seriously skint, and it hadn't done him any harm. Quite the opposite in fact. He knew how to value thrift and hard work.

'I wish she would find someone nice though Paul, I really do,' Beth moaned. 'You know, someone who will be kind to her, look after her. I do worry.'

'Well, I wouldn't hold your breath dearest. No doubt she'll eventually find someone, have a brood of viruses, get divorced and end up dumping all the little bastards on us. It's the way of this new world we live in, I'm afraid.'

'Maybe.' Beth said quietly. 'Now then, what has your day been like, dear?'

Here we go again, Paul thought. Evening ritual time: Who did you talk to? How are they? How are the children? What did so and so have to say? It was all total bollocks of course, men just didn't operate along such idiot lines. As usual he shut down his brain, tolerated and grunted the odd word here and there. Female trivia drove him nuts. Women just didn't get it. Men lived in a different world. They weren't the least bit interested in what their friends got up to with their families, neither were they interested in shops, shopping, hairdressers and fucking shoes – at least men of his vintage anyway, the new lot coming up through the ranks seemed more interested in removing hair from their arseholes, moisturisers and hair gels. Being a man just didn't come into it and as for his politically correct children Jesus, he would go out of his way to be as sexist, racist, homophobic, chauvinistic, shortist and as discriminatory as possible, just to annoy the hell out them. None of it seemed to stop them loving him though, so maybe he was doing something right after all.

Paul had learnt a long time ago that female bullshit and domestic tittle-tattle were to be avoided at all costs. Just look interested and don't listen to a bloody word. Bethan could talk for Wales, she was always on air and he had given up years ago trying to fight it.

CHAPTER 9

Porto, Portugal

Porto is Portugal's second largest metropolis. It has kept its grip on history and to a certain extent, it has also managed to avoid the concrete heresy that the grand European project has inflicted on so many of Europe's great cities.

Unlike Lisbon, the politics of concrete together with its clarion calls for bankruptcy and the exodus of youthful ambition, Porto has at least kept something of itself in its architecture and thriving side streets.

It was in one of these bustling side street bars a few months after the assassination attempt on his mother that Jolyan found himself serving coffee, beer and cakes. He still didn't quite know how he had ended up in Porto but maybe it just had something to do with the fact that grass huts on idyllic sun-drenched beaches didn't quite do it for him. Apart from anything else, getting pissed and doped up all day long just wasn't his style.

He needed to be doing something. He was always trying to learn, to gain more knowledge. It was a thirst, an appetite, for the unknown that he couldn't resist.

Jolyan knew that money was never going to be a long term problem for him. He would inherit more than he could ever spend, but his mother and Joel had always kept a tight rein on the Trust that had seen him through his education and would continue to do so until he graduated.

He had never been spoilt or overindulged. He had noticed the way some of his school friends were turning out. Right shits some of them. Their sense of ownership would some-

46

times irritate Jolyan; they took happiness and inherited wealth for granted, a weakness that in his view, would one day be their downfall and which was probably why he had decided to travel alone. He enjoyed his own company and yet he would never have described himself as a loner. He just managed well enough being on his own, providing he always had his Kindle with him that is.

A life without reading was inconceivable.

His mother and step father had made certain that his feet were firmly imbedded in terra firma, anything else just wasn't up for negotiation. They had taught him to be self-sufficient and to stand on his own two feet.

If he got into trouble, tough. Get on with it and don't come bleating to us, thus his mother's refusal to have anything to do with his drunken antics or pay the fine. He hadn't dared suggest that she pull a string or two, notwithstanding that the thought had crossed his mind, she was a Supreme Court judge after all but he knew his old girl, any such suggestion would have resulted in a clout around the ear and to hell with Amnesty International. He might have been bigger and taller than his mother but that wouldn't have made much difference. It hadn't done so to date anyway.

Jolyan was enjoying a coffee break. It was mid-day, the sun was creeping through the roof tops and just about managing to hit the table he was sitting at. It was early October, so warm enough for an open necked maroon shirt, pair of lightweight linen trousers and some proper leather shoes, no trainers. People strolled by Jolyan with an awareness, it seemed to him, that he rarely encountered in London. For some unknown reason they seemed more interested in what was going on around them, more relaxed. There wasn't that blankness of self and disinterest or rabid ambition that was always so souring, on the faces of Londoners.

Slightly taller than average, with a slim body and muscles in all the right places, Jolyan didn't have to try too hard at good lucks. He was a natural and as such, had avoided the conceit of trying to be something he wasn't. Pale skinned, he always had to watch out for the more dangerous intentions of sneaky sunshine but as long as he was careful, his skin would usually go a healthy brownish colour, but not so brown that he looked as if he had spent too much time frying himself under some pay as you go sunbed.

His hair *was* the colour of a gold sovereign. A sovereign that his mother had been banging on about for as long as he could remember, more out of fear of his tuning into a Billy no mates carrot head with freckles to boot, as far as he was concerned.

Well that hadn't happened and he had to admit, he was grateful.

For a few minutes he ignored the fascinating exercise of people watching and thought about what he was really going to do with his life. His nineteenth birthday was just around the corner. Jolyan was undoubtedly mature beyond his years which meant that he didn't quite take callow immortality for granted, although sometimes it did slip through his defences.

In some ways he was spoilt for choice. Law, business, academia? All his family were involved in one of these areas in some shape or form. He knew there was plenty of help out there if he chose to use it. The thing was, he didn't want to. He wanted to find his own way and do his own thing.

He had already decided that the law was out, with the business world not far behind it. There was something about making money that simply didn't appeal. He couldn't quite put his finger on it, but money-making seemed too rough, too nasty somehow. Shallow even, apart from anything else any fool could make a few quid; he'd seen plenty of that at public school. As for the law, having a couple of heavies watching his every move for a couple of months had put him right off the idea. As far as he knew, his mother's attacker hadn't been caught and no-one seemed to know who was behind it all. The authorities had finally given up, at the same time leaving Jolyan to his own devices.

Academia was a strong contender, his cousin Angharad seemed to have been happy enough all these years digging around ancient burial sites and so on, so maybe history was his way to the future?

Taking a sip of coffee, he finally decided bugger it. There was plenty of time to make up his mind. He was young and as fit as a fiddle, so for now careers and being a responsible adult could wait. Besides, there were far too many pretty girls walking passed him to worry about all that crap.

Far too many.

'Excuse me. Do you know where I can find some work?'

Jolyan turned his eyes away from all the tight bodies stretching Levi jeans to their limits. A boy about his own age was staring down at him.

'Sorry?' Jolyan replied, unsure of what to say next.

'Work. Do you know of any café, restaurant, bar anywhere, that might have some work for me?'

'Umm . . . not off hand.' Jolyan said, a trifle taken aback by the sudden intrusion. He saw the disappointment in the boy's eyes and for some unknown reason felt rather sorry for him. A thought suddenly crossed his mind. 'On the other hand, my own boss might be looking for someone. Only this morning he was moaning about not having enough staff. He doesn't pay much though. He's a mean sod.'

'Do you mind if I sit down?' The boy asked a little hesitantly. His English was perfect and yet there was no accent to identify his origins.

'Of course not, help yourself.' Jolyan replied. The boy sat down.

'Could you ask your boss for me then, please?' The boy smiled.' I'm travelling around like you, I think? I'm getting short of funds so some work would help'. Well, this was one problem Jolyan had never had to worry about. Money. He didn't have loads of the stuff, his mother saw to that, but providing he was reasonably careful he didn't have to beat himself up about it either.

The boy was certainly direct, Jolyan had to give him that. Some might have taken this the wrong way and yet there was something in the deep brown eyes that Jolyan warmed too. The boy wasn't begging, neither was he looking for sympathy. All he could see looking at him, was an unmistakeable sincerity, even kindness.

'Look . . . er . . . ,' Jolyan began to say.

'Alvand Asadi, just call me Al. I'm Iranian, born and bred in London though. My family took off when Khomeini took power.'

'Right Al, I'm Jolyan and from London too. Come back here at five, say. Give me a chance to have a word with my boss to see if he's got something for you. Is that ok?'

'That's great. Thanks.'

'Good, well I have to go. He goes mad if I go one minute over my beak time. See you later.'

With that Jolyan disappeared into his place of work, while Al carried on where he taken off, looking at all the girls that swayed and poured down a side street on its way to somewhere he didn't quite understand.

Alvand Asadi was one of those people whom one met and then quickly forgot. He looked so normal. Jeans, trainers, check short sleeved shirt and classic Arabian black hair, a general swarthiness and outsized nose put him firmly in the ranks of 'other ethnicity' and to hell with you if you wanted to know anything else.

He wasn't handsome but then neither was he particularly unattractive, he just didn't swing one way or the other and this included his sexuality. Heterosexual, if slightly reluctant when one took his shyness with girls into account. He certainly had none of Jolyan's confidence when it came to 'pulling' and getting a girl's knickers off.

Al tended to reject the infantile vacuity and playground antics of his social media obsessed peers. There had been drama in his family and tragedy, but nothing that had had any lasting effect on Al personally. Flight and refugee status, the executions of a distant family member or two, had all happened way before he was born and had only ever registered on his mind as figments of distant family history.

His family wasn't short of money, but whilst it despised the Jews with a vengeance, it wasn't short in imitating their reputation for meanness, true or false, or for that matter accumulating wealth, thus Al getting pretty desperate to earn some money. His wealthy grandfather had seen the 1979 Revolution coming and had made sure that his wealth had kept going – out of Iran and into London.

His father still ran the business that dealt primarily with investment banking, specifically for Iranians.

Like Jolyan, Al had been privately educated and like Jolyan, he had already won a place at university – in his case at a London medical school.

On learning of his intentions to be a doctor, no-one would have been surprised as there was definitely something of the healer in his dark brown eyes. There was also an unmistakeable capacity for giving and as Jolyan had immediately noticed, a certain kindness.

Al had been brought up in one of the wealthy suburbs of London. Well-adjusted and bright, he had followed the 'must do' student path of travelling around the world if only to see what all the fuss was about. The whole idea seemed slightly juvenile to him and he wasn't sure that travelling was going to help his world view much but then a year out from exams wouldn't do him any harm so deciding to go with the flow, here he was in Portugal trying to bum some work off a fellow Brit.

Who knows where he would end up next?

CHAPTER 10

Two weeks had passed since Al and Jolyan's first meeting. Al's luck had been in and he now worked alongside Jolyan in the bar.

To begin with Jolyan had found Al's shyness difficult to deal with, being the outgoing and take it or leave it sort that he was. Al's self-containment had been difficult to penetrate, if not downright annoying. Getting any kind of lively response seemed nigh on impossible. There was the odd smile even a grunt or two, but that was about it. Jolyan couldn't help but be reminded of his mother's constant ranting about doctors and particularly surgeons of the heart and brain variety, being nothing but a load of autistic buggers who simply had no idea how to communicate with mere mortals.

He was beginning to see what she meant. If Al was like this now, fuck knows what he would be like in a hospital or GP's surgery. It didn't bear thinking about!

Anyway Jolyan, being the tolerant sort and not easily put off, had made allowances and bit by bit had managed to make Al come out of his shell. This usually involved plying him with a few stiff drinks but never mind, when needs must.

Al was really quite likeable in that quiet way of his, and now and again he would come out with a one liner that would make Jolyan burst out loud laughing. There was a sense of humour there, it just needed being teased out from time to time.

Just as they were about to finish for the day, Jolyan had an idea.

'Look Al, I know you haven't said much about where you are staying but I bet it isn't as good as my place. Company apartment, all mod cons. There's couple of rooms going begging, so I thought you might like to move in. I could use the company and of course there's no rent to pay.' This was one of the few concessions he had managed to drag out of his mother. 'Anyway, how about it?'

Al looked at Jolyan, in that quizzical way of his, as if an act of kindness was something to be suspicious of, no doubt this had something to do with his family's history, not that Al had ever said anything but Jolyan had already learnt that where his friend was concerned only God knew what he was thinking most of the time.

'Ok, I'll take a look.' Al replied non-committedly, making sure there was nothing he couldn't get out of.

'Bloody hell, Al. Don't overdo the gratitude now will you? I'm offering you some free luxury board and all you can do is say, "ok, I'll take a look!"

Al went into sulk mode. His eyes dropped as he looked at Jolyan.

'Um . . . sorry, didn't mean to offend, Jolyan. Thank you for the thought, appreciated.'

'Accepted.' Jolyan replied. 'Come on then, it's within easy walking distance, I'll take you for a look and you *don't* have to move in. It was just a thought. I will understand if you want stay where you are.'

'Er . . . can we leave it for now?' Al replied, in that guarded way of his. 'I need to get back, see to some messages. Maybe at the weekend?'

Jolyan couldn't believe what he was hearing. What was the matter with the guy? Messages? Who the hell did he think he was, the chairman of Goldman Sachs? Jolyan gritted his teeth.

'Ok, the weekend it is but the offer isn't going to last for ever, right Al? It's take it or leave it, no skin off my nose either way. Come to think of it, it's a good job it isn't the skin off your nose though, you've got far too much of it!'

Jolyan couldn't resist and even Al managed what appeared to be a smile, even if it did look as if he was in pain.

'Right then, I'm off. See you tomorrow Al. I'm on a date tonight, so who knows I might get lucky!'Jolyan didn't notice the slightly disapproving look on the face of his new friend, as he walked away. Had he done so, he might have had second thoughts about sharing the apartment with him.

CHAPTER 11

Adina Berezin took one final look in the mirror. Yes, she would do she thought. Natural brunette hair verging on blackness, depending on which way the sun was shining, fell around her shoulders not caring much where it landed.

Her Christian name meant 'gentle' in Hebrew and she liked to think that this is exactly what she was. Gentle. Although it must be said, that sometimes this gentleness could erupt into an occasional bout of fiery, but always passionate temper. As a Sabra Jew, this probably had something to do with the Sabras who fought in the Jewish resistance movement back in the 1950's but she, like most of her generation, tended toward a more conciliatory world, a world where people of all religions and ethnicity could live side by side and in harmony. Naïve perhaps but then her twenty one years had yet to gain a firm grip on reality. Not that Adina cared much about all this, right now and in spite of herself she was getting rather excited at the prospect of meeting this young British boy from London.

He had walked into the travel agent's where she worked, with a certainty in his step and looks that had made the other girls stop what they were doing for a moment or two. For some unknown reason he had made straight for her desk – Adina had yet to fully realise how beautiful she was.

The boy had wanted to know about some flights to London and then mid-way in their conversation he had said with a boldness that she wasn't used to, 'do you have a boyfriend?'

Adina had replied simply, 'no.'

The boy had smiled, 'ok, how about a drink when you finish then, my treat?'

For a few seconds Adina had had to stop her jaw dropping. The cheek! His smile was irresistible though she had to admit, so she had straightened her back, looked at the boy straight in the eyes and said, almost by way of challenge, 'alright, 5.30 at the bar opposite. I'm making it early because if I don't like you, I can leave and still have the rest of the night to enjoy myself.'

Jolyan smirked. 'My name is Jolyan. Jolyan Treharne and yours is . . . ?'

'Adina. Adina Berezin.'

'Right Adina, 5.30 it is. Oh and you will like me, I promise. You might even want to hang around and have something to eat with me. See you later.'

With that he had walked out of the office, leaving a slightly bemused Adina wondering who the hell he thought he was, but more to the point why she had agreed to meet him?

Later that day, Jolyan had concluded that the trendy but dirty looking designer stubble bit was out. He had given it a go but his reddish credentials had merely resulted in his face looking as red as a baboon's arse. Not a great one for Facebook fashion crap, he had always gone his own way and sod what everyone else was doing. He had decided on a pair of cream chinos, not white far too flash and a navy blue shirt, no breast pocket. Breast pockets on shirts always looked so cheap and as for the short sleeve variety, forget it.

Before leaving the apartment, he had already concluded that this Adina girl merited some extra input. Of course it never occurred to him that she might stand him up, not out of any kind of conceit, it was just something that rarely if ever happened to him. God though the girl was bloody gorgeous. Her hair, olive skin and almost black eyes had caught him completely off guard and this rarely if ever happened where girls were concerned.

She wasn't a local, he knew that much. Her accent and general appearance were all wrong. Her English had been excellent, fluent and easy. There was something thoroughly intriguing about her. Different. He had already noticed an intelligent maturity about her and a femininity that he didn't often encounter in his day to day ramblings around the female of the species.

This particular date was giving him a jumpy stomach. Stupid he knew, but he couldn't help it.

An hour later he was sipping a Coke in the bar opposite the travel agent's. At 5.30 Adina showed up. Hair blowing around her face and displaying a figure that even Jolyan hadn't thought was possible, after all she had been sitting down at a desk when he had met her. She was wearing tight jeans and a white cotton top. Simple but devastating. A colourful canvass handbag hung from one of her shoulders.

Jolyan immediately stood up, he had been brought up to be a gentleman and couldn't help himself.

'Oh, a young man with manners', Adina commented as she sat down at Jolyan's table. 'That makes a change. I see you're on Coke, well I've had a long busy day, so how about sharing a bottle of wine? It's not bad in here and quite cheap. What do you say?'

A bossy bugger, Jolyan immediately thought and she didn't even know him. Interesting.

'A bottle of wine? I suppose a bottle of beer is out of the question? Sorry, forget I said that. Ok. Sit tight. What do you fancy? Like I said, my treat.'

'A Chardonnay.' Adina replied without pausing. 'The house version is good enough, trust me.'

'Chardonnay, it is then.' With that he went off to the bar to order the wine. When he returned and before he could get a word in, Adina said,' a Brit in Portugal. Not quite the normal 'gap year' beaten track, is it?'

'No, I suppose not.' Jolyan then added mischievously, 'not much gets passed you, does it?'

Ignoring the cheeky sarcasm, Adina took a sip of wine. This might prove to be an amusing evening if nothing else she thought, assuming it lasted that long.

'Now, before going any further . . . Jolyan, I just want you to know that I have never done this before. Accepted a date that is, without knowing anything about the other party I'm dating.' Jolyan couldn't help himself, somehow this Adina demanded argument.

'I've heard that one before,' he interrupted. 'Usually in a bedroom and first thing in the morning.'

This stopped Adina right in her tracks and for a moment there was absolute silence, then she suddenly started to laugh. A lovely, throat throttling sound that forced Jolyan to join in.

'That's true, I bet you have.' Adina finally managed to say. 'Stupid thing to say really, true though, trust me.'

'I don't doubt it,' Jolyan grinned. The ice had been broken and the boxing gloves taken off. Over a supper of salami, olives and freshly baked bread, they got to know each other.

Adina had been born and bred in Tel Aviv, it was her intention to return home once her 'gap year' agenda had been completed and train as a lawyer, to which Jolyan had immediately thought oh God no, not another Charlotte Treharne! She was quick to tell Jolyan that she was a firm believer in the Three State Solution to the Israeli-Palestinian Conflict.

Her passion and strength of purpose soon became clear as she held Jolyan's attention with a tirade of Sabra intensity.

'The only way for a lasting peace Jolyan, is for Israel to go back to its pre-1967 borders, the return of the Gaza Strip to the bosom of Egypt and the same with the West Bank and Jordan.'

'Yes but . . .'Jolyan tried to interrupt but got nowhere, unlike most of his generation he did take a keen interest in world affairs. Facebook and Twitter or Twatter as he liked to call it, didn't quite cut it for him. It was the same for this

Adina it seemed. Well thank God for that he thought, at least she wasn't one of those airhead girls that spend their lives attaching false nails to their fingertips, drooling over celebrity peccadillo and just waiting for some blond headed Maserati driving pop star to fuck them silly on some sun drenched beach.

He was soon able to determine that whilst she was an Israeli on a mission, she was no zealot. A peacemaker at heart, she wanted the killing to stop and if it meant giving up some territory then so be it.

Adina was two years older than Jolyan. They were both mature beyond their years, but in different ways. Adina generally took life more seriously than Jolyan (her two years conscription in the Israeli Defense Force probably had something to do with this), who was still intent on enjoying it to the full. He could exercise depth of character but only when it suited him and only when it fitted in with his *joie de vivre*.

They were both strong, independent characters but they had some mutual weak points – youth and a naïve belief that kindness would solve any problem.

They soon discovered that on the surface they had very little in common, apart from a genuine concern for their fellow men. Their tastes in music were at the opposite ends of the spectrum. Adina hated sport, Jolyan loved it, squash and tennis in particular. She loved wine, he preferred beer. He liked lounging around in bed, she liked the great outdoors and on and on it went.

And yet . . . there was an indefinable communion of spirit between. A something that drew them together. It couldn't be touched. It couldn't be explained. It was just there in their eyes and their smiles. Neither was self-obsessed and neither had been permanently damaged by an indolent social media narcissism.

They simply wanted to be together, albeit that neither was entirely sure why.

At the end of the evening, Jolyan found himself standing next to Adina outside an old building that had been converted into apartments.

'Well, here we are Adina. You're home. I kept to my word. I promised you would like me.'

'Yes you did.' Adina replied thoughtfully. She couldn't help looking into his eyes, green one minute, brown the next. 'But as far as I'm concerned the "liking" bit remains to be seen, so don't get above yourself and if you think you're going to be invited in for some coffee, forget it. Rampant sex is out.'

'As if I would!' Jolyan retorted.

'Good. Then you won't be disappointed if I say good-night. Give me a ring, I've given you my number.'

With that, she disappeared without even giving him a chaste, good night kiss on the cheek.

While Jolyan and Adina were having their maturity tested by a callow innocence that defied it, Al was tapping away at his tablet. There were messages that needed to be sent. An only child, he kept in touch with his parents in spite of finding the whole thing thoroughly boring. He really wasn't that interested. Family ties were all very well but being the self-contained character he was, as far as he was concerned friends and family were mostly an inconvenient nuisance although he had to admit he quite liked Jolyan. Some of the time, anyway.

Al found his 'friend's', a word he was always inclined to use with a certain reluctance, preoccupation with girls irritating. For Al, girls seemed to be so feckless, so unerringly shallow. He had yet to meet one who could match him in intellectual depth and perception, and this included his equals when it came to top exam grades. Somehow he just couldn't take them seriously, and their incessant giggling annoyed him intensely. He realised that he was being intolerant even unkind but he really didn't care, in fairness though he found boys his own age equally suspect.

So far, no girl had had any lasting impact on him. He had lost his virginity in an attempt to understand all the extravagant claims made about sex and had been profoundly disappointed. As far as he was concerned, sex was just a messy exercise in farcical contortion and nothing more. It was certainly nothing to get worked up about.

He was still thinking about Jolyan's offer of accommodation. He would take a look but if they were going to be on top of each other, then there was no chance. Al liked his privacy and space and neither were up for negotiation.

He carried on tapping away, he was back in his own rarefied, non-physical world and extremely comfortable in it.

CHAPTER 12

Al looked around the sitting room and kitchen, it was an up-market apartment alright. Plenty of space and light, expensive furnishings.

'Let me show you your bedroom, Al,' Jolyan said enthusiastically, which as expected didn't even raise a smile from Al, miserable sod. 'That's if you fancy taking up my offer.' Jolyan added, he was beginning to wonder why he was bothering.

Al walked into a bedroom that had its own sitting area and of course a luxurious en suite bathroom built for two. Jolyan couldn't quite see Al making full use of a double shower and tub, although his friend might surprise him yet . . . chance would be a fine thing!

'So. What do think, Al? ' He asked.

'Ummm . . . it's very nice, I must say.'

'Nice? Bloody hell Al, its pure luxury even I know that. How much would you have to pay for this lot on the open market eh? All I'm asking for is some contribution towards the utility bills, my mother is insisting on it.'

'Oh money isn't a problem now that I'm working. Right then, thanks. I'll need a few days to think about it, if that's ok?'

'What's there to think about, for fuck's sake Al?' Jolyan was usually quite restrained when it came to the effing and ceeing, he really was the laid back sort but even he was beginning to get fed up with Al. What the hell was the matter with him? Most people wouldn't be able to move in fast enough.

'Look, Jolyan,' Al replied as he started to look at the floor again, 'it's not the apartment, honestly and I appreciate the offer but I'm not sure whether we would get along so well under the same roof as it were. You're a party animal Jolyan and all for the girls, I'm not. Sorry but there it is. I like my privacy. So, if you don't mind I'll pass.'

Jolyan looked at his new friend. His words seemed genuine enough, which immediately soothed any kind of anger that was beginning to boil up in him, not that he ever got angry about much anyway.

'Ok Al, fair enough and understood. You're probably right. Let's forget the whole thing.' Jolyan smiled. 'How about drowning my sorrows in a couple of beers then?'

'Why not.' Al grinned, which didn't happen very often.

The following afternoon Jolyan and Adina were staring at the walls of Sao Bento Railway Station, or at least its vestibule. Originally a Benedictine monastery, King Carlos I laid the first stone of the station in 1900.

The young couple stared at the 20,000 tiles that depicted various scenes from Portuguese history. Dated from 1905 to 1916 they were all the work of Jorge Colaco, the most important *azulejo* painter of the time. There were landscapes and scenes from the past plastered all over the place. The Battle of Valdevez (1140), the meeting of knight Egas Moniz and Alfonso VII of Leon (12th Century),the arrival of King John I and Philippa of Lancaster (1387) and the Conquest of Ceuta.

For Jolyan, the fascination was complete. He had already learnt that history should teach but never rule and as his eyes absorbed the violence and comity of the past, as usual he wanted to know more. The artistic brilliance that combined blue and creamy white tended to pass him by, he was far more interested in the historical detail. For Jolyan this was where true art lay; the human condition, warts and all.

'Brilliant, isn't it Jolyan?' Adina said, her words more a statement than a question.

'You could say that.' Jolyan replied, as he tried to consider the real import of the events being depicted before his eyes.

The historian in him was never far away. Untested and raw it may have been, but it was there albeit that his interpretations were unsophisticated and certainly needed some fine tuning.

'Come on, I'm thirsty,' Adina ordered. 'Let's go and find a Coke somewhere.' She took Jolyon's hand and led him off down a steep road back into Porto's City Centre. It suddenly occurred to them both that this was the first time any physical contact had taken place between them. They had been out together a few times over the past month but there had always been something of the tenuous about their meetings.

Reserved even.

It was as if neither wanted to frighten the other off. For all their youthful certainty, in some ways the deeper puzzles of human emotion remained unknown quantities, at least in respect of unbidden mutual attraction if not hunger. Both knew all about dating and neither was a virgin, but there was a difference when they saw each other. A new dimension, which both excited and intimidated.

They were both treading carefully. Prodding here and there to find out more. They couldn't help looking into each other's eyes whenever they could, as if seeking out some kind of confirmation or approval of the next move.

As they jostled between the crowds, Jolyan stopped abruptly.

'Oh stuff this,' he said as he put his hands on Adina's shoulders and pulled her face and lips to his. He looked into her eyes and saw for the first time in his young life, a light that outshone all his previous adventures with young women; the passing fancies and here today gone tomorrow rumpled up bed sheets. He saw a wonder and feeling that he had only ever heard about in songs and read about in books. Adina's eyes caught his heart and moulded it into her own. He had never before felt so hopelessly drawn, so awkwardly possessed by a young woman in his life. All he could do was place his lips on hers and try to stop himself from eating her alive.

He wanted her so much.

At that time and in that place, it was a most perfect kiss.

More perfect than either of them had ever known.

Later that day, when Jolyan and Adina slid into bed naked, there was a reluctance to touch out of hand. They both wanted and yet they both exercised caution. They thought they knew it all and yet when faced with something beyond them they were at a loss. Their body's wanted to absorb, to feel everything no holds barred but each was unsure of what to do next.

Refined sex takes time but a first love rarely recognises the fact, nor indeed does it even want to. It is crowned with a halo of naivety and gentleness that is seldom repeated in life no matter how many times love strikes, consumes and breaks.

They kissed and kept on kissing.

Their tongues and lips not wanting to let go, as their fingers searched and stroked with an anticipation hanging on some edge that they had yet to define. There was uncertainty in their fingertips, as they moved into each other whilst at the same time trying not to unhinge the communion of this first, appalling love.

Neither knew the other's body. Neither knew what was good or bad. It was a time to explore, to test. Clumsiness was ignored along with any attempt to be masters at the game. All they wanted was each other, as soon as possible.

First love again.

Magnificently untried, innocent and so impossible.

Everlasting and hall marked onto memory for a lifetime.

CHAPTER 13

Charlotte Treharne was no right winger, neither indeed was she a bleeding heart liberal who felt that people couldn't help themselves and that society was to blame for everything. 'There is no such thing as society' was stretching it, on the other hand Thatcher's words were always being taken out of context by the Guardianista and Channel 4 news viewers and never quoted accurately.

If anything, Charlotte would have described herself as a social democratic Tory, in other words she was all for the strong looking after the weak and a fair distribution of wealth but she also believed in small government, a thorough rejection of the nanny state and a free market, though not an unregulated one.

The banks had made sure of that.

She was a judge who sat in the highest court of the land. Impartiality was her raison d'etre but this didn't mean to say that she didn't have a personal view or opinion. All judges did, they just kept quiet about it. They were human like everybody else, and like everybody else they had prejudices, foibles, likes and dislikes.

The post war years had seen an explosion of whining, weepy 'victimhood' and middle class, London metropolitan, dinner partied redoubts of liberal, self-righteous smugness. Everyone else was to blame. Drunks, drug addicts, fat pizza guzzling indolence were all excused by the fact that none of these people could help it. They were all victims of society's cruelty and lack of care and it was their human right to be a burden on the taxpayer.

Well Charlotte was having none of it. In her view, people, individuals were responsible for their actions. They *chose* to pick of the bottle, the syringe and the monstrous boxes of multiple coated cheese pizza.

They *chose* to be who they were.

It wasn't society's fault and they did not have a human right to demand that society pick up the bill for their chronic weakness, self-indulgence and bleating, outright selfishness.

If they had had no choice, then this of course was a different matter and Charlotte was always the first to recognise the fact, sometimes with the most extraordinary degree of understanding.

At the moment she was sitting in her office trying to work out how she could bring her judicial colleagues around to her way of thinking. At the moment it was two to one, Charlotte being the one.

Human rights law was in dire need of reform. It was complicated and tortuous. It needed simplifying. There were far too many layers of appeal for foreign nationals to avail themselves of, when the State wanted to deport them – for very good reasons.

This Atallah case was one such example.

The man had been preaching his hate around UK mosques for years. She and the other Justices had all been given sight of the Secret Service's dossier on him. It had made for frightening reading. The evidence had been clear and unequivocal: The man had been the main player in a number of terrorist atrocities in the Middle East but herein lay the problem.

He hadn't committed any outrages on British soil – yet. There were suspicions but nothing concrete. However, this hadn't been the main thrust of his defence to deportation – enter the Human Rights Act. His lawyers were convinced that if he was returned to Lebanon, his place of origin, he would be tortured and unlikely to receive a fair trial. In other words, the sanctity of his human rights would be breached and we couldn't have that now could we?

Responsible for the murder of God knows how many innocent people and yet Her Majesty's Government couldn't get rid of him. It was ridiculous.

Already fired up, she entered the Atallah case review meeting with the two other Justices, in no mood to listen to apologist cop out nonsense. There were times when she despaired at the spineless whimpering of her male colleagues. It seemed to her, that most of the time the only other Justice who had any balls was Baroness Cynthia Wilmott. Charlotte had always been able to count on her fellow female Justice when masculine idiocy raised its simpering head.

Women and periods? How about men who were too lily-livered to stand up to wifely tyranny and domination? Far more dangerous in her view. No wonder so many judges got up to all kinds of sordid diversions with boys and whips?

Dumping her files down on the meeting room table she looked at Lords Reed and Salmond or Nick and David to her.

'Right gentleman, what are your views at the present time? We have the hearing coming up next week, and it is my considered view that we should grant the government its deportation order.'

'Before we begin Charlotte, how are you since your ordeal?' David Salmond asked in that judiciously sincere way of his, 'I have left some messages with your secretary.'

'I'm fine, thank you David.' Charlotte replied curtly.

'Forgive me for presuming otherwise, Charlotte,' Salmond said quietly.

'Pardon, David?'

'Nothing Charlotte. Now, shall we get down to business?'

Charlotte quickly realised that she had been unnecessarily dismissive and rude.

'My apologies David if I sounded impolite, it was not my intention.' Charlotte said with a sincerity that was both genuine and compelling. 'Forgive me.'

'Forgiven,' Salmond smiled. Bloody woman, she could get away with murder. Beautiful and untamed, outspoken and on occasions outrageous but few men were able to resist her charm and he had to admit, integrity. He was also aware that she was capable of the most extraordinary compassion where her fellow human beings were concerned. A truly brilliant legal mind, and yet she enjoyed a common touch that the people loved and respected her for.

'For want of stating the obvious,' Charlotte continued, 'I don't have to tell you where I stand gentleman. On this occasion at least, let's try to avoid making ourselves a laughing stock where our masters are concerned, that is the good people out there on the streets, just in case you need being reminded of the fact.'

'I assure you Charlotte, we do not need to be reminded of anything, least of all by you,' Nick Reed bristled. 'As usual you are getting above yourself. Justices of the Supreme Court we may well be but it is not within our remit to interfere with primary legislation. Points of law of general public importance yes, but we are not Parliament and it is Parliament that makes law not us.'

'Rubbish Nick and you know it. What about the Common Law?'

'You are being frivolous, Charlotte.' Reed said with a withering look. 'You know exactly what I mean.'

Nick Reed couldn't stand Charlotte. Her looks did nothing for him and he despised the mythology that had been built up around her. In his view, hers was a token appointment to keep the feminist lobby happy – as usual, at any cost.

'I assume then Nick, that you are going to allow the appeal?'

'I am.'

'And you David?' Charlotte looked at David Salmond. They had always got on well and rarely disagreed on matters of law. Nick on the other hand, she knew was an out and misogynist. She had yet to work out whether he was old Queen material, albeit that rumours had abounded for years.

'I remain unconvinced by your legal arguments Charlotte, which we have been through already many times before.' Lord Salmond replied cautiously. 'This case is of considerable public interest I know, and I take your point about the judiciary becoming a laughing stock. Nevertheless, I wish more time to consider.'

'Oh come on now, David. You've already had plenty of time and if I know you, you will already have looked at all the legal options and for that matter implications.'

'True Charlotte, but I still want to sleep on my decision.'

Charlotte didn't always get her own way, even so there was a mischievous twinkle in David's eyes that told her he was more or less on her side. Years ago when they had both been young barristers they had enjoyed a fling together. Charlotte had always known that David would have loved if she had given him the chance but it was not to be.

He had been a lovely man then and still was, unlike the surly shit sitting next to him, whom she knew would go against her on principle if nothing else.

Charlotte looked at her old boyfriend. She still had a soft spot for him even after all these years. She demurred.

'Very well David, but for Heaven's sake let me know when you have made up your mind, oh and don't let that Warrior Queen of a wife of yours make it up for you!'

'God forbid Charlotte,' David grinned. 'Although, I believe you are both from the same stable, no disrespect to the horses of course.'

Marc Rey was waiting for Charlotte outside the meeting room. It had been three months since the attack and no-one had any idea as to whom was behind it, let alone the identity of the perpetrator. The protection for Jolyan had been called off, but the Home Secretary had insisted that Rey continue to keep an eye on his charge.

'Hello Lady Treharne. Home?'

'Oh, I do wish you would dispense with the formalities Marc. God knows you've been interfering in my life for long enough. You see more of me than my dear husband does. How many times do I have to tell you, Charlotte will do when we are on our own. All this 'Lady' crap is fine in its place, at least for all the formal nonsense and I'm not even sure about this, but when it's just you and me or family, Charlotte will do.'

'Very well, Charlotte. You're the boss.'

'Yes I am and don't you forget it.'

Rey smiled, he couldn't help it. Lady Treharne could be an awkward, prickly cow but he couldn't help liking her. Clever and brave, not to mention that she could still turn the heads of men his own age, she had a down to earth way about her that was both endearing and yet provocative.

'Where to then . . . um . . . Charlotte?'

'That's better. The apartment then I suppose. I need to track down that miscreant son of mine. God knows what trouble he's got himself into. The boy should be licensed.'

'Very well.' Rey replied all business this time as he opened the Exit door for Charlotte. The streets were dangerous places and his masters had told him that Lady Charlotte Treharne was still at serious risk.

An hour or so later she was relaxing with a vodka, tonic and a cigarette. Bruch's Violin Concerto No 1 was playing in the background as she kicked off her shoes and lay back on a settee. The sitting room or drawing room, as those of an adolescent Tatler magazine disposition were inclined to call it, always calmed. The gentle pale yellow of the room, together with Victorian landscapes and oriental rugs gave it a human, lived in touch, albeit an upmarket one.

The apartment had been owned by the Treharne's for years, yet another astute investment made by her mother, Lise Treharne. Charlotte still missed her mother, her strength and wisdom, particularly during those times when her own wavered, and they did waver from time to time. She was a deeply sensitive woman, she cared about people and knew how to love. She also knew that in her job any kind of craven sensitivity would have been a sign of weakness and in a man's world this was unacceptable.

Charlotte had known heart wrenching tragedy, she knew all about the terrible betrayal of love. She knew how to laugh and cry, but the real Charlotte, the real Lottie was reserved only for those she knew she could trust and those whose love would never be found wanting.

Sometimes the romantic, sometimes the hardnosed lawyer, it depended always on whom she was dealing with and whom she was fighting for, and when it came to the law by God did she fight. Always the underdog's champion and always a courageous critic of the Establishment even though she was a prime mover in it.

But then she had always known that one could create far more change from within than without.

Joel was down in Wales for a few days. Paul had asked for a meeting. Her husband saw to all their business interests and general financial well-being. The arrangement worked well as it allowed her to concentrate on her own career without being burdened by the minutiae of property, investments and general money management. Apart from anything else, Joel was better at it than she.

For a few moments she thought about her Welsh roots, such as they were. She was half Danish on her mother's side and half Welsh on her father's. William Treharne, a self-made Welsh industrialist now long gone, had built the family fortune from scratch and her mother had carried it on.

Charlotte was a London girl through and through, since arriving there as a law student all those years ago. Born and bred in Wales but schooled in England, her 'Welshness' was nothing but a romantic figment of nostalgia. She had always described herself as British first, European second and a rather confused citizen of the world, third.

A 'Welsh' identity meant nothing to her, neither indeed did any farcical Welsh nationalist fantasies, she was far too cosmopolitan both in experience and worldly endeavour, apart from anything else there were a good few pints of Danish blood running through her. As for the Welsh language, well it was simply a quaint and rather amusing subject to talk about at a dining table and that was all, as indeed was its 'nation' creating irrelevance and intent.

She pulled herself up from the settee with a sigh and headed for the drinks cabinet. She allowed herself two good sized vodkas and cigarettes a night. Wine with food. As usual she missed her husband. The bed always seemed so cold without him, so empty. She knew Rey was hovering around somewhere in the street, if not Rey then some faceless replacement. She also knew that she would have to put up with all this bodyguard nonsense for a while yet. The government couldn't allow a Supreme Court judge to be knocked off, that really would have been too much.

She sat back down, whilst feeling perfectly safe in the apartment, she knew she was in danger as soon as she stepped outside the building. Rey was a capable man she had no doubt about that and so indeed was Joel, but she also knew that no-one could stop a determined terrorist or someone intent on a suicidal attack. The thought made her shiver for a moment and think of her son. She had been assured that he was under no threat but she still had her doubts.

The world was more dangerous now than it had ever been but what could she do? Jolyan was a young man enjoying life, in his mind he was immortal. Charlotte knew otherwise and it frightened her to death but there was nothing she could do about it short of placing him under house arrest and she couldn't quite see her wayward son wearing this somehow.

She resigned herself to the situation but it couldn't go on forever, there had to be a reckoning and she knew it.

While Charlotte was considering her position, Rey stood next to his car, an unobtrusive black Ford, and watched. His eyes were everywhere, missing nothing. Throughout his military career he had relied on instinct, for him it was a sixth sense. He could see trouble coming before it happened. In this respect he and Joel Samson had a lot in common. So far they hadn't fallen out over anything. Samson had a reputation not be trifled with but then so did Rey. Even so, he was younger and fitter, so in any firefight he would have the edge, in his view anyway.

In fairness to Samson, he hadn't tried to pull rank once. They were both pro's and worked things out together. One thing Rey did know, he could trust Samson to watch his back and come up with the goods if needed, and this was the most important thing of all.

Right now everything looked normal. There was nothing out of the ordinary going on. Even so, Rey didn't relax his guard for one second. One mistake and that could be the end of Lady Charlotte Treharne and he knew what that meant.

He looked at all the other apartment windows. It was a residential street. Property was extremely expensive here. He immediately noticed how so few windows had any light shining from them. Overseas investors, buying and never living in the bricks and mortar they had invested in, apart from maybe the odd weekend visit once or twice a year. Alright for some he thought but certainly not alright for the many born and bred Londoners who had been squeezed out into the property buying cold.

For all his alertness, even Rey couldn't see into a darkness four stories up. He was good but not that good. Neither could he see the military night vision goggles staring down at him with an untroubled ease.

The woman behind the goggles watched for a few moments more. She had seen enough for now. She put the goggles into a rucksack and let herself out of the luxury apartment she had broken into. No-one would have found any trace of her, she was covered head to toe, so no DNA evidence would have been left behind.

Not one fleck of skin, not one hair.

Before walking onto the pavement, she removed the ski mask and walked straight passed Rey. Her body was lithe, skinny even, there was certainly nothing in her movements that would have made her stand out in a crowd.

Even Rey only just noticed her passing by.

CHAPTER 14

'How is that 'aunty' of mine, Joel? Christ, I nearly died when you told me about the shooting. She's already had one attempt on her life for God's sake. Mind you, when I saw her a couple of months ago, she was her usual calm and collected self but I know Lottie.'

'She's fine Paul. Like you say, calm on the surface but a frightened kitten underneath and who can blame her? By the way don't forget the incident is under wraps, so no talking out of school. Very few people know about it.'

'Of course. Any progress on who was responsible?'

'Nothing, I'm afraid.' Joel wasn't one for small talk even when it involved the life of his wife. 'Now then Paul, what's so urgent that you needed to speak with me in person?'

'There's something going on with the shares of Treharne Holdings.' Paul said seriously. 'There's a smell and I don't like it.'

'Explain.' Joel replied, he wasn't questioning Paul's judgement. He knew only too well how astute the man's business acumen was. He had proved it many times over the years. If Paul reckoned something was up, then it probably was.

'Well, I suppose it *could* just be normal stock market movement but there's been a pattern over the past few months. Treharne Holdings shares are being bought up by one entity I'm sure of it and this means one thing: a hostile takeover attempt. I've tried buying some shares up myself, but no-one is selling. So far, whoever it is now has 49% of Treharne Holdings shares. I'm worried '

'Any idea who?' Paul asked.

'None. I've had our London people look into it and all they've come up with is a load of offshore shell companies, buying and selling to each other. A sophisticated and impossible to pin down chain of buyers, at least in respect of who exactly is pulling the strings.'

'Where do we stand in the overall scheme of things then, Paul?'

'Well, as you know, between us the family owns 51%, a controlling interest. Lottie, Angharad and my good self, hold 45% of these shares between us. The other 6% is spread around our children, my three and Jolyan. Mostly in trust funds and untouchable until they all reach 21, which won't be long.'

'So where's the problem? No-one is going to sell out Paul. You're a tight knit family.'

'Yes we are Joel, but there's youth involved here and this is what worries me. It will only take a 1-2% shift in share ownership to tip us over the edge and you know how fucking silly young 'uns can be. They probably wouldn't even know what they were doing, if some letter came through the door offering them shed loads of money.'

The two men were sitting in Paul's office. A spanking glass and white statement of modernity, change and innovation. Paul had fought his predecessor Lise Treharne tooth and nail to drag the hotel chain into the 21st Century. He had eventually succeeded but only when Lise had finally given up her objectionable ghost and died.

Sometimes though, he still felt her caustic glare stabbing him in the back.

'Look Paul, I think you're worrying unnecessarily here. None of the younger members of the family would sell anything without coming to one us of first. Don't underestimate the wisdom of young people today. Granted, in some ways the internet has infantilised them but in other ways it has made them far better informed than we were at their age and don't forget they have all had the best education money can buy. None of them are stupid.

'I think we ought to just wait and see. Right now, I don't see any clear threat to Treharne Holdings. Even if the other 49% of shares are owned by one institution, company whatever, they still don't have a controlling interest. Presumably there haven't been any overt attempts to buy any family owned shares?'

'None. Not yet anyway. But I have a feeling that it won't be long. You know the sort of thing: 'An offer we can't refuse time or else.' And it's this that is worrying me, Joel.' Paul looked Joel right in the eyes. 'How far will these people, whoever they are, go to own Treharne Holdings plc? It's a highly successful company and makes a hell of a lot of serious money.

'I don't want to sound melodramatic, but there's something else Joel, something that is giving me far more cause for concern. The attempt on Lottie's life. Now before you say anything, yes I know, Lottie's death would achieve nothing in respect of her shareholding, they would simply pass down through her estate but why now? I don't believe in coincidence.'

For a moment Joel felt a cold fear come over him.

The attempted murder of the only woman he had ever truly loved came back to him in a shudder of foreboding and to date no motive had been established and neither had there been one shred of evidence to point to whom exactly was behind the attack. Islamic terrorists? No-one could be certain about anything.

Suddenly, Joel wanted to get home and fast.

'Yes Paul, I agree,' he responded calmly. 'The attempt on Lottie's life does add a new dimension to things but let's not get above ourselves. Look, keep an eye on things. I'll do some digging of my own, I have plenty of contacts in the financial world and beyond. We'll meet up again in a few weeks' time; if anything crops up before then let me know, ok?'

'Will do. Keep in touch, but I must stress Joel that I am worried . . . for the well-being of *all* the family if nothing else.'

As Joel drove back to London and began to absorb what Paul had told him, a doubt that had been niggling away at him, gradually began to take shape. There had been something wrong with the motorcyclist's attempt to kill and it hadn't just been in his (or her, Joel remained unconvinced either way) failure to complete his objective successfully.

Whoever it was, knew what they were doing. There was top drawer military training in the equation and he knew it. The way the motorcycle had been manoeuvred for the attack, the bullet proof vest, the planned getaway and disappearance without a trace. This was no amateur and it was precisely this fact that had been bothering Joel for the past few months, not that he had said anything to Lottie.

Their attacker had had the advantage, he had known what he was doing, so why hadn't they both been killed? Admittedly, Joel's well-honed instincts had seen it coming but even so, the shooter's line of fire had been all wrong.

Joel had taken a look at the car after the incident and he had known then that something was wrong. The bullets had somehow been off target. He couldn't have been sure what with all the shattered glass but his instincts had rarely if ever been wrong. He had been a Special Forces combat soldier, an expert in the art of killing for far too long, to be fooled by some rogue bullets.

The more he thought about it, the more convinced he became that the attack had been some kind of warning.

Paul Treharne hadn't been at all melodramatic; he had just scared the shit out of Joel and put him on high alert. After the incident with Lottie, Joel had reached out to old comrades in the SAS.

They had come back with nothing.

A hostile takeover of Treharne Holdings? If this was the case, then it would certainly explain a few things. Intimidation and threats to life and limb were not unknown in the dark world of international finance and mergers.

CHAPTER 15

'I think you and Paul have been reading too many novels.' Charlotte observed in that authoritative way of hers. 'What you are saying is a trifle far-fetched to put it mildly.'

They were sitting in the apartment's sitting room. The atmosphere was tense in spite of the vodka and cigarettes.

'Really?' Joel replied. 'So now, not only are you an expert in the law and just about everything else, you are also an expert on corporate skulduggery and personal security. Oh and of course not to mention, firearms, terrorist tactics and violent intimidation? How stupid of me.'

'Alright Joel, there's no need to be so sarcastic, I get the point.'

'Good. You had better get it because believe me on this occasion your instincts are wrong. I said immediately after the shooting that something didn't add up. It didn't have the hall marks of your average bog standard terrorist. You didn't listen to me and you didn't listen to your pal at the Home Office. As usual, Lottie is right in all things and bugger anyone else's opinion.

'Well you listen to me Lady Treharne, someone who really does know what he is talking about where matters like this are concerned. The jury may well be out in some respects, but Paul is no fool and neither am I. The attempt on your life was a scaring tactic. You weren't meant to be killed. The bullets were too off target, the person firing them knew what they were doing. If the shooter wanted to kill, then he could have done I'm sure of it . . . and I'm still not sure it was a man by the way.

'No, if there is an attempt to take over Treharne Holdings then all this fits. Simple as that. I'm not saying any of this is conclusive but right now, it's the best we have. None of my contacts have come back with anything. Whoever attacked you was outside talent, way outside, an independent contractor off the UK's security service's radar.'

Charlotte remained silent.

There were few people in the world who could silence her, if any, apart from Joel that is. This had been one of the reasons she had fallen so hopelessly in love with him all those years ago. He challenged her and she also knew she could never dominate him. Like all strong women, Charlotte needed a man who could stand up to her. To her imperious will. She had tried the accommodating 'we are both equal' types but they had just bored her to tears. She enjoyed a fight, she thrived on verbal combat. The new metropolitan man with his effeminate, compliant insistence on being empathetic, sympathetic and more caring than Mother bloody Theresa just made her want to weep.

She had to have a man who, when all was said and done, was tougher than she. It was just the natural order of things.

Equality between men and women, certainly of the loving kind, was a comic fantasy. A strong woman demanded a stronger man, a man she could respect. Anything less or even in between, resulted in female domination that was both repugnant and extremely unattractive.

Men should be men and that's all there was to it. There was no such thing as 'equality' in a relationship and if there was, it usually ended up in the divorce courts.

'Alright Joel. I accept what you say. This being the case, what about Jolyan, Paul's children, the rest of us? How safe are we all . . . in your *expert* opinion that is?' She couldn't resist the dig. Charlotte never gave in gracefully.

'Look Lottie, if we assume all this has something to do with Treharne Holdings, then whoever they are, they are not out to damage anyone permanently. Let's face it, this would just make the purchase of any more shares to hold a majority stake more complicated. Wills and all the legal stuff and so on. All this is about intimidation. Keeping us all off balance. In other words, we are going to buy you out and take over your company or else.

'I don't believe Jolyan or anyone else is subject to any immediate threat. It's been three months now and nothing. Not a twitch. If there was any kind of determined effort to kill you or any member of the family, they would have struck by now.'

'Are you sure?' Charlotte needed further reassurance.

'As sure as I can be, Lottie.'

'Well, losing the family's control of Treharne Holdings is just not going to happen, Joel. None of us will sell our shares and if these people have done their homework they will know that.'

'Precisely, and they obviously have done their homework thus the attack on you.'

'Yes . . . Indeed. Well, where do we go from here?'

'We wait and watch, Lottie. There will be another move, I'm sure of it. We have to be diligent and your personal protection must continue, whether you like it or not.'

Charlotte sighed. She knew when negotiating with Joel was out of the question.

'Very well, Joel. Now, let's have another drink before going to bed. It's been a long day.'

Later that night, Charlotte and Joel tried as always to eat each other alive. When it came to sex, familiarity resulted in an implosion of monotony and monotony heralded dissatisfaction, so even after ten years of marriage, they copulated with an enthusiasm that would have shamed even the most adventurous of alley cats.

Few things were off limits, sado-masochism being one of them. Charlotte enjoyed the odd spanking with a ping pong bat but this was as far as Joel was allowed to go, not that he minded, lacing the wonderfully edible arse of his wife off had never quite appealed.

There had been occasions when she had dressed up in wig and gown to stave off 'familiarity', but such inventive departures from the law had only resulted in laughter and a total cooling of any ardour about to raise its sexually, titillating head.

They poured sex over each other with a wantonness that was intolerably uninhibited. They both knew when to charge and when to reign in. Fingertip, tongue and lip, always ensured happy sex, and thus a happy marriage.

The love between Charlotte and Joel was a certain love. There was never any doubt. There was a strength in its maturity that allowed them both to mock insecurity and constant reassurance. Neither needed to check up on the other. Neither needed to explain.

The love was just there.

Volatile and passionate, it could explode into mutual temper and even plate throwing, but nevertheless they both knew that life would be a hopeless cause without the other. Their 'togetherness' didn't need to be restated or re-blessed. It didn't need to be shown off to anyone else. Their love for each other was theirs and no-one else's and this was all either of them needed to know.

Demand didn't come into it either, neither did expectation. Domination by both sides was tolerated from time to time as long as it didn't go beyond reason and knees were sometimes bent but never without just cause.

They loved each other, full stop.

CHAPTER 16

A month had gone by and Paul was now sure that one single entity had been buying up the shares of Trehrane Holdings. There was simply no doubt about it. He had tried buying shares through family trusts and so on and nearly but not quite, breaking company law rules but whoever had bought 49% of Treharne Holdings wasn't selling, even with an inflated offer. Apart from this, wherever he turned he came up against brick walls. Whoever was doing the buying were powerful bastards in the money game.

He sat in the rose garden trying to work out his next move. Puffing away at a cigarette, he had to admit he was scared. Scared of losing what had taken two generations to build up, and in many ways a great deal of tragedy. Treharne Holdings had a come at a price. His family history was riven with loss and tears. Happiness and joy too, but always and whatever the circumstances the Treharne's had prevailed. No matter what life had thrown at them, they had fought back, endured and won out in the end.

Always.

Now though, Paul was experiencing a most profound sense of the inevitable. He seemed powerless to stop the demolition of everything his family had strived to achieve for nearly one hundred years beginning with his grandfather, William Treharne.

The hotel chain had started with Ragged Cliffs, its beauty and sense of history whispered from every wall, nook and cranny. The house, because that's really what it was in the family's eyes, had seen so much. It had retained an elegant mystery unspoilt by the whims of modern vandalism. It had always refused to give up its hold on the past, and yet this was part of its allure and why guests kept coming back time and time again for its five star luxury.

Paul finished his cigarette and threw it into the flower pot, this time there were no other butts. As he looked down at the pot, he smiled. The staff might well call him a right royal shit behind his back but he knew they respected him and some even cared about him, on a good day anyway. They rarely left his employ, they all knew where their bread was buttered. Treharne Holdings was a generous employer, it always had been right from the early days. It looked after its staff from cradle to grave and everything in between.

Content staff, successful business and the Treharne's had never strayed from or compromised, this mantra of honourable intent.

Just as he was about to make his way back to the apartment, a voice stopped him.

'Mr Treharne?'

Paul looked around to see a middle aged man who looked as if he had just stepped out from a tailor's emporium in Savil Row and Paul knew a bespoke London suit when he saw one, he had a few of them himself.

There was a distinguished air about the man and yet Paul was quick enough to observe the difference between the real deal and the contrived and practised. This man was definitely not the genuine article. His unkempt button down shirt collar and schoolboy knotted tie was all Paul needed to know. The man's navy blue suit may have been top drawer but the man himself certainly wasn't.

It was late afternoon, spring had yet to arrive so daylight was already starting to say kiss my arse. For a moment Paul paused, he always tried to avoid guests, whining buggers most of them. He only dealt with them when he had to The rose garden had always been his place of respite and a sly fag for the very reason that late at night or when it was cold, guests rarely came anywhere near the place.

'Hello, yes I'm Treharne' Paul replied, with his best false smile and dropping the 'Mr', using it as an introduction always sounded so bloody presumptuous and pompous. 'May I help you?' He quickly eyed the man up and down again. Plenty of bucks here, he concluded. Handsome too. He looked the sort who was used to giving orders not taking them but then this was the general profile of most guests who stayed at Ragged Cliffs; who the hell else could afford to pay their prices, if it wasn't the rich and successful?

'Ah good. My apologies for disturbing you but I wonder if I may have a word?' Suave, American gentry. East Coast. WASP time. Paul spotted it all in seconds, he had dealt with this sort plenty of times along the way. 'Perhaps buy you a drink?'

What could this Yankee beauty want? Paul immediately thought. His radar was up and it was bleeping faster than a chambermaid trying to run away from him in his younger days, albeit that she never got very far.

'Um . . . how do you do, Mr . . . er?' Paul went straight into 'Mine host' mode. All charm and bullshit.

'Goodwinson. Fred Goodwinson. Call me Fred, here's my business card.'

'Well, how do you do Fred.' Paul smiled as he took the card and shook the man's hand. 'Now, what would you like to speak with me about?'

'A private matter, perhaps we can retire to the bar?'

Private? Paul thought. His radar really was bleeping now. The man might have looked all gentrified but there was something else. It was in the eyes. Always the eyes. An intensity of purpose that belied any sense of the kind or compassionate.

'A private matter, you say?' Paul smirked in that engaging way of his. 'Not the FBI are you?'

'No.' Goodwinson replied with a smile that appeared to have been brought out of cold storage and needed time to thaw properly. 'A business matter.'

'Ah, I see.' Paul mused as he looked at the name on the card: R&ZR Capital, Manhattan. 'Well then, perhaps my office would be the best place. More private. Please come with me.'

A few minutes later the two men were sitting in Paul's office.

Goodwinson was holding a glass of malt whisky which he had yet to touch. Paul hadn't poured himself a drink, he wanted all his wits about him. There was something dangerous about this man and he knew it. He also knew that the mysteries of the past few months might finally be cleared up.

'Er . . . Paul . . . ,' Goodwinson began, 'you may have noticed considerable movement in the share ownership of Treharne Holdings over the past few months?'

Paul's face went into immediate business mode. Tough and ready for anything.

'I have and before you go any further . . . Fred, the Treharne's 51% is not for sale. I repeat, not for sale and I don't give a flying fuck who you are, where you come from or who's behind you. No doubt you, whoever you are, now own 49% of the shares, well let me tell you now, that's as far as you are going to go.

'Treharne Holdings is not for sale and believe me I've encountered harder bastards than you in my time. Now fuck off out of my office and hotel or do I need to call security?'

Goodwinson remained still. He took a slow sip of his whisky. As he suspected this Paul Treharne was no fool but everyone and everything was for sale, sooner or later. Where Treharne Holdings plc was concerned it was just a matter of time.

'An unhelpful attitude Paul, if I may say so. My company is prepared to make you and your family an offer way above market value. You will all be very rich indeed.'

'We are already rich, Goodwinson. Now, I repeat fuck off out of my office.' Paul picked up the telephone on his desk. 'Get me security,' he growled into the mouthpiece.

At this point, Goodwinson finally stood up and walked to the door. Before opening it, he turned around and said, 'I fear you will regret this Paul, you do have a charming family after all. A great pity if anything . . . er . . . remiss should happen to one of them, don't you think?'

Paul immediately stood up. His squat frame moved surprisingly quickly for a man his age. Before Goodwinson knew what had hit him, a hand with the grip of a cast-iron vice had him by the throat.

'Now listen to me, you Yankee cunt. If anyone goes anywhere near my family, I'll personally see to it that you pay. Permanently. You're not the only master of dirty tricks and you had better believe it boyo. I didn't get where I am by being a fucking boy scout!'

Goodwinson was starting to go red in the face, as he choked for air. Paul finally relaxed his grip. 'Now, get out of here,' he sneered as he pushed Goodwinson through the door and onto the corridor floor.

The eyes that stared back at him, left Paul in no doubt that yet again the Treharne's were in a fight for survival and as usual there could only be one winner.

As he sat back down at his desk, he quickly reached for the Nitromin spray in his pocket. His heart didn't take kindly to sudden bouts of violence and at his age too!

CHAPTER 17

Goodwinson sat opposite his boss, massaging his neck.

'I told you they wouldn't give in easily, Dan.'

'I didn't expect them too. The Treharne's have quite a reputation.' Seloski's jowls looked particularly full today, Goodwinson thought. They seemed to be drooping further and further over his shirt collar every time he saw him. God the man was an ugly son of a bitch. 'It seems to me we have to apply more pressure.'

'I would counsel caution, Dan. Frankly, I have come to the conclusion that we can do without Treharne Holdings. They are too much trouble and whether you like it or not, they are a powerful family, both in the law and business. Not to mention Charlotte Treharne's government connections. They could give us a lot headaches. Is it really worth it, Dan?'

Seloski fell silent for a few moments, his small dark eyes seeming to turn in on themselves.

'Yes it is,' he finally confirmed. 'I want that company, it's as simple as that. So what if they want a fight. Let's give them one.'

Goodwinson still wasn't sure. 'How far do you want to go?'

'As far as we have to. If they can't be bought then other methods must be employed. Just get on with it, Fred.'

Goodwinson knew when his boss was beyond any kind of persuasion.

'Very well, Dan.' He said with a note of resignation, although not regret.

Later that day, Goodwinson was in his own office. Cell phones, land lines, emails, anything on paper or recordable was out of the question. He knew his trade.

One phone call from a cheap Pay As You Go cell phone which would be dumped later on, was as far as he was prepared to go. No details, just a few words which would be meaningless to anybody listening in.

As his chauffeur driven limo drove him home later that night, he was still massaging his neck. In some respects he had approved of his bosses decision, at least now he would have a chance to get even, and Christ wasn't he going to get even.

The Treharne's would be suffering more than sore necks by the time he was through with them.

CHAPTER 18

Charlotte, Joel and Paul were sitting down in Paul's office. The atmosphere was serious, this time there were no irreverent jokes coming from Paul or cynical remarks from Joel.

Just as Charlotte was about to speak, the door burst open.

'Sorry, I'm late all! Bloody weather, I'm afraid. The site is a quagmire and I had trouble getting the Land Rover to move. Never mind, I'm here now.'

Angharad Treharne, Charlotte's niece, as usual was all scruffy Barbour jacket with plenty of mud splattered all over it. Her jeans weren't much better and the hiking boots were even worse. She was in her early forties and as rebellious as ever, a typical Treharne with the good looks to boot underneath all the mud.

'How are things in the archaeological world, then Angaharad?' Charlotte asked as she hugged her niece.

'Old and messy, Lottie.' Angharad giggled.' Bit like me really! Now, what's this latest Treharne drama all about? You all look like a vicar who has just farted at a Welsh politician's funeral, not that that lot deserve anything less.'

'Sit down Angharad and for once be serious.' Paul ordered firmly. 'Treharne Holdings is under threat, allow me to explain.'

Paul told Angharad everything, including the attack on Charlotte. As the press had yet to get a sniff of the attack, no-one had deemed it necessary to inform Angharad. Security had to come first.

'So, who exactly are these people?' Angharad finally asked, as she smiled nervously and brushed some dirty blond hair out of her eyes. 'Have to admit, all this stuff is a bit beyond me. All men and mud me, as you know.' There was a worried expression on her face, if not fear. She had encountered violence only once in her life and that had been enough, thank you very much.

'Manhattan venture capitalist's,' Paul replied. 'They will massacre our chain of hotels, destroy everything we as a family have built up over the years. Strip every single asset that can be parcelled up and sold at a profit and treat our people, our staff, like dogs. We have always looked after our own, from cradle to grave. Profit hasn't always come first, not where our employees are concerned. America has worse problems with inequality in wealth than we do here in the UK, if they're not careful there really will be blood on the streets. God knows we're not far off it here.

'Does that answer your question, Angharad?'

'Oh' she replied quietly, she didn't know what else to say. This was not her world. All her adult life had been spent digging around for ancient artefacts and forgotten civilisations. She was learned and intellectually sophisticated, and yet the brutally of mankind never failed to astonish her. 'Are you saying that we are all in danger then, Paul? That these people will stop at nothing to achieve their ends?'

'No.' Paul replied. 'I'm not saying that. We at least now know who they are and we can fight back. The police have already been informed but frankly there's not much they can do. The threat by this Goodwinson man cannot be corroborated, and there is nothing to connect them to the attack on Lottie – yet. Joel is working on this. For now, we just have to be vigilant. All of us. These people are a different breed. They are utterly ruthless. Lottie is looking into their legal status, using her connections, maybe there is something there we can use.

'Like I say, for now we just have to be careful and watch our backs. I don't honestly believe that these people would be stupid enough to try anything physical on us. Threats are one thing, action quite another. We are a powerful lot in our own right and they must know this.'

Angharad seemed to look unconvinced. 'Are you sure, Paul? I mean really sure. Jesus Christ, all this is beyond me. I'm a dirt and mosaic merchant, not a fucking business woman or lawyer for that matter!' If nothing else Angahrad was her father's daughter. Kristian Treharne, now six foot under, had been a character and full of hell and his daughter was no different once her mettle was up.

The Treharne's just couldn't help it.

'As sure as I can be Angahrad but you know as well as I do, that life sometimes deals out unpredictable cards. Look, right now there's nothing for you to be unduly concerned about. The rest of us will deal with all this. Just make bloody certain you don't go flogging off any of your shares. In the meantime, keep an eye out for anything unusual and let Joel know if something is bothering you, ok?'

'There is still the possibility that someone one else is behind the attack on me.' Charlotte observed quietly. The other members of the family looked at her.

'What do you mean, Lottie?' Paul asked.

'In spite of what Joel thinks and indeed the Security Services, I refuse to rule out the possibility that Islamic terrorists were behind the attack on me, or for that matter some criminal who I have put behind bars in the past. Until I see concrete evidence to prove otherwise, as far as I am concerned, these other possibilities remain on the table.'

Joel looked at his wife and noted the firm set of her lips. He knew that expression, he also knew that nothing would change her mind. Once the lips went into set mode that was it. Nothing would budge her.

'Alright, Lottie,' Joel said, 'let's just suppose you are correct, it doesn't alter one jot the fact that the family business is in dangerous territory, does it? 'You're just going over old ground, Lottie. The fact is, we don't know who the hell it was who tried to kill us but we do know that some bastards are trying to take away the business and sell it off!' Joel was losing patience with his wife. 'Let's just deal with what we know for God's sake, everything else is just academic!'

Charlotte looked at Joel. He didn't often lose his temper, in fact such outbursts were extremely rare. He had always been the calm and collected one. The pressure must be getting to him, she quickly thought, as she immediately remembered Tricia Mayhew's reference to his age.

' Alright Joel, I'm sorry if you think I am being difficult but the Atallah case seems to be finally coming to an end and it looks as if the government will get its way.'

'What you mean Lottie,' Joel said drily, 'is that you and another judge have decided in the government's favour. Well, isn't this just going to help the situation?'

This time it was Charlotte's turn to get angry.

'Well, what the hell do you expect me to do, Joel? Give in to a bloody terrorist! The bastard is a mass murderer for God's sake!'

The other members of the family kept quiet whilst all this was going on. Charlotte and Joel were always sheer entertainment when they got going and they didn't give a damn who was listening either. The pair of them rarely agreed on anything. They would argue about two flies crawling up a window pane if it suited them.

'Alright, alright.' Paul interrupted. 'Can we keep the domestics for another time, please?'

Joel and Charlotte glared at each other. In a few minutes, it would be all lovey dovey time again. Their marriage thrived on conflict, it always had done.

'So, we are all agreed then?' Paul concluded. 'We keep a watching brief, this is all we can do for now. We are all also agreed that selling isn't an option?'

'Agreed.' Everyone replied in unison.

Later than evening, Paul was walking his two dogs along the sands of Three Cliffs Bay. He looked at the three cliffs that stood together in an uneven symmetry, as if unable to come to terms with the cards nature had dealt them. There was a stubbornness about them, even anger as they tried to reach up to a sky that wanted nothing to do with them. Glory? Majesty? Beauty? These were all fine words that as far as Paul was concerned were best kept to some daft Poets and Pints do at a local boozer. A few years back he had been fool enough to accept an invitation to one of these poetry do's. Dear God what a sorry lot these 'poets' were, he had concluded. All on the dole, all depressed or suicidal and all spouting the biggest load of self-indulgent crap he had heard in a long while.

He had always been suspicious of the arts, particularly the state funded variety but he could recognise the good stuff when he saw or read it. He wasn't as much of a philistine as he made out but neither was he one of those pretentious dullards who tried to convince everyone that they were the only ones with an intellect superior enough to recognise true shit.

He quickly gave up on his artistic musings and let his two dogs off the leash. One a greyhound, the other in Paul's words, a cross between a jackal and fuck all or if he was feeling polite, a Staffy and Border collie cross. He loved his two dogs more than the poetic bollocks that faced him now. He was all for enjoying the uneven drama around him and being absorbed by it, but to hell with using fancy words to describe it all.

The greyhound was as black as the skies that were about to open up and give him a bloody good soaking and faster than his wife's gob on a good day, and that really was saying something. It was always raining in Wales, always wet and yet as far as Paul was concerned this was the best time to walk around the bay. Cruel, unforgiving skies and plenty of rain kept people away. He would have the whole place to himself and thus be free to think without distractions.

The greyhound raced off after some seagull but Lucy, the part this and part that mongrel, stayed close. She was never far from her master's side. She followed him everywhere. Intelligent and responsive, Paul had never had cause to shout at her. She always did as she was told. The greyhound on the other hand, one Raven, was a different ball game altogether. A right royal lazy sod, who would eat lying down give half a chance. A law unto herself, Raven was the older of the two and Beth's favourite, not that his wife would ever admit it but then Lucy was Paul's pride and joy so there wasn't much he could say. He loved the bloody silly animal, well he loved both dogs but Lucy was just a little more special and she never answered back, argued or fuss arsed about things, unlike his wife.

There were times when Paul genuinely dreaded the thought of losing Lucy, it would be worse than Beth divorcing him. He could always get another wife but another Lucy? No chance. On second thoughts another wife really didn't appeal, one was enough for any man and Beth was all wife, bless her.

As he walked, his mind continued to trouble him. There was so much at stake. It wasn't about money, it wasn't even about power. The threat to Treharne Holdings was a threat to his very existence, his way of life.

It was emotional.

Paul had given so much to the business. In many ways more than the rest of the family put together. The business was him, it got him up in the mornings. He knew for a fact that if the business went, so would he. His doc had always been going on about him easing up on the stress, but Paul didn't see it like that that. For him, Treharne Holdings was a labour of love. It really was his life. He knew that without the challenges, the mental stimulation, he wouldn't last long.

Either his brain would succumb to critical senility or his heart would finally give up due to chronic bloody boredom.

As he watched Raven race around at 35 mph, the only time she did move was when there was something to catch, he knew he couldn't go on forever but he would die with Treharne Holdings intact and controlled by the family come hell or high water.

CHAPTER 19

The House of Commons Chamber echoed with cries of dissent, insult, mockery and of course the occasional bout of laughter. It was not a place for the feint hearted or for that matter those of a sensitive inclination and tending to worry about their self-esteem. It was a gloves off place where politicians could have an unrestrained go and quite right too.

There were some, particularly those in hard done by feminist circles who, rather like that Japanese soldier found in the jungle years after the ending of World War II and who still believed the war was going on, felt that the male bullying and aggression was all too much and should be banned. It was all such a frightful attack on female sensibility you see. In other words, democracy should no longer guarantee passionate debate and where necessary, unbridled verbal attack but should aspire to be a prissy little tea and cucumber sandwich get together where no-one would offend and where everyone would have a silky apology just waiting to appease and prevent pitiful tears of self-righteous but spineless boo-hoo offence.

As far as Tricia Mayhew was concerned and naturally in her private moments, these people were an affront to democracy and freedom of speech and if they found the Chamber too hot to handle then they should piss off and go and work for *Liberty* or something.

As soon as the Speaker had started going hoarse from yelling 'Order! Order!' too many times, Mayhew stood up and faced the Opposition benches. A bunch of emasculated Beaujolais Nouveau Day enthusiasts the lot of them as far as she was concerned.

'As you are aware, yesterday the Supreme Court delivered its judgement on the Abdul Mani Atallah case. He is to be deported back to his place of origin, Lebanon, as soon as is practicable.'

Before Mayhew could go any further there were the expected catcalls of 'Torturer!' 'What about human rights?!' on and on it went. Ignoring the tumult, Mayhew continued. 'It has been a long and tortuous process and one I must add, that has been a considerable drain on the public purse. It is the government's intention to enact legislation to stop this kind of legal gerrymandering in future.' More wails of outrage. 'The Human Rights Act has turned our judiciary into a Laurel and Hardy spectacular and I will not have it. Other countries have ignored the European Court of Human Rights, indeed over 8000 Strasbourg judgements have been ignored to date, without said countries turning into 'failed state' status, economically or otherwise.

'Our masters, the people, are demanding that this Human Rights farce be stopped in its tracks, and I am determined to make sure that we honour our obligations to the people, whether some in this Chamber like it or not.'

Mayhew sat down on the green leather bench behind her. This time the clapping and 'Hear, hears!' outgunned the shouts of dissent from the other side.

Another victory for Home Secretary Tricia Mayhew.

Another victory for Lady Charlotte Treharne.

Later that day, as Patricia Mayhew was being escorted to her ministerial Jaguar, a bullet smashed into her skull killing her instantly.

She was dead before blood started to pour out of the entry wound.

Her protection team had seen and heard nothing.

Walking casually away from the scene, the shooter smiled: the Brits were so easy to kill, so much for pretty, liberal politics.

CHAPTER 20

'Some breakaway Islamic group is claiming responsibility, Prime Minister. Unfortunately there are also two other groups of a similar profile claiming the same thing.'

The Head of the Security Services looked at Prime Minister Damien Carlton. For once, the Head was rattled. Normally a man of extreme self-control, the assassination of the Home Secretary had sent both himself and all the other British arms of security into a spin. Not since the IRA's mortar attack on 10 Downing Street back in 1991 had there been such a direct attack on the British political establishment.

Sir Henry Davidson pushed back his mop of silver hair with slim fingers that had only ever known pen and paper. A man of considerable distinction and ability in the opaque world of secrecy and on occasion's dirty tricks, he looked at the PM and waited for the questions that he knew must come.

'And who exactly is this "breakaway group", Sir Henry?' The PM asked calmly.

'An offshoot of Islamic State . . . we think.'

'And the others?'

'Frankly, anyone's guess.'

'I see Sir Henry, well thank you for being honest. In other words then, we have no idea, as is the case with Lady Treharne, correct? And thank God we've managed to keep that one quiet.'

'I'm afraid so, sir. For now anyway.'

'Your thoughts please, Sir Henry . . . off the record. You are the expert in these matters after all.' The PM smiled ruefully. 'It wouldn't surprise me if you have my own office bugged.'

'Perish the thought, Prime Minister,' Sir Henry smiled back. 'Now my thoughts . . . off the record. As with Lady Treharne, both attacks were sophisticated and professional. We are pretty certain foreign talent is involved. Islamist talent? Who knows, we simply don't have enough evidence, in spite of all the internet claims being made. Certain terrorist groups could just be exploiting the Home Secretary's killing, after all either way it's a massive propaganda coup for them, although note that to date none of them have declared responsibility for the Treharne incident. In both cases, the assassin has disappeared into the ether again. No trace, not even a hair.

'On the face of it, neither shooting falls into normal extremist territory be it organised, say ISIL (Islamic State of Iraq and the Levant) or local, British born and bred. There are simply none of the hall marks. There is one thing we can be pretty sure of though. The assassin or shooter, is a loner, a clean skin, which of course makes our job more difficult. To date we have been able to prevent a repeat of 7/7 or the operation of a terrorist cell comprising three or more people, but we are defenceless against some pathetic inadequate intent on murder and using extreme Islamist ideology to justify whatever crazy notions are going through his head. Frankly, where the random and unpredictable are concerned we are powerless.

'Is the same person responsible for both attacks? Answer: we can't rule anything out. Who is behind the shooter? Again, we can't rule anything out.'

'Perhaps they are just changing tactics, Sir Henry?' Carlton replied. 'Keeping us on the back foot? They're resourceful bastards as you well know and clever.'

'It's possible, Prime Minister. My instincts tell me that it is one shooter, as I say a loner if you will, the most dangerous of all terrorists. There's just one problem though, actually make that two. The forensics on the Treharne attack are now clear. The shooter didn't intend to kill. The ballistics are all wrong apparently. So there's this and the fact that no-one has claimed responsibility. There's been nothing, not even a whisper from GCHQ (Government Communications Headquarters) or anywhere else for that matter, and this includes all the other international security services. Nothing.'

'Charlotte Treharne has many enemies, Sir Henry. Personally, I've always liked the woman. I would have her in my Cabinet given half a chance. She's tough and yet I've always found her to be remarkably in touch with the people. Dig beneath the surface and well . . . I remember, not so long ago at some function or other, when she described herself to me as a 'social democratic Tory', if you can work that one out.

'Do you have anything concrete at all, on who is behind all this? I accept that where Treharne is concerned it's open season. Tricia? Most likely terrorists of whatever hue, they could even be a breakaway, die hard IRA splinter unit?'

'Indeed Prime Minister, we are not ruling anything out at the present time. Um . . .'Sir Henry paused as he collected his thoughts. This was going to be difficult. '. . . There is one other possibility.'

Carlton immediately picked up on Sir Henry's reservation.

'Go on,' Carlton urged, 'you quite obviously have something else on your mind.'

'Well, we have been keeping an eye on some old school back bench Labour MP's recently.'

'Have you now, within the law I trust Sir Henry?'

'Naturally, Prime Minister.'

Carlton refrained from asking any further questions. National security was sometimes best left to its own devices. Deniability was everything.

'Continue.' Carlton ordered.

'There are three opposition MP's, one a peer of the realm no less, who have been attracting our attention for over a year now. Champagne socialists you might say of the worse kind, if you will excuse the clichéd crudity. One of them is extremely wealthy, aristocratic background and so on. Well connected. The other two are out and out die hard ideologues. Marxist by inclination, frightfully working class but shrewd political operators and influential where the Unions are concerned. Dangerously so, in my view. They have been playing out their left of left wing views for years. Indeed the modern Labour Party views them as a liability but they still maintain high majorities in their constituencies.'

'Hold on here, Sir Henry.' Carlton interrupted. 'This is beginning to sound like Harold Wilson's bloody great black spiders in the corner of the room?'

'Please Prime Minister, allow me to finish.'

'Very well, but this had better be good. I'll have no truck with fanciful conspiracy theories.'

'Their views are shall I say, somewhat extreme even for the Labour party's more radical elements. They want a return to the pre-Thatcher days of wholesale state ownership and a state controlled economy, and believe me they are serious.'

'You have evidence to support these conclusions, Sir Henry?'

'We do.'

Again, Carlton knew better than to dig any further.

'Are you saying that they would go as far as assassination to destabilise the government? That's ridiculous.'

'Ridiculous? I think not Prime Minister.' Sir Henry replied cautiously. He knew this was going to be difficult. 'Politicians are no longer trusted. Capitalism has been discredited on a grand scale, the banks have seen to this. We still face financial turmoil for many years to come. Poverty is on the rise but more crucially the gap between rich and poor has become explosive and a focal point for social discontent, particularly amongst the urban working classes. The middle classes are also restive and they can be the most ferocious of all when they have the bit between their teeth. Anti-austerity has become the calling card of Marxist far left parties in other parts of Europe. Greece, Spain, Portugal, to name but a few and not to mention the rise of a left wing politics even in Germany.

'Both here and across the rest of the European continent an insidious nationalism is also being celebrated and the horrific lessons of history ignored yet again. Scotland and Wales are following suit in their determination to break up the United Kingdom.

'Also anti-Semitism both here and abroad is at record levels.

'There is a vicious struggle for dominion taking place between far right and far left political parties and both are gaining traction amongst the people, particularly the young. And America isn't immune, it is experiencing another Boston Tea Party, of a different political character perhaps but no less revolutionary and dangerous. Liberal dogma has become the battle cry of arrogant and unlistening righteousness, particularly in American academia. Catching 'em early has become a religion for their liberal left wing. As always the young are the assault troops, the cannon fodder, while their professors sit on top of out of range grassy hills, directing operations and grinning with glee at the carnage.

'This gang of three see an opportunity and if I may say so, it is not without merit. The political landscape here in the UK has been concentrating on the far right anti-immigration agenda, no-one is keeping an eye on the extreme left, and I'm not talking here about the metropolitan soft left liberal glitterati, who believe their views and opinions to be sacrosanct. I am talking about the re-birth of a Marxist socialism.

'The far left SNP in Scotland, the Welsh anti-austerity party in Wales, Plaid Cymru (the Party of Wales), the mad Green Party; anti-establishment parties they may be, but they are gaining support.

'They are under the mainstream political radar, apart from the SNP, one might even hazard that 21st century Western politics has forgotten all about them, and this is precisely where their strength lies. Their danger. The three I speak of have the financial means and in my view the motive, to carry out these deadly attacks on the State.'

Politics was about expecting the unexpected and not for the first time since the assassination attempt on Charlotte Treharne, a cold fear ran through Carlton's veins.

'So, you're telling me we have new 21st century fifth column in our midst?'

'I'm telling you that it's possible Prime Minister, and that it cannot be ruled out. As you well know, Islamophobia is becoming more and more toxic. There is the more recent outrage in Tunisia and Calais is becoming more and more of a security risk. The British people are starting to renege on their usual moderation. There is fear, a growing fear and the assassination of the Home Secretary has inflamed matters.

'I do not wish to sound alarmist Prime Minister but all my departments are reporting the same thing. The three I speak of, and no doubt there are more, see this rise in hatred and insecurity as an opportunity to create public hysteria and thus political mayhem. Conditions you will agree, that lend themselves to drastic political change, at least their kind of change.

'It might only take one more terrorist outrage for the people to finally snap Prime Minister, and what really worries me and you can mark my words on this, *there will be another outrage.*

'We in the security services, no matter what we do, no matter what the resources at our disposal, cannot possibly hope to defend the country against some suicidal terrorist maniac's intent on social chaos and murder.'

Carlton stood up from his desk. Early forties, he was one of the youngest Prime Ministers ever to hold office. His shirt collar was undone, no tie. He was the new, 21st Century breed of politician, Sir Henry Davidson observed. Good looking with an easy way about him, he enjoyed the essential qualities of being able to draw people in and make them see his point of view. He was TV and media friendly, a brilliant communicator, always smiling, always charming but Sir Henry knew there was another side. A ruthless, unforgiving side. One didn't become Prime Minister without having both in equal measure.

He led a centrist government with a small majority but nevertheless a democratic mandate to rule.

'Very well, Sir Henry. The country's terrorist threat level has already been raised to critical. I want the people who are behind all this, whoever they are. I want their heads on my desk fast, not yesterday not even last week. Tricia was not only a colleague, she was also a friend, a good friend Sir Henry. More to the point, I will not have law abiding citizens of the UK being slaughtered at will. The government is here to protect them, this is our duty and this is exactly what we shall do . . . at any cost. You have my full authority to do whatever it takes, just find them and neutralise them Sir Henry. No trials, no media circus.

'Do I make myself clear?'

'You do, Prime Minister.' Sir Henry replied quietly.

'The people are getting restive, frightened I know.' Carlton continued. 'No matter what we say, the politicians and media, no matter how many times we ask for calm, I can feel it in my guts that the people out there are at breaking point.

'Financial stress, terrorist carnage and the immigration 'diversity' illusion make an explosive cocktail. Hatred toward Muslim communities and of course ignorance, has been underneath the surface for a while now, justified or not. You know and I know, that most Muslims are peaceful and law abiding. They are a beautiful people, I know I have lived amongst them. The Koran teaches peace not violence. We both know too, that it is an extreme minority that is causing all the trouble and if there are some in Parliament who are trying to exploit this terror then they must be stopped . . . without mercy. There is also of course the anti-Semitic element to all this. Thousands of Jews are already moving out of Europe and back to their historical birth place.

'I too fear, that it will only take another atrocity to set off mass riots. Then, God help us a state of emergency will have to be declared and the army called in. Some cities in Europe have already had to mobilise the military and our friends across the pond believe they have licked Islamic extremism with their calm multi-ethnic integration?

'The Americans are being complacent. Extreme Islamic terrorism couldn't care less about integration or for that matter, assimilation. One would have thought they had learnt that after 9/11. If they think they are immune, they had better think again. Isolationism is a flawed premise, particularly in the small technological space we all now live in.

'You are of course aware, that contingency plans are in place for mass internment of our Muslim citizens, for their own protection as much as for ours.'

'I am, sir.'

'Let us hope then, that it doesn't come to this. It failed in Northern Ireland, I see no reason to suppose that it will succeed a second time around. Now, come along, we have a COBRA (Cabinet Office Meeting Room A – a civil contingencies committee which leads responses to national crises) meeting to attend. Oh and one thing Sir Henry, before we go. No-one and I mean no-one, must know about your suspicions where our very own MP's are concerned, apart of course from those who need to know. If the press got hold of the things we have just been discussing they would have field day and the consequences simply do not bear thinking about.'

'Yes, Prime Minister'. Sir Henry had been left in no doubt as to what he had to do. Decisive and unscrupulous when required, it was no wonder Carlton had got to the top of the tree.

The two men left Carlton's study with heavy hearts and a supressed anxiety that both could almost touch.

CHAPTER 21

'The Guardian newspaper is going soft, Mike. It's becoming more Tory than the bloody Telegraph.'

'Soft or just middle ground, John? It's the way of politics these days. The sons and daughters of Thatcher don't know anything else. Blair and Brown both sold us down the river with their third ways and look what we've got now? A spineless fourth way twat who wouldn't know a working class pay-packet from a bag of fish and chips.

'We've lost the voters who always counted on us, who founded the fucking party for Christ's sake. The working man has been sent to hell in a handcart.'

The two Members of Parliament, Michael Meechan and John Griffin, were sitting down in a greasy spoon café in one of Soho's side streets. Far away from the Westminster village and prying hacks.

'Mayhew's ambitions have come to an abrupt end then.' John Griffin said with a smile as he stopped reading the Guardian and looked at his friend, well 'friend' was probably pushing it, there was no such thing as friendship in politics, allies yes but friends . . . ?

Before Meechan could reply a man sat down opposite them. Tall, distinguished and with plenty of greying hair at the temples, he was immaculately dressed in a double-breasted chalk stripe suit, silk shirt and tie, handmade black brogues, topped off with a permanent expression on his refined face of sheer contempt for the lower classes.

'Gentlemen, could you not have chosen somewhere a trifle more salubrious?' George Eden remarked. 'Working class romanticisms are fine in their place, but really.'

'Oh shut your pie 'ole, Eden.' Meechan snarled in that offensive way of his. 'Now, what have you got for us?'

George Eden MP, came from true blue blooded stock. He had dropped his title upon discovering the virtues of a communist state. Karl Marx and Royal connections did not make easy bed mates, so in order to achieve a modicum of success as a politician he had opted for the Labour Party, without of course ever revealing his true political persuasions. Change had to be treated carefully, but he fervently believed that the country was now ripe for a born again socialism no matter what the cost.

Eden was a fanatic of the first order but a clever one and not to be underestimated. It was a pity the two working class MP's facing him were too stupid to recognise the fact. He nearly responded to Meechan with one of his best aristocratic sneers but thought better of it. He needed them, for now anyway.

Eton, Cambridge, London tailors and exclusive gentleman's clubs, Eden was a product of his background and upbringing but somewhere along the way he had gone rogue and he wasn't the first of his kind to do so.

An ideologue to his core and with an intellect that was so acute and finely tuned that most of his political brethren tended to give him a wide berth, to avoid being made a fool of if nothing else.

He looked at his two fellow MP's. Vulgarity in extremis he mused. In their middle sixties and older than him by a good stretch, they were political ruffians. Uncouth but nevertheless necessary. Cheap shiny suits, polyester ties, rubber soled shoes and faces that looked as if they had been hacked from some long gone coal face, their lack of breeding and secondary modern education was distasteful but he had no choice. For now anyway.

'Right, before we go any further,' Eden immediately took charge of the meeting, 'we are agreed on the view that in the present political climate, the people are ready for radical change. Islamist terrorism is making them vulnerable and scared. We must exploit this situation as much as we can to achieve our ends. We must stoke the fires in the press and media. Mayhew's assassination has provided us with an admirable opportunity, the media are already fanning the flames of extreme Islamist terrorism.

'The more hatred of Muslims we can incite the better. The people are ready for re-nationalisation. Particularly of the utilities, gas, electric, water, railways etc. As for the banks, well they are target No1. The people are sick of capitalist short term profit and monopoly, even if they don't understand it. Fed up of allowing the market to decide their futures and financial well-being. Tax evading greed and the widening gap between rich and poor has become the lightning rod for political change. Agreed?'

'Agreed. Fuck free markets and neo-liberalism shit. Look where it all got us?' Meechan responded without pause.

'This being the case,' Eden continued, 'we must up our game and quickly. We must start getting our colleagues truly on board. Our leader must be undermined and discredited whenever possible. We must do our level best to create as much political upheaval and chaos as possible. Once this is achieved we can move into the political vacuum that will undoubtedly result and achieve our aims: Destruction of the present capitalist model and culture of greed.'

'Fine words Eden, I'll give you that,' Griffin said, 'but what about all the other fuckers in the House? They'll need some convincing, you know what they're like. Holding on to their seats comes before principle.'

'They'll join us as soon as they see which way the wind is blowing don't worry about that. Like you say, holding on to their seats comes before principle. My own soundings tell me that at least 70% are already ripe for the picking. We'll get the party on our side, don't worry. Now then, both you and Michael have strong Union ties. You John, I believe are extremely friendly with the Police Federation. Now is the time to start using your influence to full effect. We need the Unions on board.'

'I don't think there's any problem there, Eden.' Griffin observed. 'Union leaders are champing at the bit for some payback time. We're pushing against an open door.'

'Good, but keep pushing all the same. We must leave nothing to chance.' Eden replied. There was silence for a few moments as all three men dared to allow themselves a future that hitherto they had only been able to dream about.

Griffin finally broke the silence. 'A stroke of luck that hard-nosed bitch Mayhew getting topped, wasn't it just. She had it coming if you ask me. Any idea who was behind it? The press is full of fucking silly conspiracy theories, the usual old garbage but it's not difficult to see that they've got nothing and this includes the government.'

'My contacts tell me that there is very little evidence to conclude who was behind the killing.' Eden replied carefully. 'No doubt the Government will continue to spin Islam being responsible, which suits our aims. Like I say, the more hatred that is stirred up against the Muslims the better. It just means more unrest, more opportunities for us, and more political instability.' He knew more than he was letting on but there was a limit as to how far he would take these pig ignorant morons into his confidence.

'So gentleman, for now we must leave events take their course. You both know what you have to do. Now I must go, a dinner engagement you understand.'

Meechan and Griffin looked at each. Bloody typical, for Eden's sort, it was always dinner or supper whereas for them it was 'tea'.

"Social mobility?" In your fucking dreams.

CHAPTER 22

'Dear God Joel, what is happening to the country? Tricia and I were close. We had been friends for years. I will miss her terribly. The brutality of her death leaves me cold.'

Joel looked at his wife. He wanted to calm her fears, wipe them all away but he knew he was powerless. Even in grief her beauty confounded him, as she tried to push her auburn curls away from the tears that wouldn't stop. This was the real Lottie, the sensitive, caring woman who took on all comers no matter what.

They were sitting in the Chelsea apartment. Normally the sitting room calmed with its gentle colours and easy furniture, but right now it all went unnoticed as a hectic confusion challenged them both.

Joel put his arms around his wife.

'My darling Lottie, I just don't know what to say. I really don't. I can only look after you, protect you with my life if I have to. There are things going on here that just don't make any sense.'

'Joel, I am frightened for the country. Our country. For law and order. Should this break down, then only anarchy will prevail. Saudi Arabian Wahhabism will have won, the worldwide Caliphate maniacs will have achieved their aims, and it's not only this. There is civil unrest in the air, hatred, I can feel it. We have lost all sense of certainty. This Islamic State has declared responsibility for Tricia's assassination. Whether this is true or not, is irrelevant. Perception is everything. The internet has a great deal to answer for.

'We cannot, must not, allow this to happen. As much as I hate to even consider it, but radical threats require radical responses. Reasoning and conciliatory objection has failed and yet we must not allow ourselves to sink to barbaric levels.

'We must not.

'How we reconcile a radical reaction whilst holding on to our principles of liberty, free speech and fair play is, at the moment beyond me. As you know, I have never agreed with the dismantling of habeas corpus or giving too much power to the state but now I'm not so sure. It is being mooted around the powers that be, that the mass internment of our Muslim communities may well be the only option.

'In other words, take away the liberty of citizens regardless of whether they are guilty of any crimes and even where there is an absence of evidential suspicion. And before you say it, the Attalah case was clear and unequivocal. The evidence was there in black and white, he was a murderer and a threat to our national security, no question.

'If we are not careful we will have another Guantanamo Bay fiasco on our hands. That awful place is a profound insult to the fundamental principles of common law and the foundations of a civilised, democratic society.

'I will never allow such a hideous abuse of an individual's right to a fair trial to take place while I sit in the Supreme Court. Holding someone without trial for years is anathema to me. It disgusts me and flies in the face of everything I believe in as a lawyer. The Americans have become nothing better than the very people they are trying to protect themselves from.

'Without the rule of law a society is nothing!'

'Alright Lottie alright. I'm no lawyer and you know if it was me I would fight them all bullet for bullet. Get boots on the ground, plenty of them, and have done with it. Either this or just let the whole lot fight it out amongst themselves without any Western interference at all.'

'That would result in the wholesale slaughter of innocent people and you know it, Joel.'

'Isn't this precisely what is happening now?'

Charlotte remained silent.

'As for the violent, lone wolf fanatic and suicide bomber,' Joel continued, 'you know as well as I do, there that is no protection. None. We live in a society of open streets and public places. Fertile ground for anyone determined to kill and maim without restraint.

'The Security Services can do their level best, but this simply isn't going to be enough, now that the terrorists have raised the ante. How the hell can they keep tabs on every bloody maniac running around our streets? It's impossible. Someone will get through our security again, you can guarantee it, Lottie.

'As far as I am concerned, the war really has reached our shores and there can only be one winner, come what may.'

Charlotte pulled away from her husband and looked him in the eyes.

'What about the future, Joel? What about people leading lives without fear or commuters travelling to work never knowing when a bomb or bullet will strike? What about parents and their children? The school runs, the play grounds, fairgrounds, the theatres, museums, all easy targets?

'Our fundamental sense of freedom of movement, of expression and liberty are under attack. Everything the West stands for, has developed over hundreds of years and not without paying an extremely heavy price, is under threat from an extreme few who merely contaminate the peaceful theology of a world religion. Perhaps we have become *too* spoilt in our affluence, in our taking for granted the good life and demanding everything yesterday?

'Look at politically correct farce or the suppression of truth, if you like. Where has it got us? Islamist extremism has been allowed to thrive and flourish because we who should know better have been cowards, scared of speaking out for fear of offending or upsetting the sensibilities of some crazy minority point of view. The judiciary and this includes me, the politicians, are right up there when the accusing chickens come home to roost.

'Outspoken I may be Joel, but believe me there have been many, too many, times when I have kept quiet, when I should have spoken out, to my eternal shame I may add.

'God help us, is all I can say.'

'I wouldn't beat yourself up about anything on that score, my darling.' Joel said gently, as he kissed her cheek. 'You are a courageous woman Lottie, always have been. You have spoken out more times than I can remember when most have hidden behind veils of apology and timidity. You have absolutely nothing to upbraid yourself about. Nothing. Do you hear me?' He placed one of her hands in his. He knew only too well that his wife for all her strengths and capabilities, suffered from self-doubt and insecurity on occasions. She was a human being after all, a fact that sometimes the press and those not personally involved with her tended to forget.

'Now Lottie, to change the subject, have you turned up anything on these R&ZR Capital people?'

'I've made some enquiries and called in a few favours, yes. There are plenty of powerful people out there who know better than to get on the wrong side of me.'

'I don't doubt it, Lottie.' Joel grinned.

'Well, at the moment I'm waiting for them to get back to me. I can tell you that R&ZR are big players on Wall Street. There have been rumours about the CEO, one Dan Seloski. An unsavoury and ruthless character I'm told. Dangerous. I presume you have yet to unearth anything to connect them to the attack on us, Joel?'

'Nothing.'

'Well then, we must wait and see what my own endeavours come up with. This Seloski man apparently has a lot of enemies, I'm told. There are plenty of people in the financial world who would relish his downfall, so we may well discover something useful. The man certainly has a reputation for being unscrupulous and sailing close to the legal wind but to date the American financial authorities have been unable to make anything stick.'

'Very well Lottie, but let's not take too long about it please. You are still in danger and don't you forget it.'

CHAPTER 23

Jolyan and Adina were in the throes of a first love, in other words they couldn't keep their hands off each other. It was sex, sex and more sex, anytime, anyplace and anywhere. Practise makes perfect and they were certainly getting plenty of it.

It was after one such bout of body fluid exchange and greedy skin eating, that they lay exhausted in Jolyan's bed. A knock on the apartment door suddenly brought them to their senses.

'Who can that be, Jolyan?' Adina asked as she sat up, her perfect nakedness unashamed and poetic without the self-pity. 'You're not expecting anyone are you?'

'No. I'm not. God, I hope it's not my mother! She's pulled tricks like this before, turning up unannounced. Stay there Adina, I'll go and see who it is. It's probably someone from the company checking up on me. Bloody mother!'

Jolyan jumped out of bed and threw on a bath robe. A moment later he was looking at Al on the small closed cicuit TV screen.

'Oh, it's you Al.' Jolyan said into the intercom. 'I thought it was my mother or one of her spies. Come on up.'

Jolyan was indeed surprised to see his friend. Al never came around to the apartment without arranging something first. Spontaneity wasn't his style and as far as Jolyan could see, this applied to just about everything else in his life too.

Al walked in without saying anything. As usual, smiles of greeting were absent, there wasn't even a friendly 'Hello'. Sometimes Jolyan wondered what kept their friendship going, if it could even be called that. Wasn't friendship supposed to be all about give and take? Sharing, support and the exchanging of confidences? Al didn't seem to need any of these things.

'What's up, Al?' Jolyan asked in his usual casual and friendly way. 'Must be something for you to pop around here unannounced.'

Before Al could answer, Adina waltzed into the room with nothing but a towel wrapped around her naked body.

'Hi Al. How are you?' Adina asked, unconcerned by her towelled immodesty.

'Oh, er . . . look I'm sorry for the . . . um . . . intrusion.' Al stuttered, as if this was the first time he had ever seen a young woman half naked. 'I'll . . . er . . . come back later.'

'Oh don't be silly Al,' Jolyan said, 'we were just having an afternoon nap. Now sit down, can I get you something to drink. A Coke, a coffee?'

Suddenly Al's voice hardened. Jolyan was used to his moods but there was something different about the expression on his face. There was a rigidness he hadn't seen before as Al's eyes sliced straight through him.

'No thank you, Jolyan.' Al said curtly as his eyes quickly looked at Adina then darted back to Jolyan. 'Look, Adina shouldn't be wandering around like that in company. It's wrong. It's indecent. I'll see you at the café tomorrow. Frankly, I find the way you and Adina behave quite disgusting. You should be ashamed of yourselves.'

With that he walked out without saying another word.

Jolyan remained where he was, his jaw starting to drop with shock. 'What the hell was all that about?' He said as he turned to Adina, who looked as bewildered as he did.

'Don't ask me, Al should chill out if you ask me. I've told you before Jolyan and I know he's your friend and all that, but he really does give me the creeps. The way he looks at me sometimes is really quite unsettling. There's something not right there. He's not gay is he? After all I've never seen him with a girl, certainly since we've been together.

Come to think of it, I've never seen him with a boy either. Weird.'

'Gay?' Jolyan replied. 'I don't think so. At least I've never noticed anything. On the other hand you are right, he's never shown much interest in girls, almost seems frightened of them. I've always put it down to shyness, I mean not everyone is a confident sod like me are they?'

'No they are not, Jolyan,' Adina smiled. She then undid the towel wrapped around her body and let it drop to the floor. 'Come on, let's go back to bed, to hell with Al. If he wants to behave like a child that's up to him. We have more important things to do, like trying out a different position or two!'

Adina's body would brook no argument. Her full breasts stared at him, the dark nipples ordering his penis to attention. There was nothing he could do. Her hips and waist, discreetly lavish in intent, demanded touch and tongue. There was nowhere else to go.

He took Adina's hand and led her back to the bedroom. He would find out what Al wanted tomorrow, right now, touching and kissing the girl he loved was far more important.

Adina had always rejected the so-called glory of the female form resembling the emaciated tragedy of a drug addict or the anorexic wisps of flesh that pranced around the pages of fantasy fashion magazines and flashing catwalks. She believed that a woman should look like a woman, not a boy whose buttocks disappeared into one long streak of bone. She loved her curves. Her breasts were perfect, round and firm, without any hint of collapse. Her waist was narrow and sculptured by a master into buttocks that could make any man plead for mercy.

She was an unapologetic specimen of femininity. A young woman with a will of her own, determined and with a body that would stretch the imaginations of most men. She knew where she was going but more importantly for her world of online culture, love and sex, she knew who she was and she knew how to give and take.

As she gripped Jolyan's back and dug her tongue into his, she gasped with the sheer delight of it all. She just couldn't let go of Jolyan's lips as they both began to realise that a kiss could be more intimate and stimulating than sex itself. They were fixed in a sensory hiatus of craving, where love transcended all things, all emotions and all intentions.

They were one as their bodies joined together in a piquant, ridiculous dream that both believed would go on forever.

Never to be forgotten, never to be resisted.

Later that night, Jolyan and Adina were walking back to the apartment. Over a few drinks, they had decided that Adina should move in with Jolyan once and for all. They were both aware that this could only ever be a temporary arrangement but being young and in love, the future could go and hang itself.

They had yet to realise that love needed more than touch and kiss.

As they were walking along the pavement, some late night drinkers were falling out of a bar behind them. They were making so much noise that Adina stopped to see what was going on. In the split second it took her to turn her head, she saw two huge headlights coming straight at them.

There was no doubt in her mind that they were in immediate danger.

'Look out!' she screamed as she pushed Jolyan up against a wall, her own body crashing into his as she did so. The vehicle missed them by a hair's breadth as it raced off down the quiet street. All Adina saw as the vehicle disappeared from view, were the red brake lights of what looked like a black 4x4.

'That that was a close shave, Adina.' Jolyan just about managed to mumble. 'The bastard could have killed us. What the hell was he playing at? Drunk no doubt.'

Still in shock, Adina whispered, 'I don't think so, Jolyan. I saw him coming straight at us. It was intentional.' Jolyan looked at her, her deep brown eyes and face, serious and frightened. He immediately took her hand and put his arms around her. God, what if she had been hurt or worse killed? It was typical Jolyan to ignore his own well-being.

'Don't be silly now, Adina.' Jolyan said as calmly as he could, albeit that he was as shaken as she. 'It was just some boozed up idiot trying to find his way home that's all, no harm done is there?'

'Jolyan, for God's sake the driver came right at us!' Adina shouted. 'He mounted the pavement! He was trying to kill us for fuck's sake!'

'Calm down, Adina. Please calm down.' In a split second the attempt on his mother's life came back to him with a vengeance. No, there couldn't be any connection, surely? He hadn't told Adina anything about the attack on his mum. She knew something of his background, what his mum did and so on but not much more. Jolyan was not secretive by nature, it simply hadn't entered his head to go into the all the detailed ins and outs of his family. Why would he?

'We must go to the police, Jolyan.' Adina insisted. 'We must!'

Jolyan immediately, more by instinct than design, decided that this was not a good idea. He knew that any contact with the Portuguese police would result in his mother knowing about the incident within a few hours and this was the last thing he wanted. Before he knew it, he would be escorted on to a British Airways flight back home and he sure as hell wasn't about to leave Adina – for anyone. Besides, he couldn't help feeling that she was exaggerating things a bit.

'I don't think that's a good idea, I really don't Adina.' Jolyan tried to sound firm but as soon as he looked at her his voice wavered. He hated seeing her so scared. 'I still think it was a drunk driver. For a start why us? We're a couple of nobodies.'

'I might be Jolyan but you're not,' Adina interrupted. 'Your mother is a Supreme Court judge, I've been reading up on her. Quite a woman I have to say and from what Google tells me, she's upset a lot of people. We must go to the police.'

'Have you now.'

'Oh don't be stupid Jolyan, of course I did some Googling. Your family has a worldwide reputation, what else did you expect? Apart from anything else, I'm entitled to know what I'm getting myself into, aren't I?' Suddenly Adina's voice softened. 'You're very modest though, I'll say that for you and not at all spoilt.'

It hadn't taken Adina long to get a grip on herself. The panic and fear had almost totally evaporated, instead there was a slow aftershock of relief that neither of them had been hurt.

'Alright, alright.' Jolyan replied with a note of resignation in his voice. 'Being as you're such a bloody smart arse, what do you propose telling the police anyway, have you thought of that? Neither of us has been hurt in any way. Did you catch the number plate or even the make of car . . . ?'

Adina slowly began to realise that Jolyan was right. What *could* they tell the police? Nothing, that's what. A black 4x4 maybe but that was it. It had all been too quick for her to catch the number plate or even for that matter be sure about the make of vehicle.

She couldn't help herself but some untidy tears starting rolling down her cheeks. This was the first time Jolyan had seen her cry, and he hated it. All he wanted to do was protect and shield her. He held her tight, not quite knowing what to say. He had seen female tears before, but this was different. This time they cut him to shreds and left him feeling so utterly useless.

'Come on Adina,' he said gently, as he touched her tears and took her hand. 'Let's go back to the apartment. A glass of your favourite wine won't do you any harm.'

Adina looked at this British boy who had somehow managed to capture her heart. She squeezed his hand and said, 'Yes, that sounds like a good idea. Come on then, let's get away from this awful place.'

'Oh and one thing Adina. Not a word about this to anyone. My mother will go nuts if she hears about it, so no telling friends or family and no internet stuff, ok? Promise?'

'Promise, Jolyan.' Adina replied reluctantly, although she still wasn't sure whether someone had just tried to kill them or not.

CHAPTER 24

Dan Seloski looked at his swimming pool.

This was as near as he ever got to an actual swim, looking that is. He puffed away on a cigar that made his face look smaller than a pin head, which was quite a feat bearing in mind the size of his fat-filled jowls and neck the size of a side of beef.

There was something about the shimmering ripples of the water that always forced Seloski to remember. He didn't like looking back, it served no useful purpose and yet there were times when he couldn't resist it. He had loved once. Christ had he loved. He had been sixteen the other boy seventeen. There had been two summers of passion and glorious infatuation, until his God fearing Mormon parents and community found out.

Cruelty and ferocious religion had driven him out and away from the place he had once called home. Away from the boy he had loved so much.

He had never forgiven.

The bitterness had brought him untold wealth and power. He had bought up all the land where his persecutors had thrived and eventually evicted them all without mercy. For a moment he smiled, it was a rare and momentary concession to his own humanity. Brief but there.

The fake Italianate glory that surrounded him now left him cold. The mansion, a simple tax dodge, sprawled across five acres of top drawer Los Angeles real estate. Ten bedrooms, fifteen baths, gyms, tennis courts, you name it and none of it used. Seloski vaguely considered the fact that the estate also had three guest houses and parking for thirty cars. For a moment, a sneer forced his lips to bend in a way that shifted some of the fat around, bringing it some light relief if nothing else.

"Guests," he pondered. Suckers more like. He hated people. Take that Bernie Madoff, he had known him personally in the early days. The man had been a fool then and even bigger fool in later years. He had committed the cardinal sin of being caught out so he deserved all he got, as did all the other stupid sons of bitches who had fallen for his bullshit.

Seloski walked away from the swimming pool and into a vestibule that would have shamed the most extravagant outrages of Cosimo de Medici. It was bloated with crystal chandeliers highlighting loud, uncouth frescoes of flouncing twentieth century celebrity, intended to declare and announce the echoes of a mockery that never kept still and celebrated the obscenity of such fierce decadence.

Seloski didn't give a shit. Fuck people. If they were too weak to make it, tough.

A servant who was only occasionally seen and certainly never heard, appeared from nowhere.

'There is a call for you, sir. Mr Goodwinson.'

'I'll take it in my study.' Seloski replied. The only thing he had ever studied were share prices, even so he liked the room. The walls lined with books and old world oak were somehow comforting, not that he really knew what this meant and as for the books, he didn't even know what their titles were, let alone what they were about.

'What is it, Fred?' Seloski said in that abrasive way of his.

'The Treharne's, Dan. We've made another more than generous off, they won't move. If we go any higher the whole project becomes seriously untenable. What do you want me to do? And before you say it, we have tried er . . . More subtle forms of persuasion. Nothing doing.'

'Right, let me think about it. I'll get back to you.'

Seloski banged down the phone. Who did these fucking people think they were?! No-one defied Dan Seloski, no-one. They were going to pay for this and pay in a big way. A few moments later he rang Goodwinson back and gave his orders.

CHAPTER 25

'Ask Khunti to collect me at the office in five minutes, will you please Jane? Oh and take Lucy over to Beth when you have a minute.'

Paul replaced the telephone and put some papers into a briefcase. He looked down at Lucy who was in her favourite place underneath his chair; wherever Paul went Lucy went too. As soon as he went for his briefcase the stupid dog would know something was up and go into one of her anxious states. It was always the same, ears back and eyes begging for some reassuring deliverance. It never worked of course, but like all females she would try it on all the same.

Paul had a meeting with their London bankers that evening. He had made sure that Treharne Holdings had nothing whatsoever to do with the Welsh Labour government or for that matter Welsh business organisations. The former could run a sweet shop into bankruptcy in quick order and the latter didn't fart without taxpayer subsidy backing them up and thus were in the pockets of those Labour clowns in Cardiff Bay, even the multi nationals didn't 'invest' in Wales unless they received ridiculous tax breaks and grants. It was pathetic, unsustainable bribery all along the way and when the gravy train stopped, as usual all these companies would take off back to where they came from.

There had been a time when Paul had considered building a hotel in Cardiff Bay. Initial discussions with the Welsh government had made him run a mile. The officials had all come from Welsh university madrassas, where Welsh speaking nationalism was all that mattered and where their knowledge of basic business practice could have been written on the back of a stale Welsh cake.

When they had started comparing his financial projections to the score board at some international rugby match, he had walked out in disgust, never to return.

Wales had become a taxpayer junky, no-one moved unless the taxpayer paid for it. Chronic dependency was the name of the game. It sickened Paul to see what had happened to Wales since devolution. The principality was now run by a Welsh speaking elite who believed the world stopped at the Severn Bridge and who were intent on taking Wales back into the Dark Ages.

Would Wales ever flourish, would it ever aspire to genuine entrepreneurial ambition and innovation?

Not in his life time or his children's Paul concluded, all of whom had done the sensible thing and refused to seek a career in Wales. None of them would have got very far anyway – they were too anglicised and didn't speak Welsh.

None of the Treharne children had ever been allowed to go anywhere near a Welsh school, be it English or Welsh medium and for good reason. The Welsh education system was a disgrace, full stop. All it did was celebrate failure.

Thinking about Wales was depressing Paul finally decided, so he tried to think about something else while he waited outside the office for his driver.

Colin Khunti had been with Paul for more than twenty years. From Tipton in the West Midlands, Khunti was a mix of yam yam Black Country and Hindu Vishnu. Most of the time, he wasn't sure what the hell he was but he did maintain certain standards. One of them being "Any hole, is a goal!" He fancied himself as the only truly authentic, lady killing Boy Bander in town, albeit that his hair, or at least the odd wisp of it, had gone as grey as a badgers arse and had receded all the way back to the nape of his neck.

Only once in his life had a woman been daft enough to marry him. One week after the wedding the bride had discovered Khunti in bed with another woman, three times her size (and she wasn't petite by anyone's standards), with a hair lip and no teeth. In quick order, Khunti's few belongings were dumped in some black refuse bags and thrown out of an upstairs window.

Divorce had quickly followed but Khunti being the resilient sort, had merely refined his "Any hole is a goal" motto to excluding toothless women. He had at least learnt something then, although it should be noted here that even in late middle age he would certainly not be considered as the discerning type when it came to his choice of female companionship.

Before long a classic 1960's bright red 3.8 Jaguar pulled up in front of Paul. Jaguars had been his choice of vehicle for as far back as he could remember. He had always found the Mercedes' and BMW's of the world a trifle uncouth and flawed by an unrelenting, nouveau riche dilettantism.

Seconds later Khunti jumped out of the driver's side.

'Yum ready then boss?'

'Oh Christ, speak English will you Khunti? Any more 'yum' this and 'yum' that and you'll be out on your arse. Now come on, I'm late already. The station, fast.'

As always, Khunti met the rebuke with a grin that was irresistible. 'Don't start now boss, you know you'd be lost without me. Anyone else would have you up before an Employment Tribunal before you could say "Yum, yum fucking Black Country!"

'Station it is then.'

Khunti was wearing a check shirt hanging out of his trousers, jeans and trainers. Before Paul got into the passenger seat, he said, 'most men, when they've just had a bowel movement, tuck their bloody shirts back into their trousers Khunti. Jesus, I'm not going anywhere with you looking like that, you bloody oaf!'

'Ahh get in now boss. It's the fashion.'

'Fashion?! You look a right idiot. Now tuck your shirt in or you're sacked! Oh and what's this I hear about you having a tattoo inscribed on your arse? Dear God, you're nearly sixty?'

'Body . . . um . . . something or other they call it, boss. Only a small one, a heart with an arrow going through it.'

'Original then? And what's the point in having one done if you can't see it?'

'For the ladies boss, you know, gives 'em something to talk about when all the work is done, if you know what I mean.'

'Oh I give up. The last 'lady' I saw you with, would have needed a face transplant and a violent dietician to make her look even half presentable. She was an absolute bloody disgrace, Khunti. I don't know how you do it, I really don't.'

'Well boss, its simple enough. The more beers I drink the prettier they look. There's always the morning of course but I'm gone before daylight, so no harm done eh?'

'Indeed not, now can we go? I have a train to catch.'

Colin Khunti was far more than an employee of Treharne Holdings. He had become a firm and loyal friend to its CEO, thus the familiarity he was able to exercise without restraint. He watched Paul's back with a handy pair of ready fists and a manly love that knew no boundaries. Paul Treharne had given him a chance all those years ago when no-one else would even look at him. Boozed out and down and out, Paul had given him back his dignity, hauled him out of the hell he was living in and given him back his life.

Khunti would risk everything for Paul Treharne if he had to, no questions.

Just as Paul was about to get in the car, Jane his personal assistant came rushing out of the office.

'Mr Treharne! Mr Treharne! Stop, please stop!' Jane was in a state, not like her at all Paul quickly observed, she was always extremely calm and collected. She had to be working for him.

'What on earth is the matter, Jane? Now calm down and tell me what's wrong?'

'It's Mrs Treharne, she's in a terrible state. She just called the office looking for you. You must go home straight away. I couldn't quite make out what she was talking about. She seemed so upset but I think something awful has happened. You really must go home, Mr Treharne. Now.'

Paul knew his PA well enough that if she said something was wrong then it most certainly was.

'Come with me Khunti and Jane, if I'm longer than fifteen minutes ring London and postpone everything, alright?'

'Yes, of course Mr Treharne.'

With that they took off to the apartment. Beth could be a bit of a drama queen now and again, but phoning his office direct was unusual, it was usually nag by message. As he tried to run to the apartment his chest started to hurt but he ignored it as a deep sense of foreboding cut into his stomach. If those Yankee bastards had hurt his wife then it really would be war, money no object!

When he pushed open the kitchen door, Beth was sitting on the floor sobbing her eyes out. She couldn't speak to him, all she could do was point to the table in the middle of the room. He followed her fingertip and stopped right in his tracks.

There was blood all over the table's surface, some of it had started to drip onto the floor.

Right in the middle of this horror, was their greyhound's hacked off head.

In a few split seconds Paul pushed all emotion aside. There would be time enough for this later.

He turned around and faced Khunti. 'You clean up here while I see to Beth. Not a word to anyone about this Khunti, understand? Not even Jane. As far as anyone else is concerned, Raven just passed away suddenly. Got it?'

'Understood, boss. Do you want me to look for . . . er Raven?'

'Yes, you can try but I doubt you will find anything. Whoever did this must have taken her from the garden without Beth realising. I doubt they will have left any evidence anywhere, they will be long gone.' With that, Paul went over to his wife and gently picked her up from the floor, shielding her eyes from the table as he did so.

'Come on Beth, my love.' He coaxed. 'Let's get you away from all this'. Beth was still sobbing and beside herself with shock and grief. Raven had been her companion for eleven years. There first thing in the morning and there last thing at night.

'Who . . . who could do such a thing Paul? Who . . . who could hurt my lovely girl like this? Who, for pities sake?!'

Paul knew but said nothing, instead he sat Beth down in the sitting room and poured her a neat whisky. 'Drink this Beth, in one go please' His wife did as ordered. She didn't know what else to do.

He let her cry her eyes out as he sat next to her and held her hand. As he came to terms with what had just happened, he knew that now was not the time to think about reaction and what to do next. He was too shrewd an operator to make decisions at a time of extreme anger and emotional stress.

This terrible event demanded cold eyes and an even colder heart.

For now he would comfort Beth and bring her round to accepting what had just happened to her precious Raven. He knew this would be difficult as he couldn't tell her what he knew. He had always kept Beth away from Treharne Holdings, not for any reasons of secrecy or exclusion, it was just that he believed in keeping his business and home life separate.

When he opened the door to their apartment, he was firmly closing the door on Treharne Holdings. Beth, his home life and his privacy kept him sane. It was a rule that had never been broken until now.

R&ZR Capital had hurt his wife, a Treharne, and brought business into his home.

There had been many occasions in the past when powerful people had tried to harm his family. They had lost and suffered the consequences. These American bastards were no different.

They would suffer, by Christ would they suffer.

CHAPTER 26

There was a time when Paul had enjoyed the frantic indifference and chaotic unknown of London's shifty streets and the tortured history that lurked around every corner ready to pounce.

Now he detested the place.

There was a ruthless, cruel and inhuman magnetism about the metropolis that left him cold. On a daily basis he dealt with the London business world, its people. He knew they would wine and dine him one minute, cut his throat the next. It was no wonder he had refused to move out of Wales. He may have deplored its politics but its beauty calmed, and its people were softer, gentler and more inclined to kindness than brutal avarice.

London had changed.

It was now a confused miasma of vicious intent Paul concluded, run by a soft left, politically correct bunch of simpering degree holding do gooders, who loved criminals, tree hugging and immigrants. The London media was no different. Its effete hacks and staffers were exactly the same as the very people they were supposed to scrutinise and hold to task: middle class, Oxbridge, smug and nauseatingly self-righteous; they had no idea how the real world and real people worked outside the bubbled-up obscenity of Westminster and the Home Counties.

The United Kingdom had become a battleground of London against the rest and it was usually the rest that lost out. The sweet talking lefty Bolsheviks, Bowel bashers and Cunts (the BBC and BBC Wales in particular), was a public broadcasting disgrace and an affront to the common man, as were the rest of the bleeding heart liberal commentariat, who pontificated from unrepentant, empathyholic towers of intellectual elitism and a sickening belief that they were the Chosen Ones and in the vanguard of a new Politically Correct Enlightenment.

Of course, your average Joe had no idea what they were going on about and Paul knew it. He may well be a wealthy man but he had started out at the sharp end, no father helping to bring him up but with a mother who had loved, cared and fought.

He despised this new breed of London puppet masters who slithered around in Islington and Hampstead, who knew fuck all about real graft and fuck all about the people they dared to speak and write about; who lionised self-pity, victimhood, pathetic public emoting and grand standing 'entitlement' for all.

As he walked along the platform in Paddington Station he took out some written directions that Jane had given him earlier. He used a mobile phone but only when he was away from home. He was always within easy reach of the office, so had managed to avoid becoming a victim of technical domination. All this 'App' stuff was beyond him, instead he relied on his PA to do all the computer stuff and more to the point, provide him with directions that he could easily access – like the written word on the piece of paper that he now held in his hand.

As far as he was concerned the modern internet world was something to be feared and he genuinely believed that one day there would be a price to pay. A high price, he only hoped to God that he wouldn't be around to see it, his children would though and this disturbed him even more.

Man was creating a monster, the likes of which had never been seen before. One day it would turn and eat him alive.

He arrived in Paddington's main concourse and stopped. It must be age he thought. How could a man change so much in his disposition toward a city that in many ways was so like every other? He remembered his days as young man, when London had been a scathing opportunity for adventure, girls and booze. His father, when he had finally decided to show his face, had sent him there to learn about business, to learn about life. Paul had played hard and worked hard for a few years:

He had learnt.

Now though, the world had changed and he hadn't. He was aware of this but still he refused to bend, to play the game. He realised that he had been softened by the peace of a rural life, albeit a life that was constantly in the middle of unrestrained financial grandiloquence. He was also aware that his determination to remain apart made him the subject of youthful mockery. He was probably being mocked right now by all these flash London bastards walking passed him with bits of metal welded to their bloody ears, what with his piece of paper and bashed up old leather briefcase.

Who the fuck used paper these days? He could hear them sneer as they waded through lives of complacent idiocy. Didn't they realise that happiness usually demanded the human touch?

Paul felt intimidated if not slightly scared by the crowds, the people and their inability to see beyond their mobile phones and themselves. Their tiny, insignificant lives had suddenly been given a counterfeit validity through the conduit of a cruel, computerised pseudoscience that would one day be their downfall.

As he walked to the taxi rank, two young men brushed passed him. They were holding hands and chattering away like two old crones in Swansea market. Their high pitched voices, ballerina style body language and feminised exaggeration nearly stopped Paul in his tracks.

What the hell was going on, he almost pleaded? Boys trying to be girls, girls trying to be boys, it was all too much.

The world had gone mad. Bloody great pansies he thought, they all needed a kick up the arse, on second thoughts if he tried that he'd probably lose his shoe!

Young men had become so feminised, so female. Their sissy, compliant ways and creeping appeasement of female domination made him sick, and not to mention the fact that they now took longer to dress than their girlfriends. It was all the cosmetics they used apparently.

Christ.

In a state of utter confusion, he finally found the certainty of a black cab and jumped in, thanking God as he did so that he didn't have the slightest trace of a Welsh accent. If this had been the case, no doubt he would have be given a tour of London's side streets and charged a hundred quid for the privilege.

He gave his destination and off they went, well this sod had better not try it on because Paul knew exactly where he was going and the best way to get there.

Charlotte was sitting at a corner table in a swanky West End restaurant. As soon as she saw Paul, she stood up and held out her arms.

'How are you then, Paul? Come here and give me a hug!' Paul did as he was told, Charlotte was always ordering, sometimes he obliged sometimes he didn't.

As always he couldn't resist her smile, maturity and age had somehow enhanced her beauty. Gone were the pristine fads of youthful hope, instead she had managed to exploit a new beginning in wisdom and perception and it showed in the gentle lines around her mouth and eyes. He knew that she had never fallen for the bloated, lippy confidence tricks of Botox or the absurd scams of cosmetic butchery and celebrity insecurity.

As always Charlotte was dressed in a way that only sea-soned beauty could get away with. A tailored navy blue suit that accentuated her curves without throwing them in everyone's faces. Paul suddenly remembered her brother's nick-name for her. Dear old Kristian, a character if there was now sadly gone, had always called her 'Bigjugs'. The nickname was still used by the family now and again if only to make sure that Charlotte never forgot where she came from. In fairness though, she would always laugh along with the rest of them.

Paul noticed a handy looking chap sitting on his own at a table two doors away from Lottie's. He had been warned.

After a genuine kiss on Charlotte's cheek, neither of them were into all this lingering air blowing crap, they sat down. A waiter arrived at their table with a couple of menus and a carafe of iced water.

'Before we get down to business Paul, how is Beth? That was awful, how low will these people sink? A dumb animal for God's sake? I assume you believe it's this R&ZR lot?'

'I haven't got over it yet Lottie, if you must know. I loved that dog. That's the trouble, we get so attached to the silly animals whilst at the same time knowing full well that we will probably out live them. Beth and I have decided not to have any more after Lucy. Who would look after them when we are gone? We're both old after all. As it is, I couldn't bear the thought of Lucy being with someone else. There's no-one out there who knows her the way I do. Damn, I'm getting all maudlin over a dog! Now I don't really want too talk about it, it's still a bit raw Lottie.'

'Understood.' Charlotte said quietly. She loved dogs too, she would have had a house full of them given half a chance but the life she and Joel led just wouldn't have been fair on them. Maybe one day, when they were both retired. If that day ever came.

'Now Lottie, to come back to your question about R&ZR. I might have rubbed the odd dull bugger up along the way but I've never really hurt anyone, as you well know. Our company has been built on integrity and honesty, I don't have to tell you that. It's them alright.'

'Mmmm . . . Well, we had better order don't you think? I'm on a tight schedule.'

'Jesus Lottie are you asking?' Paul remarked. 'That makes a change.'

'Now now Paul, don't start being belligerent.' Charlotte replied. 'This meeting is about business *and pleasure* and I have to say, as always it is a pleasure to see you even if you are becoming more of a crotchety old curmudgeon by the day.'

'It's called age Lottie, and intolerance. Don't worry, you'll be there yourself before you know it. You're not that far behind me after all. Wasn't it one of your erstwhile star Law Lords who said, "With age I have become more tolerant of some things but more intolerant of others" or something like that? The chippy Lord Denning if I remember correctly.'

Nothing surprised Charlotte where Paul was concerned. He really was remarkably well read, he just didn't advertise the fact, believing as he did that intellectual showmanship was for pompous and inadequate prigs who knew nothing at all about life. Those who can't teachers and highbrow academics were usually first in the firing line.

'Yes, I do believe you are right Paul,' Charlotte grinned. 'Now come on, let's order and then we can talk.'

'I thought Joel was joining us?' Paul asked before taking a look at the menu. Not that he ever bothered much with menus, he knew what he liked and if the restaurant couldn't come up Bird's Custard or HP Sauce then he never went back. As for the cord en bleu sensibilities of prima donna Chef Outrage, bollocks to 'em. He employed some of the best in the world and as far as he was concerned they were all first class prats. The same with wine: no pretension, no bullshit.

He ate to live, he didn't live to eat.

'He'll be joining us later, Paul. Now, let's order?' Paul looked around for a waiter, he finally managed to attract the attention of one with a discreetly raised hand. The clicking of fingers was abhorrent to him and nothing but a display of ignorant contempt for those who worked hard for little money. A man had tried such antics on with him once in the Ragged Cliffs restaurant. Paul had picked him up by the lapels and thrown him out of the hotel, he had been younger then of course.

'Fair enough, I'm looking forward to seeing him Lottie.' Paul said. He then looked at the waiter who was hovering. 'Right young man, I'll have the rack of lamb, with some Jersey new potatoes and asparagus please. Nothing else, oh and do make sure the asparagus is well cooked and drowning in butter. We'll have a half decent bottle of claret to go with it, I think. I'll leave the choice to you young man, just make sure that's it's a good 'un.' The waiter was in his forties but Paul reckoned that anyone under fifty was young. Age again.

'Of course, sir,' the waiter smiled. A no-nonsense customer for once, it made a pleasant change.

'Paul,' Charlotte interrupted, 'shouldn't you be avoiding butter, let alone heaps of it? I mean . . .'

'Oh do be quiet Lottie. I'm having a day out, I'm entitled to indulge myself now and again. Dear God, there isn't as much as a sliver of the stuff in our kitchen, Beth sees to that, bloody fascist.'

'Oh Paul, I give up. Oh and you might have asked me about the wine?'

'Don't be silly now Lottie. I should know by now what tipple tickles your palate. I don't need to ask.' Sighing with resignation, Charlotte ordered some lobster with a green side salad, having any influence over Paul Treharne had always been a touch and go business, her son was no different.

'So Lady Treharne, what have you got for me that you couldn't talk about over the phone?'

Before Charlotte could answer, the waiter returned with the bottle of claret.

'Sir . . . ?' He said expectantly, as he tipped a couple of drops of wine into Paul's glass.

'Oh no need for all that nonsense, young man.' Paul said quietly. 'Thank you, just pour away.'

The waiter smiled, this gentleman really was a pleasure to serve.

'Some rather interesting facts . . . ,' Charlotte replied when the waiter had gone, 'but before I go any further, Joel has also been doing some digging. Frankly Paul, there are certain areas that I keep clear of where Joel is concerned. His background is hardly what one would describe as pedestrian is it? Sometimes I dread to think what he gets up to. Anyway, be that as it may. We have been investigating R&Z Capital in tandem as it were.

'The CEO is one Dan Seloski, an unsavoury sort if ever there was. Connected to Bernie Madoff back in the early 90's but when the scandal blew up, he came out squeaky clean. The US Securities and Exchange Commission have been after him for quite a while. I don't need to tell you Paul that all this is strictly confidential. I've had to call in some favours from my friends across the pond and believe me it took some shall I say, unorthodox persuasion to obtain the information.'

'Of course Lottie, that's a given. I know about Seloski, I've been doing my own research. Go on.'

'On a number of occasions, the SEC have had enough evidence to indict him for false accounting, serious breaches of American antitrust laws and insider trading – *insider trading is the trading of a public company's stock or other securities (such as bonds or stock options) by individuals with access to non-public information or confidential information of said company* – and out and out fraud on an industrial scale but just as they have been about to arrest him, witnesses have clammed up or simply disappeared.

The man is a consummate fraudster I'm told but extremely slippery. They are however, in the process of building another case against him, one that will stick. Insider trading again. Quite obviously they are playing their cards close to their chest on this, it is critical to their case that Seloski doesn't get wind of anything, they know what will happen if he does.'

'Details?'

'My friends won't tell me Paul, there is only so much arm bending I can do, the same for Joel'

Paul took a sip of his wine whilst he absorbed everything Charlotte had just told him.

'There is something else, Paul. Something that might explain the attack on me.'

'Oh yes? Do go on, this is getting better by the minute, Lottie.'

'When I was sitting on the Court of Appeal, a case concerning the merger of two multinational telecoms companies came before us. Billions of pounds were involved. The Competition Commission as it is now known, it was formerly the Monopolies and Mergers Commission, wanted to stop the merger, as in their view it would be against the public interest, seriously so, for such a merger to go ahead.

'We in the Court of Appeal found for the Commission and stopped the merger. Frankly, I had forgotten all about the case until Joel flagged it up following his own investigations; you can imagine it was hugely complex and God knows how many names were involved.

'Well, guess who was behind the attempted merger?'

'Don't tell me, R&ZR Capital Manhattan, namely that bastard Dan Seloski.'

'Correct.' Charlotte confirmed. 'How I missed the connection is beyond me but there we are, I suppose I'm human after all.'

'Oh you're human alright, Lottie.' Paul smiled. 'So, I assume you are putting Seloski as the front runner for the attempt on your life? The man certainly fits the bill, particularly when one considers his track record. Witnesses disappearing and so on.'

'Well . . . ,' Charlotte said uncertainly, 'I will not believe anything until I see hard evidence. All we have is speculation and circumstantial evidence, certainly nothing that would stand up in a court of law. Admittedly, Seloksi is a strong candidate for the attack on me but as you know Paul, there are also of plenty of others who would wish to do me mischief. Seloski is trying to take over our company, we are refusing so yes, he has a motive to intimidate and threaten us. He may also be extremely bitter about the Court of Appeal's decision but I remain unconvinced. Killing a Supreme Court judge? We must have more evidence, Paul. It's as simple as that, which of course Joel is looking into.'

Paul remained silent for a few moments. As far as he was concerned legal niceties could go to hell in a handcart. He had been told all he needed to know nevertheless he kept quiet, Lottie was one of the most senior judges in the land after all and hardly likely to condone anything that had a whiff of the illegals about it.

'Well, it all seems pretty cut and dried to me. What does Joel think about it all?'

'He can tell you himself, when he decides to eventually grace us with his presence. He's not in my good books at the moment. He just doesn't listen to a word I say. Last night . . .'

'Yes, yes Lottie,' Paul immediately interrupted, 'before you go into one, men don't listen for a reason, you know. You women nag the shit out of us and most of the time you talk a load of drivel, so what do you expect?'

'What! Drivel! Dear God, you've got a nerve! We're in the 21st century for God's sake, Paul Treharne. Really! You are impossible! You're a dinosaur and a rude one at that! I suppose you'd like me to be seen and not heard too!'

Paul loved winding Charlotte up. She rose to the bait every time.

'Now you mention it, that's not such a bad idea.' Paul smirked. 'Ah, here's the grub. Now, eat up. I'll have a chat with Joel when he arrives.'

Charlotte simmered for a few seconds as she quickly decided that Paul was a lost cause. An outrageous throwback to another time, she knew that arguing with him would get her nowhere. She also knew that he was just playing with her. A modern metropolitan man he was not, but he did respect women and their brains, most of the time anyway.

Just as the coffee arrived, Joel turned up.

'Oh, so you've finally managed to extract yourself from whatever meeting was so important then, have you?' Charlotte said sarcastically as he pulled up a chair. 'I really don't know what the United Nations would do without you.'

'Oh they'll get by without me for a few minutes I expect, Lottie.' Joel grinned as he shook hands with Paul and ignored his wife's ill humour. 'Now then, have you filled Paul in on what we have so far?'

'I have.'

'Good.'

'Unfortunately, I am going to have to leave you boys to it.' Charlotte said. 'I really do have an important meeting to attend.' She stood up, slung her handbag over her shoulder and paused. Waiting.

Both Paul and Joel stood up at the same time. They were gentlemen after all, at least when it mattered. Joel looked at his wife and smiled in that annoyingly, captivating way of his. It worked every time. It infuriated Charlotte but that was love for you. Her anger disappeared as she went to her husband and kissed his cheek.

'I'll see you later and don't concoct anything with Paul that I may consider questionable or even remotely illegal. Do you understand, Joel?'

'As if we would, my darling. Now don't work too hard and I'll pick you up at the usual time.' With that Charlotte headed for the restaurant door. As always Marc Rey wasn't far behind her. He was instructed to be unobtrusive but this didn't mean to say that he was any the less deadly for it. Wherever Charlotte went, his eyes and trigger finger went too. Always alert, always ready. As he walked out he turned around to look at Paul. Words or a nod of acknowledgement were unnecessary. They both knew their duty.

Joel turned to Paul.' Sorry to hear about your greyhound.' He said calmly, 'although I'm not surprised. We are dealing with some nasty people Paul.'

'You don't have to tell me that, Joel. Beth is still beside herself and I'm not far off. I can only hope the bastards didn't torture the poor animal before they killed her, I wouldn't put it passed them. We still haven't found her body. So, now that law fearing Lottie is out of the way, what are we going to do to stop this madness? She's filled me in with what you have come up with so far but no doubt you have a different take on things.'

'Well now Paul,' Joel replied, 'unlike Lottie I'm not a "beyond reasonable doubt" merchant. I understand her insistence on irrefutable evidence but she's a lawyer through and through and I wouldn't expect anything less, but I'm not and neither are you.

'My own view is that the situation requires some direct action and fast. We have to stop R&ZR before someone really gets hurt. And sooner or later this will happen, it always does in situations like this. Things escalate.'

'I agree. So what do you have in mind, Joel?'

'We have to be careful and we cannot involve Lottie in any way. This is what I have in mind . . .'

An hour later Paul sat back in his chair. 'Unimaginative Joel but no doubt effective I'll say that. I've racked my brains for solutions and come up with damn all.'

'The more imaginative a plan Paul, the more that can go wrong. Believe me, I learnt this the hard way. Simplicity is always best and the fewer the number of people involved the better. Right now, that means just you and me and I see no reason why it shouldn't be kept that way. Lottie must know nothing. I take it you are behind me on this? It's no good if you're not.'

'Of course Joel and don't worry about keeping things between you and me. I've got more secrets knocking about in my head than you'll find in MI5's archives, so don't worry about that.'

'No phone calls, no mobiles, no emails, nothing. I'll come to you when I think we need to talk, is that ok?'

'Fine with me. Isn't there anything I can do to help, what you are proposing is dangerous as you know better than I?'

'Nothing.' Joel said firmly. 'If there is, I'll let you know.'

'Do you know something, Joel?'

'What?'

'Your calmness about all this is scaring the shit out of me. *You* are scaring the shit out of me.'

'Nothing for you to be scared about, Paul.' Joel replied coldly and with a detachment that in itself intimidated. 'You're not the enemy.'

Later that day, Joel was on a flight to New York. Charlotte had been told it was a necessary business trip following his lunchtime meeting with Paul. The security arrangements at one of their American hotels needed reviewing due to the fact the President was attending a summit at one of them.

It was not unusual for Joel to take off to America at short notice and Charlotte was aware of the summit, even so there were times in their marriage when she knew it was best not to ask too many questions.

She might not have liked the answers.

CHAPTER 27

'Goddamn Jo, you're getting a bit wrinkled up for the old action man stuff aren't you?'

'Don't worry, I'm not intending to do anything too strenuous, Bill.'

They were sitting in a Brooklyn diner. Glass, chrome, brash zig zag lighting on the outside, red vinyl seat coverings, piles of apple and chicken pot pies, pastrami and burgers on the inside, in other words as far as Joel was concerned, there was too much of everything but then New York prided itself on being too much full stop.

Bill Klosky, big, loud and all American, was ex-SEAL, ex-CIA and ex-husband a few times over. He read the piece of paper Joel had given him, whilst trying to demolish a corned beef sandwich the size of a canoe.

'Ummm . . . well, the information you want shouldn't be too difficult,' Bill managed to say in between bites, 'a couple of calls will get you that. The other items? A bit tougher in these days of post 9/11 paranoia but you know me Jo, I'm a can do kind of guy . . . pity my ex-wives weren't but what the hell.'

'How long?' Joel asked.

'Ooooh . . . I'd say 48 hours.'

'Sooner?'

'Jesus Christ Jo, I'm out of the game you know! We're ol' timers you and me.'

'Don't give me that shit, Bill. You bastards are never out, you just go from full throttle to cruise.'

'Yeah yeah.' Klosky grinned. He had always liked Joel Samson but more to the point he owed him. The man had saved his life back in the first Gulf War. 'Ok, leave it to me. I won't ask what you're up to but you know how to reach me if you need any other help.' Klosky looked straight into Joel's eyes. 'Any kind of help now Jo, you understand?'

'I do Bill and thanks.'

'Right then, see you back here same time tomorrow. Now, can I get on and finish this corned beef sandwich, it's better than sex for Christ's sake! And you can tell me all about that beautiful wife of yours. Long-time no see, Jeez you struck gold there Jo, fucking gold. What I wouldn't do too . . .'

'Yes, yes Bill, eat your sandwich will you?!'

Back in London, Sir Henry Davidson sipped his malt whisky and leaned back into the scrumptious well-being of the leather armchair. His Gentleman's Club was his haven, his retreat from intemperate, hum drum inconsequence. Anachronistic his club may have been in its insistence on male only membership but if men had nowhere to hide where was the point in living?

His club was tucked away in the back streets of Piccadilly. Nothing much had changed. An institution of serene power, it had been host to some of the most momentous decisions and events in British political and world history. The place remained a constant in a world poleaxed by uncertainty and violence. Sir Henry loved his club, his refuge, his membership of an elite that ruled without question in spite of the democratic fantasies constantly being peddled and lionised by a loathsome press and media.

Just as he was about to take another sip of his drink, a note was handed to him by one of the flunkeys who were rarely noticed and only seen when required. He read it quickly, then tore it up and placed the remnants in one of the pockets of his double breasted navy blue suit to be disposed of later.

As expected Mr Samson had arrived in New York and had already met one of his erstwhile companions on the battlefield. A resourceful fellow this Samson chap, what will he do next, Sir Henry casually wondered?

As Sir Henry was pondering Joel Samson's next move, the man himself was standing absolutely still behind a concrete pillar in an underground car park. It was 4.45 am. Quiet. Joel had positioned himself right in the middle of a security blind spot. Having checked out the surveillance cameras it didn't take him long to work out exactly where he could operate unseen. Bill had provided him with the security details and plans of the luxury Manhattan apartment block. He had also given him the address of Dan Seloski – his private address that is, the one that never appeared on official documentation or database.

Joel looked at his watch.

He was wearing an everyday maintenance worker's overall and a black balaclava that covered his face but not his eyes or mouth. A few minutes tops. The dossier Bill had given him confirmed that Seloski was an early riser, a creature of habit, albeit a cautious one. The man took his personal security seriously, at least as seriously as his arrogance allowed, which in Joel's view was ideal. In his experience, those who felt most secure were the ones most vulnerable. There were invariably chinks in their armour, weak points. A belief in immortality usually resulted in death.

On time, a black limousine pulled up outside some elevator doors for Seloski's use only. The elevator led directly from the penthouse suite to the underground car park. In an instant Joel set up a small portable ladder, climbed up it and disabled the one camera that would be able to see his approach to the limo. He knew he only had only two minutes, three at a push before alarm lights starting flashing on the security console in the main foyer of the apartment block.

Before the chauffeur was able to get both legs out of his driving seat Joel had knocked him unconscious with a straight uppercut to his chin. The man hadn't even seen it coming. Placing him gently back in the driving seat, Joel closed the car door. He then made a bee line for the elevator doors. In seconds they swished open and Seloski started to walk out, before he had time to wonder why his chauffeur wasn't standing with the back door to the limo open, Joel moved in quickly behind him. A head lock and the pressure pulling up Seloski's fat throat, made sure the man stayed silent as Joel pulled him back into the lift and pressed the button to close the lift doors. Early morning it may have been but this was New York, anyone could have been walking around.

Seloski pawed at Joel's arm, struggling to breathe but got nowhere. He was totally incapacitated.

Joel pressed a silenced Sig Sauer P226 to Seloski's temple.

'Now Dan, listen carefully.' Joel whispered calmly. 'You call off the dogs you've let loose on the Treharne's, because if you don't I will kill you . . . very slowly and very painfully and it really won't make any difference how much security you have. I will get though it and kill you. Do you understand?'

Seloski couldn't move, so Joel loosened his grip, he didn't want the fat bastard dying on him. 'I don't think you understand what I'm saying Dan. A pity.' With that, Joel gripped Seloski's left wrist and shot off an index finger, this was followed up by a quick knock to the back of Seloski's head with the butt of the Sig.

In less than a minute he had rewired the security camera and was walking along the sidewalk wearing a yellow hard hat and a maintenance worker's tool belt dripping with the paraphernalia of his trade.

As Joel was walking along the streets of New York, Charlotte was in mid conversation with Marc Rey. They were walking along the pavement to her office, a short distance of about a quarter of a mile from the car park.

Suddenly and without warning, Rey threw Charlotte to the ground as he tried to cover her with his own body. A shower of bullets erupted around them and ricocheted off the concrete pavement. Rey was able to pull his own firearm and start shooting but it was hopeless. The target, a black clad motor-cyclist was gone.

This time there was no mistake.

The assassin had intended to kill.

Rey hauled Charlotte up and dragged her along the pave-ment to the doors of her office. He threw her inside as he kept his gun moving from side to side, ready to kill without the slightest hesitation.

Seconds later all hell broke loose.

Rey quickly glanced at Charlotte. She had gone white and was bleeding profusely from her thigh and chest. As he ripped open her coat to apply some First Aid he yelled, 'Call an ambulance!' to some staff who had gathered around the two of them. He was surrounded by nothing but shock, 'get me a towel and give me some fucking space, will you!'

Rey knew how to deal with gunshot wounds, he also know that Charlotte was already on the critical list. She was barely conscious.

'You stay with me now, Lady Treharne. You just stay with me.' He urged as he cradled her head in his arms. A moan escaped from her lips but that was all. He ripped off his belt and tied it around her thigh to stop the bleeding. If the bullet had hit the femoral artery then she was in real trouble.

'Where's that fucking ambulance?' he shouted again as a towel was placed nervously in his hand. He immediately used it to apply pressure to the gunshot wound in Charlotte's right upper torso.

Minutes later two paramedics were rushing Charlotte off to an emergency unit at the nearest hospital. It was only as the ambulance was pulling away, that Rey noticed the blood pouring down his hand and the pain in his shoulder.

He'd better get himself to the hospital too, but only after he'd tightened up the security around Charlotte. The woman had better not die on him, he had started too seriously like her.

CHAPTER 28

Within thirty minutes the assassin was removing her helmet and black leathers. The motorbike was up on its stand and the only noise intruding upon her determination to kill was coming from an overhead slip road onto the motorway.

The garage had come with the flat she had bought years ago in a rough part of London's East End, although these days the area wasn't so rough. London's beautiful people had moved in and property prices had soared, not that she was interested in investment returns or treacle coated Guardian reading dinner party violation.

She never stayed at the flat. Security services around the world had upped their game post 9/11 and she wasn't one to take any unnecessary risks. They were not to be underestimated. Her ownership of the flat was untraceable but even so, technology could now spot a mouse on the moon so why take any chances?

It was this caution verging on the paranoid that had kept her alive and more to the point, unknown to the security services. She had no doubt that they were aware of her but this was all they had. An awareness. She had always made sure that their files contained nothing but rumour and speculation, nothing concrete.

She placed her weapon on a shelf attached to a wall. Her hands were remarkably petite and feminine, her fingers long and elegant. In another time, another world she would have stopped men in their tracks. On close inspection her face was flawless, every feature enjoying a perfect symmetry of completeness and expressive beauty, in spite of all her efforts at facial neutrality.

For years she had supressed her femininity, knowing as she did that any such physical celebration of womanhood would make her body, her face, memorable and thus vulnerable.

She put on a grey baggy jumper and grey trousers, pulled on a short grey coat that had been hanging on a nail banged into a wall, ruffled her hair and set off to get something to eat.

Minutes later she was standing in front of a sandwich booth ordering a cheese sandwich, an apple and a bottle of water. She never went anywhere near restaurants to eat, there were too many eyes watching and observing. As she ate, she briefly wondered if her contract had been fulfilled. Her bullets had hit the judge and her bodyguard but this was no guarantee of death. In such a public place it would have been suicide to stop and make certain. She had gone into a TV shop to check the news, the shooting was being flashed across the world but there had been no confirmation of death.

If the judge had survived there could be no further attempts, she knew when enough was enough. Her own personal security depended on it.

The judge had been lucky the first time and she still couldn't work out why she had missed. She hadn't made the same mistake the second time around, so if the judge lived then so be it.

It was time to get out.

CHAPTER 29

Jolyan and Adina were discovering that first love tended to be a little more realistic when confronted with the everyday realities of close quarter toilet action, toilet seats not being put back down, covert flatulence and toothpaste tubes being squeezed at the wrong end. There were also of course, issues relating to who did the washing up and cleaning, who looked like shit first thing in the morning and who was going to do the laundry and ironing?

The everyday joys of living with someone took courage and a certain degree of mutual toleration but at least they had youth on their side and thus a natural exemption from the tyranny of ageing habit and wrinkled up stubbornness.

They were already learning how to fight according to the rules of domestic bliss but both were still keeping the gloves on – for now anyway.

They loved each other far too much to hurt.

'Jolyan come here, quickly!' Adina shouted from the bedroom.

'What's the matter, Adina? Can't I have shower in peace?' Jolyan was standing in the doorway of the bathroom, a towel draped over his head and nothing else.

'Oh Jolyan, you'd better have a look at this. 'Adina said more softly as she stretched across the bed and handed him her mobile phone. Jolyan read the news item on the small screen.

'Oh God!' Was all he could say. He stood still as he tried to make sense of what he had just read. 'What . . . I mean . . . oh fuck, the report isn't saying whether my mother is alive or dead? Wait here Adina, I need to ring my family.' The phone in the sitting room rang just before he picked it up.

It was Joel. He was waiting to catch a flight home from John F. Kennedy International Airport. After some brief words, Jolyan disconnected the line.

He turned around to see Adina standing right in front of him, her eyes brimming concern.

'Is she, well . . . is she . . . ?' Adina didn't know whether she should dare ask.

'She's alive Adina but only. I have to get the next flight back. Can you try and organise something for me from your office? It might be quicker.'

'Of course, I can make some calls from here. Let me get dressed and I'll check things out straightaway.' She went to Jolyan and put her arms around him. 'It will be ok Jolyan, I promise you it will be ok. Now, make us come coffee while I get dressed.'

He did as he was told. Right now he was in a state of utter confusion. That crazy driver, the attack on his mother a few months ago and now this. What the hell was going on? For a few brief seconds the serious possibility of losing his mother filled him with dread. She had always been so inde-structible, so alive. This just couldn't be happening. His brain was unable to grasp the events that were unfolding. They were distant and yet so near, untouchable and yet frightening.

As he put on some clothes and tried to bring some order to his thoughts, the apartment buzzer echoed through the hallway.

Picking up the intercom phone he looked at the screen above it. The camera pointing at the entrance revealed two men standing in front of it. There was something about them, Jolyan couldn't say whether there was anything threatening or even unusual in the way they stood or were dressed but they just didn't look right. He quickly realised that maybe he was starting to get paranoid but there had been that incident with the car trying to mow them down. Either way, something inside him triggered an immediate reaction of flight.

He ran into the bedroom and grabbed Adina's arm.

'Come on! The fire escape Adina! Hurry!'

Before Adina could put on anymore clothes, she was being hauled down the emergency stairway of the apartment block.

'Jolyan . . . Jolyan . . . what's going on?!' She managed to gasp as they ran into a back street.

'Not now Adina! Not now!' Jolyan shouted back. 'Come on, we've got to get away from here! Two men at the apartment door. They didn't look right, that's all I know and I'm not taking any chances!'

He kept a tight grip on Adina's hand as they ran onto a main road. A few seconds later they were sitting in the back of a taxi. Before either of them were able to look calmly at what had happened they were back at Sao Bento Railway Station, losing themselves in the crowds.

'Right, come on Adina. Let's find somewhere where we can talk.'

They eventually found a bench on one of the platforms where they could sit down and talk.

'Now Jolyan, would you like to tell me what is going on?' Adina asked, just about managing to maintain some kind of composure.

'Those two men at the apartment. I didn't like the look of them that's all, what with that car the . . .'

'Oh, you mean your drunk driver . . . ?'

'Alright, alright Adina, maybe you were right.'

'I was right, Jolyan. There's something going on here and you're a fool if you can't see it. I've lived with danger all my life and there are things going on with your family that are frightening me. What are we going to do?'

Jolyan looked at the girl he loved so much.

'Oh God I don't know but Adina, you can't be with me. Not now. If anything should happen to you because of me or my family I wouldn't be able to live with myself. I really wouldn't. You're not involved in any of this. Look, there was a failed assassination attempt on my mother a few months ago. I didn't tell you because I've been under orders to keep quiet about it. I won't blame you for getting mad but honestly, sometimes where my mother is concerned choice doesn't come into it. She's a Supreme Court judge and there is a price to pay for her family. Please don't be too hard on me.'

Adina wanted to scream and shout at him but she didn't. She could see his love and his turmoil.

'Well Jolyan Treharne, if you think you can dump me this easily you can forget it. I know how to look after myself and use a firearm. Comes with being a Sabra Jew. You're not going anywhere without me, so get used to it!'

Jolyan looked at the dark eyes staring at him. He knew there could be no argument. Not this time.

'Firearms?! Jesus Adina, hang on a minute here will you? This isn't some bloody silly Mission Impossible movie you know. We don't know anything for certain at the moment. Before we do anything I need to speak with my stepfather, so sit tight while I try and ring him. Although if he's half way across the Atlantic then there's no chance. I'll have to try Paul Treharne instead. We have offices all over the world, so maybe he'll come up with something.'

'Who's Paul Treharne?' Adina asked, as usual wanting to know everything in spite of the drama being played out.

'He's my . . . oh never mind, it's too complicated to get into right now. Now, let me see if I can find out where we go from here, will you?'

Just as Jolyan started to tap into his mobile phone two men appeared in front of them. They looked like a couple of investment bankers who had just been caught out, apologetic but without the sincerity.

'Mr Treharne. Please don't try and run away this time. Neither my colleague nor I are getting any younger and we are not here to do you any harm.' The taller of the two reached into the inside of his jacket and pulled out an identity card wallet. 'We work for the Portuguese government. If you would like to come with us, we are instructed to see you safely onto a flight back to London.'

The man doing the talking spoke perfect English and on closer inspection didn't seem at all threatening. He had the look of someone who was thoroughly pissed off with his job, not to mention wanting to divorce his wife and telling all his children to go to hell. He was one of life's victims, the sort that were always out there and always blaming everyone else for their own fanciful downfalls.

Without saying anything, Jolyan stood up to take a closer look at the man's identity card. At the same time Adina barged in front of him and snatched it out of the man's hand. She was used to intrusive authority and had learnt not to take anything for granted.

'Security?' She asked.' Can you be more specific, please?'

The man looked at her and sighed.

'Like I say, we work for the Portuguese government. SIS to be exact.'

'SIS?' Adina insisted.

'Security Intelligence Service. Internal security.' The man replied with an edge of frustration in his voice. 'Now young lady, we have a job to do, so if you don't mind.'

'Let's see your partner's credentials.' Adina stated. It wasn't a question. The man looked at his partner, whose English wasn't as good as his and said in Portuguese, 'youngsters, they're a pain in the arse. Give her your identity card.'

Adina looked at the card before handing back the other one.

'Ok, you seem kosher.'

'I'm glad you are satisfied young lady.' The one doing all the talking added, 'Mr Treharne, can we go please? I believe there is a flight leaving for London in about an hour's time. You must be on it.'

'Now hold it, hold it right there.' Adina said firmly. She was standing between Jolyan and the two men. Hands on hips and ready to fight to the death. 'You're not going anywhere without me, is that clear?'

Jolyan was starting to enjoy all this, he had never seen Adina so fired up. God she was bloody magnificent!

'Miss . . . ?' The English speaker started to say.

'Berezin'

'Miss Berezin, are you related to Mr Treharne?

'No.'

'You are aware that his life may be in danger, which is why we are here?'

'I am, which is precisely why he's not going anywhere without me. He's a city boy, I'm an Israeli Jew. He needs my protection. I'll pay for my airline ticket.'

'I see, so he needs *your* protection?'

'He does, do you have a problem with that?'

The security man rubbed his chin. A brave girl he had to admit and quite obviously one who wasn't about to take no for an answer. Apart from anything else he could hardly stop her joining this Treharne boy on his way home. His orders were clear: Get Treharne on the plane and out of our hair fast. No diplomatic incident. The Treharne's were serious commercial players in Portugal, didn't dodge taxes and so far they hadn't taken a hike out of an economy in freefall.

'Right, Miss Berezin. Come this way both of you. We have a car waiting.'

With that Adina took Jolyan's hand, who couldn't help smiling at her performance. What would she be like in a real fight he wondered to himself?

'By the way Adina and just out of curiosity, 'Jolyan said as they followed the two men to their car, 'won't your parents have something to say about all this?'

'Oh, don't worry about them,' Adina replied, 'they gave up on their wayward daughter as soon as she reached puberty. They still love me though, just like someone else I know!'

CHAPTER 30

'How is Lady Treharne?' Marc Rey asked, 'and before you say anything Joel, I fucked up. I'm sorry.'

'She's lucky. Extremely lucky. Two bullets. One went straight through her thigh. It didn't hit any bone or the femoral artery. The other, missed her heart by a whisker, nicked her lung but she should make a full recovery. They've managed to get the bullet out. She won't be so full of steam for a while but that won't do her any harm. As for any apology forget it. You saved her life Marc, simple as that. If you hadn't reacted as quickly as you did, my wife would be dead.'

Marc Rey was sitting opposite Joel in a visitor's room at the hospital. His arm was in a sling following the bullet wound to his own shoulder. Nothing serious, he had known worse. His body was covered with scars. He realised that he too had been lucky.

'Right Marc. What happened?' Joel was tired. He had come straight from Heathrow. The adrenalin was still flowing but it was starting to ebb away as his anxiety over the woman he loved so much started to take over.

'I heard the motorbike coming up behind us. The street that Lady Charlotte's office is on is quite quiet. It was a powerful job. 500cc? The sudden revving of its engine made me turn around. The rider was head to toe in black leathers.'

'Weapon?' Joel interrupted.

'MP5A3, no doubt about it.'

'SAS sub machine gun of choice for close quarters combat. Collapsible stock. Reliable and deadly. Go on.'

'He came straight at us. Short bursts. I managed to let off three rounds with my own weapon but it was pretty hopeless.

He was already on his way. There were civilians around so I had to be careful, and of course there was Lady Charlotte. In those split seconds I could see that an attempt on her life was about to be made, so I threw her on the ground and covered her with my own body as best I could.'

'You did well, Marc. Did you notice anything unusual about the shooter?'

'What do you mean?'

'From what you're saying, it sounds like the same person who tried to kill us a few months ago. Same MO.'

'Well, now you mention it the rider did seem quite small. Let me think for a moment . . . yes, the shooter was definitely on the small side. Could have been a woman. The movements of the shooter were well . . . almost graceful. Man or woman, this was no amateur job; they knew what they were doing. The attack had been well planned. We were caught at our most vulnerable.'

'As I thought then.' Joel said quietly. 'It's the same shooter by the sound of it.'

'Who's behind all this then Joel? I know you've got your contacts. Come to that so have I. The politicos don't seem to have a clue. At least there's no firm evidence pointing in any particular direction. The Home Secretary has been assassinated and my masters are running around like headless chickens. No one seems to know what the hell is going on. The money is on Islamist extremists. What do you think?'

'Honest answer? I don't know. There has been a hostile takeover bid for Treharne Holdings but I believe that has now been neutralised. In any event, it is doubtful that the people behind the bid would go to these lengths. It just doesn't add up somehow, oh and not a word to anyone about the Treharne's business dealings, I don't want the government sticking their bloody oars in. Understood, Marc?'

'Understood.' Rey confirmed.

Later that evening Rey arrived back at his London flat. A professional to his core, he was still troubled by the fact that he had failed Lady Treharne. No matter what Joel Samson said, he had failed her and there were no two ways about it.

Taking a bottle of beer out of the fridge he noticed that there was wasn't even a moulded up piece of cheese or carton of sour milk to keep it company. So much for a home life.

He sat down on a chair fresh out of IKEA and looked around the flat's statement on sheer boredom. Zero personality, minus zero character and an emptiness that would have pushed the pitiful meanderings of a poet laureate, stared back at him. In an odd way, the flat's chronic indifference clashed with the true nature of Rey. A consummate killing machine when required, he was also a human being. Human in the sense that he believed in what he did but could still question the orders he was instructed to carry out. To say he was ruthless or indeed merciless, would have been to misunderstand the man. In his lexicon of fair play, might wasn't always right.

His trigger finger did sometimes pause or at the very least reconsider. Only at the right time of course and never when life and limb were in immediate danger. An automaton he was not. He was more the warrior fighting a just cause, albeit that there were times when a natural introspection forced him to conform to a moral framework that he was unsure of.

His world of aloneness sometimes bothered him. As he sipped his beer, he wondered if he would ever find that fulfilment which he knew deep down he wanted. Wars and strange countries were all very well for the macho man carrying out the orders of democratic righteousness but what happened when the shooting stopped?

Rey was aware of the emotional chaos and social annihilation of Civvy Street. He had seen too many of his former comrades be ruined by a life without a gun and the companionship of early death possibility. Thus his refusal to turn his flat into a proper home. Whilst he remained on active service he knew that his life could be whisked away at any moment, so what good were homely possessions to him then?

The same applied to his heart. He wanted to love, to have a wife and children but how could he? How could he snatch away a good woman's love and then leave it with nothing but a memory or two? Or worse, gain the trust and unquestioning devotion of a child and then turn his back with a bullet in it?

At thirty six he was starting to want a life of normality, a life without danger but would he thrive in such a life? Was he ready?

His questions remained unanswered when later that night, he fell into a fitful sleep in an empty bed.

While Rey slept, Joel sat next to his wife's hospital bed. Two counter-terrorism officers stood outside the door, armed and on high alert. All the UK security servics were scouring London for the assassin who had tried to kill a Supreme Court judge.

First the Home Secretary, now this. Not so long ago such outrages would have been unthinkable, at least in the minds of ordinary citizens going about their lawful business. The right wing media and press were stoking up peoples' fears. The Unions were on the rampage for a new world order and far right MP's were demanding new radical policies to counter the evils of terrorism. Left wing liberalism of everyone being nice to each other was to blame for it all, the people they served had had enough.

Joel sat back in his chair and tried to make some sense of the second attack on his wife's life.

He had sounded confident enough when talking with Rey about neutralising Seloski, but Joel knew that the bastard could still have been behind the attack. The shooter was a pro, she wouldn't have needed much time to plan the hit, and Joel was now convinced that it was a "she."

Joel had heard whispers, rumours from some of his friends in the darker world of political and military expedience, that there was a woman assassin out there for hire, a woman who made your average thuggish terrorist look like a frustrated dad having a day out with the kids at Disney World. They were only rumours admittedly but nevertheless some of the people he had spoken to, dependable people, seemed pretty certain of her existence.

He was aware that terrorists could still be behind everything, including the killing of the Home Secretary. Some Islamist groups had declared responsibility although again there was little if any, hard evidence to confirm the credibility of these claims, unless of course Her Majesty's Government was holding something back. Not unknown where national security was concerned, indeed as Joel well knew, most of the time it was par for the course: Keep the great unwashed happy and quiet at all costs and screw open, democratic transparency.

Such a policy had its virtues as Joel knew only too well.

So then, as far as he was concerned the jury was still out on all possibilities and this was the problem. If not extremists or Seloski then who? It was quite possible that the Home Secretary and Charlotte were connected, both women were powerful figures of the Establishment but the trouble with this idea was the shooter. Was it the same person pulling the trigger in both attacks? He had no doubt that this was the case where the two attempts on Charlotte's life were concerned, but Patricia Mayhew? Once again there was no evidence. The more Joel thought, the more convinced he became that the key to all this lay in Charlotte's past.

Someone somewhere hadn't forgotten and they had the money to put their revenge into action.

Joel looked at his darling wife, the tubes and whirring of life giving technology moved his mind away from the present. All he could see and feel was a love stronger than anything he had ever known. He gripped Charlotte's hand and felt its warmth as she slept and healed.

Sleep the greatest healer of all.

Her eyelids flickered for a moment then opened. There was recognition in her blue eyes as she gripped Joel's hand.

'Find them, my darling. Find them.' She murmured as the drugs forced her back into a deep sleep. Joel touched her cheek and knew that a life without Lottie would be no life at all.

It would be nothing less than an existence shattered by raw agony.

He would find who had hurt the woman he loved so much and kill them.

CHAPTER 31

Sir Henry Davidson had earned his title through sheer hard work in public service; he was not one of those brash, fairground Knights of the celebrity and sporting riff-raff who obtained such honours through singing some pop song outrage, rowing a canoe or riding a push bike around some silly asphalt racing track. The private Sir Henry treated such political largesse or more accurately, as much as it pained him to admit it, patronage, with nothing less that raw contempt.

The gun room in the manor house had been in his family for hundreds of years. It had seen off Cromwell and his hordes of Republicans, it had survived venal socialist greed and it had avoided the necessity of having to allow coach loads of the ice-beam splattered and crisp guzzling curious roaming around its glorious rooms at will.

Sir Henry was cleaning his brace of Purdey's. The guns in his view, were much more than objects of game shooting. They were works of art. The classical deep-scroll engraving with the depictions of game birds and other magnificent creatures held the eyes and kept them there. Such beauty went beyond the excitement and trigger pulling sport of grouse shooting.

The guns were especially aesthetic and captivating in their intent to kill. They could be picked up at a moment's notice and do the job. Art was fine in its place but it still had to serve some purpose otherwise what was the point?

As he oiled and cleaned, his mind considered the clash between populist political expediency and ruthless reality. The mainstream political parties had all become people pleasing fools, intent on securing a future of mediocrity, pretty word speak and modern day liberal emasculation.

The passion of politics, the unkempt but effective and selfish rules of leadership had gone. Democracy had become the fucked senseless bitch of weak and spineless men. It was no longer fit for purpose. Britain's strength, its greatness had been victorious in times of undemocratic political will, when leaders had been able to ignore the diktats of indolent ignorance, mass mind fickleness and pitiful universal suffrage, the last World War being one such example.

Sir Henry despaired.

He considered the dossier sitting on his desk as he rubbed away at the shotgun barrels. The study in the house was one place where he could guarantee no-one was watching or for that matter, listening. The study was swept for bugs on a weekly basis.

'Sexing up' security dossiers had become de rigueur in recent times, he smiled to himself. 'Sexing up'? Who on earth had thought that one up? Some imbecilic media hack, looking for headlines no doubt. The words had worked too. It was now Government by 'Inquiry'. These days every citizen with a fatuous grudge to bear demanded an Inquiry, be it about their Irritable Bowel Syndrome, a fat fighting gastric band or the fact that their local public lavatory didn't stay open on Sunday's. Yet another example of democracy gone mad.

For Sir Henry, the real problem however, lay in mass immigration and more particularly those who wouldn't integrate. In his view, namely the Muslim communities. The Utopian multicultural project in Europe had failed miserably, it had simply become a lethal weapon to divide and conquer. He was an intelligent and highly educated man who knew full well that it was intellectually primitive to blame the actions of an extreme few on the law abiding and decent majority, but since when did politics and national security consider what was right and proper?

The Muslim end justified his means and that's all there was to it. Justice was for highbrow jurisprudence not the real world. Or for that matter the real Great Britain. For a few moments he allowed his more human side to take over. Whilst being an adept in the dark arts of national security, he was also an intellectual. He knew his sort, the thinkers, were always the first to be put up against a wall and shot in times of revolt and social holocaust and there were times when he experienced considerable ethical conflict in his efforts to protect the realm and its people. Which and who should come first?

In spite of himself, he felt a certain sympathy for those who felt disdain for the West. It had become an ugly leviathan of wanton secular affluence and malicious consumerism. Need no longer fitted into the Western mind-set. People were only interested in what they wanted and what they could buy, be it a new kitchen or two weeks on some ghastly Greek island.

In many respects the West deserved all it got, apart from anything else its footprint in the Middle Ease both past and present, had resulted in nothing but wholesale slaughter and tragedy.

Sir Henry knew it was time for change, radical change. His precious country was going to the dogs and quite by chance serendipity had struck and given him an opportunity to do something about it once and for all.

The file on his desk marked 'Top Secret' and 'Eyes Only' was in itself inconclusive. It did however, on the balance of probabilities anyway, confirm that the most likely perpetrators of the recent outrages on the Home Secretary and Lady Treharne were of extreme Islamist origin. No particular terrorist cell had been identified but nevertheless his security analysts, and they were the experts in these matters, had concluded that such a determination was a fair one, at least going on the evidence before them, which Sir Henry knew that at best was somewhat circumstantial. Balance of probability time again, but then if this was good enough for a civil court of law, it was good enough for him.

Civil or criminal burden of proof? This question was for lawyers to argue over, not national security.

He placed the shotguns back in their gun case, locked them up in a cabinet and headed to his study. He needed to take another look at the file and think. A plan was starting to form in his mind, a plan that was undoubtedly treasonous in the eyes of the law but his love of country, he refused to use the word patriotism, it stank of Oscar Wilde's virtue of being vicious, had gone way beyond any such ancient and pious niceties.

A few minutes later Sir Henry was at his desk fountain pen in hand, as he read every single word of the dossier for the umpteenth time. His pen didn't touch one page, it was official documentation and not to be interfered with, at least not now. As he read he scribbled some words on a notebook next to the dossier, random ideas and thoughts that he would bring some order to later. Exaggeration and spin were the names of the political game these days and he saw no reason why he shouldn't play by these rules. His masters had invented them after all.

An hour later a satisfied smile appeared on his face as he sat back in his chair. Yes he thought, it could be done. It would need some tactful and careful planning, in other words dirty tricks, but it could be done. He would need the loyalty of his deputy but he didn't consider this to be a problem. His deputy had been with him for the last fifteen years and the man's loyalty had never been in doubt, apart from anything else Sir Henry knew that he was of a like mind to his own.

The three main world religions, Judaism, Christianity and Islam were like the spokes of a bicycle wheel, they all led back to the same thing and yet they found it impossible to live with each other. In Sir Henry's view, mankind's greatest mistake and miscalculation of all.

His plan was simple. The dossier had to be cooked in such a way as to make a multiple target Islamist terrorist attack imminent. London would be turned into a blood bath, with the possibility of dirty bombs being used in the process. Mass murder would result on a scale hitherto unheard of let alone imagined.

In order to prevent this, Sir Henry would recommend the immediate internment of thousands of Muslims, in the meantime details of the proposed attacks would be leaked to the media.

The public outcry for justice would silence liberal political will and mob rule would result. As previously discussed with the PM, the army would have to be called in to restore order and a national government installed, in other words a dictatorship, a benign one but nevertheless a dictatorship.

A new beginning? All Sir Henry could do was hope. To further his cause, he almost relished the prospect of another terrorist outrage, one bloodier and with a higher death toll. The end justifying the means? Machiavelli had never been one of his hero's but on the other hand?

There was one final piece of the jigsaw sitting on his desk: Eden and his team of two pathetic Marxist MP's.

They could be used, Sir Henry decided. He already knew that they were up to something and no doubt they would exploit any political turmoil to achieve their power to the people madness. For now he would leave them alone, they could be useful. Ultimately something would have to be done about them but this could wait.

Sir Henry closed the file, it was time for dinner with Lady Davidson. As he walked out of his study he remembered another file sitting on his desk. So, Joel Samson was taking the law into his own hands again, ah well the man was best left to his own devices as long as nothing arrived on HMG's doormat then good luck to him.

CHAPTER 32

'He shot my fucking finger off, for Christ's sake!!' Seloski yelled as he waved his bandaged hand around like a demented mummy. Goodwinson sat back in his chair and allowed his boss to rant and rave. It was to be expected.' Look at my hand! Look at it, for fuck's sake! The bastard!'

Seloski was sitting behind his desk in a state of inconsolable fury.

'Well Dan, I did warn you.' Goodwinson murmured.

'What! What was that?!'

'Oh nothing Dan. Any idea who did it?'

'Are you fucking joking?! The cops are a waste of time. The bastard was in and out. What could I tell them? Some fucking Spiderman comic book hero got into my private lift, shot my fucking index finger off and then pistol whipped me! All those schmucks could do was say we'll do our best Mr Seloski and do you have any enemies? Well that was a fucking joke. What me? Enemies? I replied. I'm the fucking Robin Hood and Kofi Annan of Wall Street, what do you think? Stupid cunts!'

'Well . . . er . . . at least your attacker left your right hand alone, I mean . . .'

'What Fred?! Are you trying to say he was a considerate motherfucker! Jesus!'

'Well no, Dan. Just saying that it could have been worse, that's all.' For a few moments Seloski remained silent. His hand still ached like hell in spite of the painkillers and his head wasn't far behind.

'I can tell you one thing Fred,' Seloski said, 'he knew what he was doing and it wasn't some slob off the street after my

Rolex either. He got passed all the state of the art security. The cameras haven't picked up a thing. Didn't you tell me that the Treharne's had some ex- Special Forces in their ranks?'

'I might have mentioned something in passing, Dan. I can't remember now but I do know that Lady Treharne's husband, Joel Samson is ex-SAS. Special Air Service, considered to be the best in the business. Do you not think that the attack on you was a warning? Some counter measures from the Treharne's, perhaps? The family does have quite a reputation when it comes to defending their turf. It is quite clear to me that whoever it was who shot your finger off was capable of doing much worse.'

'Oh it was a warning alright. The son of a bitch told me to stay away from the Treharne's or he'd kill me. Not that I told the police that. Some of our own medicine? It was a pro whoever it was, not that we are ever likely to find out the bastard's true identity. Far too smart.'

'So Dan, where do we go from here, the takeover? We have been applying some . . . umm . . . subtle forms of persuasion but so far nothing has worked. They won't sell, no matter what we throw at them. I'm sorry but there it is. I warned you it wouldn't be easy. You know that an attempt has just been made to assassinate Lady Treharne? The attempt failed but she's still in intensive care. I don't have any other details. She could be comatose or only just hanging on. No-one knows, there's a media blackout on the details. Islamic terrorists are being blamed.'

'Are they now.'Seloski replied, his words were a statement not a question. He was aware of the assassination attempt on Charlotte Treharne. 'The bitch cost us millions over that telecoms merger, so I hope she meets her Maker.'

'Makes you wonder if we'll be next, doesn't it? These towel heads seem to be getting bolder. Changing tactics. Imagine if they managed to do a JFK on the President?'

'That would be no loss.' Seloski sneered.

'Maybe not but you know and I know, that what goes on across the pond usually has some kind of follow up over here. That Unholy Trinity of Bush, Rumsfeld and Cheney have a lot to answer for. If you ask me, it's been too quiet for a long time. Far too quiet.'

'That's true, Fred. But if there is another 9/11 then we'll find some way of making some bucks out of it, so let these terrorists bring it on I say. Ought to nuke the lot of 'em and have done with it if you ask me but then don't forget war is money. Profit. Always has been always will be. We've made millions out of the arms trade so the more death and destruction that goes on in the world the better and fuck the morals of it all.'

'Quite so, Dan. Still, you haven't answered my question. What do want me to do about Treharne Holdings?'

Seloski tapped the glass top of his desk with his good hand. He loved glass. His whole office was covered with the stuff. There was something about its brittle weakness that attracted him.

'Do nothing for now, I want to think about it. Treharne Holdings are not going anywhere. They are beginning to become a bad investment and I don't like bad investments. I'm not saying that they've beaten us, no-one beats me and fuck the threats, but there's no shame in retreating and consolidating. We need to take a step back and look at our options.'

'As you say, Dan.'

'I do say, Fred. Now I have some calls to make, so fuck off.'

As soon as Goodwinson left the office, Seloski put his good hand over the mutilated one. For the first time in his life he was seriously scared, not that he would ever show anyone this, least of all Goodwinson. Seloski was a coward through and through, a loud mouth and a bully, and like all bully's the world over, if his victim hit back or showed a fearlessness way beyond anything he could muster, he would run and dive for cover.

It had been his index finger this time, what would it be next, a hand, a foot . . . his fucking head?!

CHAPTER 33

George Eden sat at a semi-circle table in one of the Committee Rooms in the Palace of Westminster, in other words Parliament. Along with ten other Members of Parliament, he was a member of a Select Committee convened to investigate the public financing of the National Health Service.

Select Committees had no power: they couldn't force government policy change. They sat merely to check and report on what the government of the day got up to. Most committees were composed of a motley bunch of cross-party politicos with little if any expertise in the areas they were supposed to report on. As for any adversarial competence in the art of cross-examination of witnesses brought before them, forget it. All MP's had political axes to grind and partisan loyalties to consider, so most who sat in these talking shops were there more as toothless spectators than serious seekers of the truth.

Just as Eden, an exception to the rule of passive Committee culture, was about to lay into the government, a UKIP (UK Independence Party) MP sitting to his left started knocking the hell out of what he considered to be 'that monstrous Holy cow' known as the NHS.

'It's unsustainable, sir!' Jack Simmonds berated a junior health minister. 'Those of comfortable means should start paying a health tax, or health insurance levy if you like. The strong looking after the weak. What's wrong with that? We have an ageing population and not enough young taxpayers coming through the ranks to pay for it. When are you in government going to be brave enough to tell the people the truth, that we can no longer afford free healthcare at the point of delivery? When? The notion that this can go on forever is a fantasy and you know it.'

The junior minister mumbled a meaningless reply, knowing full well that the English NHS was a time bomb just waiting to explode, and any talk of privatising it or making people pay was also a bloody great vote loser. Jack Simmonds was right of course and every politician knew it.

'And while we're at it, why doesn't the government start imposing a modest fee for every visit a patient makes to see their doctor? This would sort out the whingers, dossers and lead swinging hypochondriacs in seconds!' Simmonds was certainly going for it but then he could, he didn't have a party whipping machine to worry about. He was UKIP's only MP.

Eden was about to intervene on behalf of the noble proletariat when the Chairman called time and everyone made a dash for the nearest subsidised bar.

Waiting for him outside the Committee Room was Michael Meechan.

'What the hell are you doing here?' Eden rasped as he looked over his shoulder. 'We can't been seen talking together.'

Meechan's lips curled with contempt.''Fraid of being seen with the lower orders are you, George? Well just remember that without us, you're fucked.'

Eden smiled as he changed his tone of voice. This time it was friendlier, less upper class. He managed to sound normal for a moment or two. 'Look Michael, why don't we meet at that nasty little café later, say 5pm? I really am extremely busy for the rest of the afternoon. We can talk privately there.'

'Ok but don't mess me about. I've got some things to tell you. Important things. John will be with me.'

'That's fine,' Eden said, looking nervously over his shoulder again. Supping with the Devil wasn't easy. 'I'll see you later, now I must go. Goodbye.'

With that Eden walked off down the corridor, relieved to get away from Meechan. As soon as he stopped needing the unctuous little man, he would dump him.

At 5pm, Meechan was scoffing a bacon sandwich with 'red sauce', while John Griffin filled his face with an all-day English breakfast ie bacon, eggs, baked beans, black pudding, sausage, fried bread and just about anything else that could be fried and drowned in fat.

Eden looked on and felt quite ill. Why did the hoi polloi have to have such vulgar eating habits, he wondered? God his two honourable friends really were an absolute bloody disgrace. Animals in suits. Red sauce for God's sake, what was wrong with tomato ketchup?

With his mouth full, Meechan said, 'one more terrorist attack. One more spark and the country will explode, I'm telling you George. The Internet is going ballistic, we'll be having our very own Arab Spring soon trust me. The hatred out there is shocking *me* and I thought I'd seen it all.

'Incitement to racial hatred? Jesus, the Muslims are really coming in for it now. The airwaves, the Internet, the odd street riot. Things are really hotting up. The government will fall before long, I'm sure of it. The people have just had enough. They've had enough of capitalism for the few fat cats and enough of kow-towing to ethnic minorities, particularly the Muslims. What's right doesn't come into it, they see the whole lot as the criminals behind the killing of Mayhew and the attempted murder of Treharne.

'We'll have a new government, a truly socialist government before long I guarantee it and when I say socialist I don't mean the poxy Labour Party that we all belong too. Let's face it, it's no different from the Tories and as for the Liberals, fucking 'ell that lot go loopy over some stupid tart having her knee rubbed up the wrong way!'

Eden listened to the tirade with detached interest. He knew exactly what was going on in the country and he knew how imminent political meltdown was. Everything he had been secretly planning for years was coming to fruition. Meechan's observations may have been politically crude but they were correct. Very soon the political void that must surely come would be crying out for a true leader to put the country back on its feet.

And who that leader would be? Well, he knew that answer to that question.

'Before you go any further Michael, what exactly were these matters of great import that you had to tell me about so urgently? So far I've heard nothing new.'

'Well now . . .' Before Meechan could go any further with his objectionable mouth, John Griffin interrupted. At least the man wasn't about to speak with his mouth full of cheap bacon and saw dust sausage, Eden's eyes observed in that superior way of his.

'It's like this George,' Griffin said casually. 'The Unions are about to agitate big time. A general strike is on the cards, it's just a question of timing. Of course, they've been very careful not to leek any kind of notice of their intentions to the media or anybody else. They are after maximum political damage and wholesale infra-structure upheaval. They might not have as much power now as they did before that bitch Thatcher went on the attack but we all know that that they can still pack a punch. The Unions are still one hell of a force to be reckoned with.

'Their agenda? Like ours. Total re-nationalisation. Of everything. The banks, the utilities, transport, telecoms you name it. They are on the same hymn sheet as we are and be in no doubt that Michael and I know what we are talking about. We both have close links with the top Union boys as you know.

'A general strike could well be Michael's "one more spark."'

'It could be, John. It could be.' Eden replied cautiously, whilst at the same time trying to hide his excitement. All this was indeed important news.' One final thing, John. Where do your Union friends stand on the country's nuclear deterrent?'

'Oh that's for the knacker's yard and sod the yanks.'

'Right,' Eden said dryly. 'So, matters are finally coming together it seems, jolly good. Well, all we can do now is wait. We have MP's a plenty on our side, certainly enough to achieve our goals. You are both certain that all those you have approached, discreetly I hope we still don't want the government to get wind of what we have in mind, are with us and can be relied upon?'

'No problems there, George. Trust me.' Meechan confirmed, to which Eden made no response. He didn't even trust his wife, the philandering trollop let alone a fellow MP. For a brief moment he wondered who she was romping around with at the moment. The gardener, the plumber, one of the estate hands? She had always been partial to a bit of rough as they say. Never mind, as long as it kept her happy and content, who was he to complain?

'Well then, we watch and wait gentleman. Now I must get back to the House, so if you will excuse me. Oh and Michael, please don't approach me again in such a situation where our, shall I say friendship, could be deemed conspicuous. Particularly now, when matters are coming to a head. Unwelcome attention is one thing we really don't need. The Security Services are not as stupid as you quite obviously believe them to be. We must leave nothing to chance and I mean nothing. Do you understand?'

The voice of the aristocrat could still intimidate and silence. Even Meechan and Griffin knew when to shut up and obey, albeit that their hearts and minds still fought against the persecution of deference.

They also knew who would be leading the new socialist Jerusalem.

CHAPTER 34

'Given up on Nelson's column then, have we Jolyan? Everest next perhaps?'

'Oh don't go on mum, student high jinks, that's all.'

'Mmmmm, so you say. Drunk and incapable for heaven's sake, have you paid the fine?'

'I have.'

'Good. The press enjoyed themselves as expected, so do try and be a little more discreet in future, will you?'

'I will mum,' Jolyan sighed. He was sitting next to Charlotte's bed. She had been moved out of intensive care and was now recuperating in a private room. 'Well mum, you certainly seem to be getting back on form I must say.' Jolyan observed in an attempt to change the subject. 'I've been in a few times but you weren't quite with it. Anyway, how are you?'

'Oh I do wish people would stop asking me that. How do you think I am? I mean, really.'

'Oops, sorry I asked.'

Charlotte looked at the little boy who had now become a man, at least he thought he had. She said gently. 'I'm sorry Jolyan. I'm just a bit irritable, ignore me. It's all this lying around doing nothing. I hate it. Come on, come and give me a hug. I need it but be gentle, this chest of mine is a bit sore, as is my leg.'

Jolyan did as he was told and went to his mother. He didn't mind the show of affection, it came naturally. As his mother had always told him, there are plenty of wives out there but you will only ever have one mother.

A moment later he was sitting back down.

'Does anyone know anything, mum?'

'If they do, I'm not aware of it.'

'Oh.' Jolyan replied simply. Charlotte knew her son and silence usually meant anxiety or guilt about something.

'Come on Jolyan, what is it? Spit it out.'

'Well . . . er I think there is something I ought to tell you.'

'Oh God you haven't got a girl pregnant have you?' Charlotte had no illusions where her son and girls were concerned. He was a good looking boy with the charm to match.

'No mum, I haven't. Although I did meet someone in Portugal. Someone special. She's staying with me in the Chelsea apartment, I hope you don't mind.'

'Of course I don't. Now what is the matter? You can tell me about your new girlfriend later.' Although Charlotte was still aching and in a degree of pain, if there was something worrying her son, she wanted to know about it.

'Well, there was an incident if you like, in Portugal. A car tried to run us down.'

'What! Are you sure? When did this happen?'

Jolyan told his mother the details.

'That's it, mum. Can't really be sure if it wasn't a drunk driver but what with, well you being shot and stuff, I thought I had better mention it.'

Charlotte remained calm but her but her insides were doing somersaults.

'Have you told Joel about all this?'

'Not yet. To be honest, there hasn't been much time, what with the quick exit from Portugal, armed minders and everything. I've hardly seen him. By the way, how long do I have to have someone watching my every move? I'm fed up with it.'

'Well my boy. What would you prefer? Lying here with a couple of bullet holes in you, that's if you are lucky? I'll hear no whining from you, Jolyan. You will just have to put up with things until the danger passes and that's all there is to it. Do you understand? Oh and don't trying giving the security people the slip, I know what you're like. This is serious Jolyan and if anything should happen to you, well . . . it just doesn't bear thinking about.'

Charlotte looked at her son, her only child. Her heart nearly broke there and then at the very thought of him being hurt in some way. It was just too horrible to even think about. She took his hand and held it tightly. 'You know how much I love you Jolyan, God I love you so much and if anything should well, I can't . . . so please listen to me and don't do anything silly. Joel will be here in a few minutes, you must tell him everything and I mean everything Jolyan.'

A few minutes later as predicted Joel walked into the room. He immediately went to Jolyan and put his arms around him.

'I'm so sorry Jolyan that I wasn't able to meet you at the airport. You've been back a day or so I know. I left the apartment early this morning but I didn't want to wake you. You probably needed the rest. Anyway how are you?'

'I'm great thanks, Joel. Mum is fussing a bit as usual.'

'No doubt with good reason. Listen to her is my advice, she's a wise old bird you know.'

'Not so much of the 'old' if you don't mind Joel' Charlotte interrupted.

'Ah, I see you are getting back to your old self, my love.' Joel smiled.

'Oh I most certainly am and don't think for one moment that I'm going to stay in here one second longer than I have to. I'm feeling much better, so to hell with the quacks and their "don't do this and don't do that's"!'

Joel looked at his step-son and lifted his eyes as if to say, "see what I mean, you try living with your mother full-time for a bit".

'Oh I don't doubt it Lottie, now let's hear what young Jolyan has been up to on his travels.'

'He has something important to tell you, Joel.' Charlotte said firmly.

'Oh not now mum. I'll speak with Joel later, alright?'

'Very well, but just make sure you do.'

For the next hour Charlotte and Joel listened to Jolyan's tales of youthful adventure. The boy was obviously deeply in love. All he could talk about was his new girlfriend, Adina. Every now and again his parents exchanged knowing looks. They both remembered, both knew, that this first love would no doubt sooner or later break his heart with a cruelty that he would never forget. They both felt for the boy and the inevitability of a parting that had to come, no matter how much he loved. They would be there for him, listen and just wait for the pain to pass, which eventually it would. The memories of course, would always remain no matter what adulthood and maturity threw at them.

Back in the Chelsea apartment later that afternoon, Joel finally met Adina. Her beauty was striking he had to admit. It was bursting with youth and untested vivacity. He had always found the comparison between the lithe and seismic enthusiasm of fresh and tight skin to the more mature and experienced vintage sort of gentle age somewhat irrational. Both could stun but in different ways, at least by eyes that knew how to discern and know the difference.

'Adina,' Joel smiled as he shook her hand. 'I hate to say it but I've heard a lot about you.'

'And I suppose I should reply "all good I hope" but I won't.' Adina giggled.

A sassy one, Joel immediately concluded, great. The boy needed a girl who could give as good as she took.

Adina liked Joel on sight, there was just something incredibly honest about his worn out face.

Compelling even.

Jolyan had already told her something about his step-father, no doubt knowing the Treharne's there was much, much more.

'Right them, I thought I'd take you both out later on for something to eat. You can tell me more about yourself, Adina.

How are you fixed?' Joel said. 'I know one hell of steak house, oh you're not vegetarian are you, Adina?'

'Definitely not. A good juicy steak sounds fine with me.'

'Good. You and Jolyan be ready by 7pm then. We'll take a taxi. Oh and Jolyan, I gather you have something to tell me? Does it need to be in private?'

'No, no need for secrets, besides Adina was with me when it happened Joel. I can tell you one thing though, I don't like all these men and women who keep watching our every move and following us wherever we go.'

'Never mind that for a moment Jolyan, tell me what happened?'

'Ok, here we go.' When he had finished Joel sat back in his chair. He could only hope that his handiwork in New York had done the trick, time would tell.

He remained calm as he said, 'look, frankly there's no knowing whether or not this Portuguese incident has anything to do with your mother. I suspect that like you say Jolyan, it was probably a drunk driver, who knows.' Joel didn't want to frighten them so he kept things low key.

Adina immediately interrupted. 'That's not how I see it, Joel. The driver came straight at us. He wanted to kill. I'm sure of it.'

Plenty of sprit here Joel noted, Jolyan was going to have his hands full alright. 'And you may well be right Adina but we still have no way of proving it. Both of you will just have to accept the protection you have at the moment, its intrusive I know but necessary. I understand that you might find it inconvenient but that's just way it is. Right now, we are not sure of anything. As for who tried to kill your mother and why, well, we have nothing but guesswork.'

Joel didn't go into R&ZR Capital. It was 'need to know time' and his step-son really didn't need to know. 'Jolyan, the danger will pass I promise you. It might already have done so, but for now we just have to sit tight. I don't believe either of you are in any immediate danger but let's not take any chances until we know what's what, ok?'

'If you say so.' Jolyan replied miserably. He didn't like the situation but he knew there was nothing he could do about it.

'Right, well I've got to out so I'll see the pair of you later, and be ready Jolyan, the same goes for you Adina.'

'We'll be ready, don't worry,' Jolyan replied, 'I should know by now that you're a zero tolerance merchant when it comes to time-keeping!'

With that Joel left them to it and he knew what that meant, he had been young himself once.

A few hours later the three of them were sitting in a restaurant that only cooked lumps of beef from Australia, America, north and south and the UK. Uncooked steaks as thick as a copy of Tolstoy's War and Peace were presented on a large platter while the waiter explained which continent they had come from and how best to have them cooked ie rare, medium or well done. He seemed to know his stuff, either this or he was a bloody good salesman, Paul Treharne would have been proud of him.

Tenderness all came down to the feed apparently, which partly explained why British beef was always so hit and miss when it came to taste and how easily a knife could cut through it. In the UK different cattle farms used different animal feed thus the notoriously unpredictable quality of British beef, this was not the case where the larger beef producers of America and Australia were concerned.

In between bites of some of the most delicious beef that any of them had ever tasted, Adina spoke about her life in Israel, her family and her intentions to be a fast talking lawyer. She was an impressive young woman who seemed to know exactly where she was going. Joel wondered how Jolyan was going to fit into all this, or for that matter how Adina was going to fit into his place at Oxford.

As he ate and listened, he saw two extremely bright young people with the world at their feet and everything to live for. He knew with a certainty that disturbed him, that their world was not his. In spite of all the bullets and twentieth century turmoil, he feared for their future in a distorted twenty first century Western culture so hell bent on mach 2 technological change, Celebrity Worship and wiping itself out.

The superficial, the shallow had become the raison d'etre of budding maturity. "Celebrity". That sickening word again. As Edward Young observed, 'Pygmies are pygmies still, though perched on the Alps.'

The young were now so caught up with technology Joel observed, that they couldn't be without it for one minute. They were obsessed with celebrities, sports, music, and their own demigod status concocted via selective self- representation on Facebook. Being alone with their own thoughts was simply unthinkable.

He knew that Toffler's 'too much change in too short a time' was accosting any sense of optimism that his no doubt aged cynicism was guilty of, but even so his anxiety remained as he was reminded of the words from an old poem:

> *"Princes we are if we prevail*
> *And gallant villains if we fail*
> *When to our fame is told*
> *It will not be our least of praise*
> *Since a new state we could not raise*
> *To have destroyed the old."*

Joel had always known his enemy. Where to aim his sights. These days the enemy, the real enemy, was the shadow of a fingertip in some darkened room, tapping away at a keyboard. Cyberspace had become the new monster of destruction, the latest top of the range high tech nuclear warhead.

Could the wheel turn full circle? He doubted it, not this time. Google and mein kampf Tweeting had become too powerful, too exhaustive and elusive.

He looked again at his two young companions and for a brief moment a spark of hope contradicted his thoughts. Both were struggling to understand the world they lived in, both had inquisitive minds untainted, it seemed, by Smartphone tyranny.

They were the future, Joel just hoped to hell they would know how to handle it.

As they left the restaurant later that evening, Joel noticed a lone diner sitting by the door drinking a cup of coffee. He also noticed a woman, standing outside in a doorway next to the restaurant.

Security.

His two young companions were oblivious to the firearms surrounding them, including his own. As they waited for a taxi, Joel nodded to the woman in the doorway and tried yet again to rid himself of a stubborn dread that just wouldn't go away.

It wasn't working.

Half an hour later when they arrived at the apartment who should be there to greet them, but Charlotte. She was sitting in an armchair smoking a cigarette and sipping from a damn great tumbler of vodka and tonic.

'What the hell are you doing here, Lottie?!' Joel exclaimed. 'You're supposed to be in hospital for Christ's sake!'

He wasn't amused as he looked down at his wife.

'I discharged myself, Joel. Don't start getting your knickers in a twist, I'm fine. I couldn't bare looking at four sterile, bloody walls any longer. They've given me some medication, so don't fuss.'

'Ah, you must be Adina,' Charlotte smiled as she ignored Joel's outburst. Gripping an ugly hospital issue crutch, she stood up slowly and shook Adina's hand, 'and what a pretty young woman you are! My son has some taste after all. Do excuse this husband of mine, he's inclined to the occasional bout of neurotic melodrama I'm afraid. Don't take any notice. Now come and sit down and make yourself at home. What would you like to drink?'

This was not what Adina was expecting at all. Jolyan's mother was so, well, normal, although underneath the normality Adina's sharp mind quickly decided that here was a beautiful woman in her prime. A woman with spirit, strength and a razor sharp intelligence that would have no truck with fools.

Before Adina could reply to her host, Joel fumed, 'oh God, I give up. I'm off out to check on our minders!' With that he disappeared leaving them all to it.

'Now, that drink Adina?'

'Oh a Coke will be fine thank you . . . um . . . Lady Treharne.'

'Lottie will do, Adina. Go on then Jolyan, see to this lovely looking girl.'

Jolyan grunted something in reply and went off to the kitchen. No doubt his mother was about to give Adina the third degree; she'd want to know the ins and outs of a donkey's arse, he knew what she was like.

'So tell me all about yourself Adina and how you came to suffer the misfortune of being with my son? I would also like to hear your version of what happened with that car?'

For a moment Adina was taken aback by Charlotte's directness, she felt as if she had just been dumped in some court room witness box and was on trial for her life. The moment passed however, as Adina saw a genuine warmth in Charlotte's eyes, if not a somewhat distracted mischief tinged with humour. She quickly realised that she wasn't being interrogated at all. Charlotte was simply being a mother and employing a natural curiosity toward the girl who had quite obviously stolen her son's heart.

193

Jolyan came back into the sitting room, handed Adina her Coke and sat down. He kept quiet and observed. He knew only too well that when his mother went into transmit mode, only the brave would try and interrupt her, Joel being one such person. He couldn't help smiling to himself as he watched Adina holding her own, his mother wasn't getting it all her own way. The confrontation with the Portuguese security men immediately came to mind.

Adina interrupted, had her say and challenged. Lawyering was definitely for her he concluded, if she could handle his mother she could handle anyone!

He had to admit that his mum was looking good, bearing in mind her body had taken a couple of bullets. Slightly off colour maybe but still in fine form. Still strong and as usual not one word of self-pity. She was a tough cookie he had to give her that. It would take more than some assassin's bullets to put her out of action.

He watched the two women prowl and explore for half an hour before saying, 'right, I'm off to bed. I'm leaving you both to it.'

They didn't even notice him leaving the room. A good sign in Jolyan's book. He wanted his mother to like Adina, he wasn't entirely sure why as he would have loved her with or without parental approval but somehow it mattered. He was close to his mother, always had been and like it not he invariably sought her approval for his choices and the things that he did. Advice? Not always but approval certainly, most of the time anyway. It was the same with Joel, but perhaps not quite as much.

Later that night as Charlotte cuddled up to her husband, she still wasn't sure whether he had forgiven her impulsive leave of absence from the hospital, she reached around him and held his hand.

'Are you still cross with me, darling?' She wasn't the only one who sought approval from time to time.

'Just about,' Joel murmured as he gripped her hand, 'but you're fucking well beyond, do you know that?'

'I do.'

'And I'm taking you back to the hospital first thing in the morning to have you checked over, like it or not.'

'If you say so.' Charlotte demurred.

'I do say so, now go to sleep. You need to rest.'

'One thing, Joel.'

He turned around to face his wife. He knew that tone of voice and it usually meant she was troubled by something and needed to talk.

'What is it?'

'Adina is a lovely girl. Beautiful too.'

'I'll go along with that Lottie, so what's the problem?'

'She's taking my son away.'

Joel looked into the eyes that even in darkness could see into his soul.

'My darling girl,' he said softly as he kissed her lips. 'The young eventually fly the nest. They grow into their own people and there's nothing we can do about it. Jolyan will always love you, always, but he's a young man now and his heart is bound to seek out another kind of love. A love that is beyond anything his mother can give him. You know that, Lottie.'

'Yes, I know Joel but I don't have to like it do I?'

'No you don't, but you do have accept it. Now go to sleep, you need it.'

CHAPTER 35

It was late morning and Jolyan was just about to take some coffee and hot croissants into Adina when the apartment entry phone buzzed. Everything was quiet. Joel had taken his mother back to the hospital for a final medical going over. She had protested but had finally given in, she usually did when Joel put his foot down.

Jolyan picked up the phone. It was Al.

'God Al, when did you get back?' He asked slightly surprised. He hadn't gone into any detail as to why he had suddenly left Portugal, but he had sent him a text message apologising for his quick departure claiming family illness. He had also given Al his London address, with the usual 'look me up, when you're next in town.'

'Can I come in?' Short and to the point as always. Al didn't change.

Bugger it! Jolyan thought. Al had a nasty habit of turning up at the most awkward of moments. He had intended to give Adina a little more than coffee and croissants.

'Yes of course, Al. Come on up.'

Jolyan opened the main entry door to the apartment block and resigned himself to some unwanted celibacy.

A few seconds later Al was barging his way into the apartment.

'You said to look you up when I was back in town Jolyan, so here I am.' Polite conversation had never been one of Al's strong points.

'So you are Al. Do you want some coffee, something to eat? I've got some croissants on the go, if you fancy some?'

'No. I'm ok. I saw the news reports on your mother. How is she?'

'She's fine Al and thanks for asking.' Jolyan was under strict instructions not to discuss anything about his mother with anyone.

Before Al could say anything else Adina appeared in the sitting room, wearing a nightdress that was struggling to cover her outrageous modesty.

'Hello Al!' she beamed. 'Fancy you turning up. How are things?'

Al's face dropped.

'Oh, you're here.' Came the surly greeting.

'Yes I am Al, sorry to disappoint.' Adina was fully aware of Al's dislike of her. She treated it with an amused acceptance. She had matured enough to know that friendship was more than a word, Facebook notwithstanding, so ignored Al's blatant hostility and said with a glorious smile, 'Has Jolyan offered you some coffee?'

'He has, but I don't want any. I only came here to see if everything is ok, you know what with his mother and so on. I didn't expect you to be here. And please will you go and get dressed, I find your brazen nakedness offensive, you're behaving like some back street prostitute!'

This time Jolyan stepped in. Al's voice had seethed with contempt for the girl he loved and he wasn't having any of it.

'Right Al, that's enough! I'm sick of your fucking rudeness. You're in my home and if Adina wants to walk around stark bollock naked that's up to her! Now, I've really had enough of your miserable face and your fucking ignorance! Now leave before I throw you out! I've had it with you!'

The silence between the three of them could have been chopped up and flogged at top drawer prices at the nearby Fortnum & Mason.

Adina looked at Jolyan, She was shocked. She had never seen him in such a rage. He had gone red in the face with anger and looked as if he was about to punch Al. She immediately stepped in front of Jolyan, with her hands raised and said calmly, 'I really think you had better go, Al. Please go.'

The raw hatred that stared back at her made her move closer to Jolyan. Al was frightening her.

Without another word, he turned around and left the apartment.

'Al's a bloody nutcase Adina, before you say anything. You know if you hadn't stepped in I would have hit the stuck up bastard. Bloody hell, I've put up with his fucking pious antics for long enough and even my 'Mr Nice Guy' has its limits.'

'Oh I think I've just seen that, Jolyan.' Adina replied with a hint of admiration. He had always come across as the unflappable, thoroughly chilled out sort. Wouldn't harm a fly. She had just seen a different side to the boy she loved. A fighting, courageous side. Now she really knew how much like his mother he truly was. 'Somehow, I don't think we'll be seeing Al again. A pity it had to end like this, but there we are. It's his own doing, makes you wonder what kind of life he has ahead of him, doesn't it?'

'A lonely one I think, Adina. I don't like quarrelling and I hate falling out with people but he asked for that. He really did. If he'd insulted me personally it wouldn't have been so bad, but I won't have anyone talking to you like that. Not Al, not anyone.'

Adina looked into the eyes that always seemed to be changing colour. God she loved this boy, she wanted to hold him forever.

'Come on Jolyan, let's go back to bed before your mother comes home. I feel like making some noise!'

Jolyan looked as his girl.

All his anger immediately drained away as he said, 'yes, come on. You make as much noise as you like but keep those nails of yours to yourself!'

CHAPTER 36

Paul Treharne was back in his thinking place.

He had always been a down to earth man, both in thought and in speech. He rejected extravagant exercises in intellectual exploitation or in his view, the nonsense of irrelevant piffle. Having said this, he had to grudgingly admit that he was as capable as the next unworthy academic when it came to thoughtful analysis of the world around him.

Paul Treharne was an extremely well read man, not that he would ever admit it. He despised the trumped up snobbery and self-important scams of artistic self-serving illusion and solipsistic ego. He lived in the real world not a cosy, leather arm chaired redoubt of idiot, unreal harmony.

He was a reactionary, a self-confessed intellectual ruffian and proud of the fact.

He would throw crude comment at those who would seek to impress with bookish tedium and glimpses into a world known only to themselves or so they believed. His contempt for sullen, highbrow superiority was always clear and present and he knew all about Oliver Wendell Holmes, Jr. too, so fuck 'em!

As he puffed on his cigarette he mused upon the fact that everything had gone remarkably quiet. Thank God Lottie had survived yet another attack, Christ the woman was a survivor no mistake. He might fight with her now and again, she was a sodding lawyer after all so what did she expect? But this notwithstanding, he would feel a huge sense of loss if anything happened to her; for all her faults she was a Treharne, family and family meant everything to him.

Whatever Joel had got up to in New York it seemed to have done the trick, although Paul wasn't fool enough to allow a brief period of respite to lure him into a false sense of security. He still remained on full alert. R&ZR Capital might well have just made an orderly retreat for the time being.

Where business was concerned, Paul had learnt to never take anything for granted until things were signed sealed and delivered.

Just as he was about to stub out his cigarette and curse all doctors en masse, Jane his PA, appeared in front of him.

'I'm sorry to bother you Mr Treharne but you are needed in the kitchens.'

'What?' Paul rarely had anything to do with the operational side of Ragged Cliffs.

'The kitchens, Mr Treharne. Apparently, we have a newly employed waitress who is refusing to carry out a guest's dining order unless it is written in the Welsh language.'

'Are you taking the piss, Jane?'

'Er . . . no, I'm afraid not.' She knew only too well her bosses feelings toward the Welsh language.

'Don't tell me, she's from North Wales.'

'I believe so, Mr Treharne.'

'Jesus Christ, well can't the manager deal with it? That's what I pay him for!'

'He has tried but she won't budge and he doesn't want us to be hauled up before the Welsh Language Commissioner. Bad publicity and so on.'

'Well bollocks to bad publicity! I suppose I had better go and sort it out then. Stupid bloody girl!'

A few minutes later Paul was in the kitchens. The manager was talking to the waitress in question. It didn't take Paul long to confirm that she was from North Wales as he had predicted. The nasal outrage of her accent was unmistakeable.

'Please Lleucu, no-one is being unreasonable here,' the manager pleaded, 'you are perfectly capable of understanding

English, both in speech and in writing, at least you were at your interview.'

'That's not the point, Mr Anthony. Welsh is my first language and this hotel is in Wales!'

'Of God . . .' The manager was starting to despair, apart from anything else the lunchtime rush was going full steam and the last thing he needed was some guest playing hell about the service he was receiving.

'What's the problem here, Mr Anthony?' Paul interrupted.

'Er . . . well, Miss Anwyl here is . . .'

'Oh never mind, right young lady. I gather you are refusing to respond to menu orders unless they are written in Welsh, is that correct?'

'I am.'

'So you are not prepared to carry out a lawful and perfectly reasonable request, as per the terms of your contract of employment?'

'Correct. ' The girl was standing with her hands on hips. Her face defiant and lips ready to snarl.

'Right, you're fired.' Paul replied curtly. 'Collect your things and leave the hotel immediately. We will send on any wages owing to you.'

'You can't do this!' The girl shouted back. 'This is blatant discrimination! I'll take you to an Employment Tribunal and I'll report you to the Welsh Language Society and Commissioner! '

'You do that, young lady,' Paul said calmly. 'I'll look forward to it. Now, do I have to call security to escort you off the premises?'

The girl's face was exploding with anger as she picked up her bag. 'You haven't heard the last of me!' She seethed as she stormed out of the kitchen.

Paul looked at his manager.

'Now Mr Anthony,' he said calmly, 'minority views are always to be respected and where possible accommodated, however such views must not be allowed to rule. God knows there is enough of this going on in Wales as it is. Do I make myself clear?

"Yes Mr Treharne.' The manager replied promptly.

'Good, then may I suggest you be a trifle more circumspect in future where your recruiting procedures are concerned.'

'I will Mr Treharne, be assured.'

'Good. I'll leave you to it, then. Carry on.'

CHAPTER 37

Seloski and Goodwinson were discussing how they could corner the market in cocoa when there was a sudden commotion in the outside office. Before they knew what was happening a team of men from the Securities and Exchange Commission and the FBI were standing them up and handcuffing them.

Seloski got as far as saying 'What the fuck!' before being given some notification of his arrest and why. Both men were then marched out of the office.

The clean shaven faces of SEC enforcement had waited a long time for this day and yet there were no smiles of satisfaction. They all knew that Seloski would have the best legal team that money could buy to try and get him off the hook, but they also knew that this time they had left nothing to chance. Their paperwork was Seloski proof.

The man was going to go down for a long time and so were some of his associates. Justice was long overdue. He was a thieving son of bitch who had had it coming. The arrogance and assumptions of entitlement in the financial services sector had already brought the country to its knees.

It was payback time and these characters were going to pay, big time. Some of the enforcement officers were aware that to a certain extent Wall Street had already gone back to its old ways. It had screwed the taxpayer but what the hell. The 1% holding more than half the world's wealth was just a process of natural selection as far as they were concerned. Their money trickled down to the lowly rest didn't it?

Did it hell.

$200,000 diamond studded watches and $300,000 super cars didn't employ thousands of people or give the 'lowly rest' better lives.

It was all bullshit.

The man leading the team knew all this but as he watched Seloski and Goodwinson being brought down once and for all, he knew that whatever the law did, ultimately their obscene wealth would just be recycled back to the likes of the very people he had just arrested.

As usual greed and venal obsession would win out, the American dream would go on regardless and the rich would get richer, the poor poorer.

Perhaps.

How long could such brazen financial inequality go on, the man wondered? How long, before the people finally rose up?

There would be a price to pay, he was sure of it. For a moment the thought made him shudder.

Beaten up bodies hanging from lamp posts . . . ?

CHAPTER 38

Joel and Charlotte had retreated to the West Sussex house for the weekend. Of late they had neglected their Georgian beauty. Old houses required constant attention, or at the very least some warming up now and again, both physically and emotionally.

A house was the portrait of the person or persons living in it. Its quirks and foibles, its furniture, decoration and bric a brack, could assassinate or celebrate a person's character in seconds.

If a house had no soul, no books or pictures, no knick knacks of personality or objects of individual character, then it was nothing but a structure of pointless bricks and mortar.

It was not a home.

They had named the house "Tether's End" and it was all "home". It was full to the brim with who they were. Elegant and refined one minute, rough and ready the next. Each room had a personality of its own as practicality merged with the romantic. Brash items from car boot sales mingled with antique superiority. English and American literature, books on world history, religion, philosophy and politics, law and the arts stuck their metaphorical fingers up at Hardy cane fishing rods and cartridge belts, statues of laughing policeman and marble busts of Socrates. The house was a beautiful mess and yet it exploded with natural charm and a certain forgiveness, leaving no-one in any doubt as to whom its occupants were.

"Tether's End" *was* Joel and Charlotte.

The grounds around the house and the general calm of the place had become a sanctuary for the soldier and his judge.

The house also enabled them to love in peace. As soon as the car passed through the iron gates mobile phones were turned off. There was a landline in the house and as far as they were concerned, this was good enough. Only those who needed to know the telephone number had access to it, mainly family and an official or two. On buying the property, Joel and Charlotte had agreed that not only would internet access be denied but so would television sets of any size or description. The only channel to the outside world they allowed was an old Roberts radio that blurted out its trouble and strife from a corner table in the kitchen.

It was breakfast time on a Saturday morning. Charlotte was leaning against one of the solid oak kitchen worktops speaking into the telephone, the crutch had gone, while Joel pitched into a traditional English breakfast. Joel loved the fatty grub and it sure as hell beat all the fancy stuff he had to endure most of the time when in London. Lethal it may be, but by Christ it did the job!

'Joel,' Charlotte said casually as she ended the call, 'how did that last trip to New York go?'

'Oh just the usual business stuff. Nothing of any note, Lottie. Why?' His wife had one of those quizzical looks on her face, the sort that said if you're lying to me, I'll chop your balls off. No anger, just a "I'm no bloody fool so you had better come clean if you know what's good for you".

'Mmmm . . .' Charlotte replied, unconvinced. 'Paul tells me that things have gone very quiet on the R&ZR front.'

'Nothing wrong is there?' Paul asked distractedly. When Charlotte was in one of her Sherlock Holmes moods it was best to display indifference and avoid eye contact.

'No, nothing in particular Joel but it does seem rather odd that R&ZR have suddenly backed away though. Odder still that this suddenness had arisen immediately after your New York trip? I gather Mr Seloski was attacked on his way to work. He had one of his fingers blown off with a firearm apparently. The American police haven't found the person or persons responsible and are not likely to either, so I'm told. The attacker is a bit of the Will-o'- the wisp character, it seems.'

'Oh, is that so? Well, the bastard had it coming so what's the problem?' Joel replied without taking his eyes away from his breakfast.

'Look at me, Joel Samson.' Charlotte ordered. This time there was no ducking and diving. Joel looked up at his wife. The quizzical expression had been replaced by one of sceptical generosity. 'I'm not stupid as you well know and I don't want to know the details but for God's sake Joel make this the last time. This is all I'm going to say.'

Joel stood up from the table and went to his wife. He placed her chin in the palm of his hand and gently kissed her lips, 'for you, Lottie. Just remember that, please. For you. The takeover bid does now appear to have been neutralised.'

'I know Joel, I know,' Charlotte said as she looked into his yes,' but if something should happen to you, I simply couldn't bear it. I love you so much.'

'Nothing will happen to me, my darling. Now, what would you like to do for the rest of the day? You're still on sick leave, so how about a long walk and some lunch somewhere special?'

'That will be nice. Just one more thing. That phone call was about Dan Seloski. He and some of his playmates have just been arrested and taken into custody. Insider trading I'm told and the authorities have a water tight case this time. I'm assured he will go down for a long time.'

'Now you tell me? That's good news, Lottie. The family can breathe easy then.'

'I hope so, but there are still the attempts on my life which have yet to be resolved. We still don't know who is behind them. Seloski isn't off the suspect list yet.'

'The security services are doing their best, Lottie. Talking of which, have our two friends had some tea yet?'

'Yes,' Charlotte replied. I took a couple of mugs out to them earlier. They seem comfortable in the cottage. There were guns all over the kitchen table and God knows what else, which makes me feel a trifle uncomfortable but there we are.'

'You must still have some protection for the time being, Lottie. I'm sorry but there it is. We have to wait until we get an official ok.'

'Very well but it can't go on forever. I simply won't have it, apart from anything else that son of mine is nagging me about being followed around everywhere. It's cramping his loved up style so he tells me and God forbid we can't have that now can we?'

'Understood, Lottie. As for young Jolyan, he'll just have to put up with it as well. It's for his own good, young love or not. Adina being with him is a worry but there's nothing we can do about it. He's a Treharne through and through and he will only wear so much. Now, go and get dressed . . . on second thoughts . . .'

Charlotte paused for a moment, deep in thought. Normally she would have responded to some early morning sex with enthusiasm but not today. This alone put Joel on notice.

'What's the matter, Lottie? Something's up. Tell me what's wrong?'

She looked at Joel, there was uncertainty, if not concern in her blue eyes.

'Joel, I'm not sure whether I want to go on.'

'What do you mean?'

'Go on, with the law that is. The price is becoming too high. The danger too much. I've been lucky and let's face it, to a certain extent so have you. There's also Jolyan. That incident in Portugal.'

'I don't think there's anything more to worry about there,' Joel said. 'No doubt Seloski was behind it and now he's off the scene, I'm sure of it.'

'Joel, how can you be sure of anything? How? There's no firm evidence pointing at anything conclusive. The who and why are as opaque now as they have ever been and you know it, so please don't try humouring me, it won't wash.'

'I wasn't trying to humour you.' Joel replied gently. 'The evidence may well be circumstantial I grant you, but it's enough for me.'

'That's as maybe but it isn't good enough. The risk is still with us and more to the point, so is the risk to my son and if anything should happen to him then God help me. I will not put him in danger merely to satisfy my own ego. I've reached the top of my profession Joel, there's nowhere else to go. My personal ambition has been fully satisfied, perhaps it's time to say enough and leave the field gracefully, while we are all in one piece.'

Joel could see the turmoil, he could also see the determination to protect her family no matter what the cost.

'Lottie, you must do whatever you think is best. You know I will always be behind you no matter what, but the decision must be yours and yours alone. All I will say right now, is take your time. Don't do anything rash. The law is your life and has been for many years. You love a challenge, a fight. Will you be happy without this stimulation in your life? There's one other element too, perhaps the most important one. If you resign your position in the Supreme Court, will you not be giving in? Will you not be surrendering everything you believe in and have fought for throughout your legal career? Will you not be bending your knee to oppression, as you have so often put it?

'Think about out it, my darling. Think long and hard.'

Charlotte looked at the face that had seen so much, and saw only the man who had been by her side through thick and thin all these years and who loved her so deeply and without question.

'Alright, I hear what you say Joel. I won't do anything impulsive but that's not to say that I won't pack it all in. Now, about your suggestion about my not getting dressed yet . . . ?'

Back in London, Adina announced that she would have to go home soon.

'Even my liberally minded parents are beginning to get fed up, Jolyan. In fairness, they haven't seen me for nearly a year.'

Jolyan remained quiet. He didn't know how to respond.

'When?' he finally asked, just the one word. He had rarely been confused about anything in his young life and he wasn't confused now, but he was trying to fight off a terrible sense of loss. Of need.

'A week, maybe two at the most.' Adina replied. 'Either way I have to book my flight, it depends on the best deal I can get I suppose.'

Jolyan took one of her hands in his and kissed her lightly on the lips.

'God, do you have to Adina? Go home, I mean.'

Adina saw the love in his eyes and felt her own longing. The months they had spent together had passed so quickly. Endings and separations had been blocked out by their enjoyment of the now.

'Yes I must. I have a career to think about as do you. I haven't told my family anything about you, as you know. Or our little adventures. I don't think they'd be too happy somehow if they knew. Doing my duty in the IDF was one thing, putting myself in danger in the big wide world quite another. Silly I know, but that's parents for you. Irrational and neurotic.'

'You can say that again. Still, I really don't want you to go, Adina. I know we have no choice but bloody hell!'

210

'I don't want to leave you either. I do love you, you know and it's going to be hell getting on that plane but there's no other way. It doesn't have to be the end, does it?' Adina smiled. "Love will always find a away" and all that crap.'

'Sod that, as Joel always says "absence makes the heart grow fonder but presence makes it stronger". I don't suppose Israel is that far away, come to think of it.'

'Three hour odd flight.' Adina confirmed.

'Well, we had better enjoy the time we have left then. Come here and give me one of your best kisses and I mean your best.'

They fell into each other's arms with an ease that only love could exploit. Their lips and tongues searched and explored with a tenderness unspoilt by the experience of life. They knew that separation and distance could destroy them and that wants and needs could go in different directions and tear them apart, but for now they had each other and this was enough.

Young love could always stick two fingers up at the real world.

It was life that fucked it up.

CHAPTER 39

The new Home Secretary was a different animal to his predecessor.

In years gone by he had been one of the standard bearers of the 'Diversity' delusion: The pan European project that believed Europe could thrive in multi-racial harmony, regardless of different skin colour, culture, tradition, history and most importantly of all, human nature.

The pipe dream had exploded with more to come, thus the European immigration chaos and terrorist backlash.

The noble mantra of "Tolerance in all things" as being the only human virtue in a civilised society and to hell with honesty and integrity, had bitten back with a vengeance.

A Patricia Mayhew he was not and Charlotte knew it, as she sat opposite him in his Whitehall study.

'Well Lady Treharne it does seem, at least so my security people tell me, that the immediate threat to your life has passed. Of course, I am aware of the shenanigans in respect of your family business . . .'

'Shenanigans?' Charlotte interrupted. 'Are you being serious Home Secretary? I would hardly call the decapitation of a dumb animal and the attempt on my son's life an exercise in juvenile mischief, unless of course I am missing something?'

Jim Davies, the newly appointed Home Secretary immediately regretted his casual comment in respect of Lady Treharne's recent travails. She was not a woman to be flippant with.

'My apologies Lady Treharne. No offense intended.'

'I hope not.' Charlotte replied, her face unmoving. She had disliked this man on sight. His suit looked as if it had been picked up from a landfill site, his hair had been spiked with product in some vain attempt to create a vision of youthful flair, he was short and fat and to cap it all his lower lip occasionally drooped – a sure sign of Neanderthal stupidity in her view. As if all this wasn't bad enough, the bloody man had managed to slither his way right up to one of the most important departments of state in the land in spite of being a talentless buffoon.

As she looked at the surly politico sitting opposite her, she was immediately reminded of Bernard Shaw's "rule by anybody, chosen by everybody." That was democracy for you, only fools got to govern.

'Quite . . . er Lady Treharne. Now, as I say you no longer appear to be the subject of any immediate threat and as I am sure you are aware, in these unfortunate times of austerity the government has to watch every penny. So, your personal security will be withdrawn forthwith. I'm sure you will understand. Of course the normal security procedures where your position as a Supreme Court justice will remain in place.'

Charlotte's eyes remained fixed on Davies. She knew there was no arguing with his decision but she didn't have to make things easy for him either. In some ways the decision was a relief, she and her family would get their privacy back but a nagging doubt remained at the back of her mind. Withdrawal of her personal security brought a new urgency to whether or not she wished to remain sitting in the Supreme Court. She had known that the security around her couldn't have gone on forever and she had never been its willing companion, but even so the speed of it all had come as a shock.

'Very well, I must put my trust in your Security Service's intelligence Home Secretary. I assume you are unprepared to share it with me?'

'Regrettably Lady Treharne, "Eyes Only."'

'There is nothing left for me to say then. Thank you for keeping me informed. I will consider my options in due course.'

'Options, Lady Treharne?' Davies immediately looked worried. This Treharne woman was a loose cannon, always had been. God knows what she was capable of and the last thing he needed in his new job was a whole load of negative press headlines in respect of one of the most respected and popular judges in the land.

'Yes, options Home Secretary. Regrettably "Eyes Only" I'm afraid. Now I must go, congratulations on the new job by the way, no doubt you will find it both instructive and edifying.

'Goodbye.'

Charlotte left the study without waiting for a reply.

Marc Rey was waiting for her. He had fully recovered and was back on duty.

'I take it you've heard?'

'I have Lady . . . sorry Charlotte.' He still couldn't get used to calling her Charlotte, it just didn't seem right. 'Today is my last day of baby . . .'

'Don't you dare, Marc! Babysitting my backside! Right, do you like champagne?'

'Well, yes . . .'

'Good, because you and I are going to go to an extremely expensive West End restaurant to gorge ourselves on some of the best food London has to offer and drink ourselves into a stupor on vintage champagne, and that trumped up Home Office turd in there is going to pay for it all, if you'll excuse my departure into crude refrain.'

'Excused.' Rey grinned. He loved it when Lady Treharne got the bit between her teeth.

'Come on then. No cars, we'll use taxis.'

Later that afternoon as the champagne started to loosen up even Charlotte's professional self-containment, Rey felt comfortable enough to tell her how much he was going to miss them all. It was at this point that Charlotte looked at her bodyguard and felt obliged to confirm one or two things.

'Now then young man, before you go any further there are some things that need to be said. Firstly, you must know how grateful I am to you. You saved my life and before you start saying "I was just doing my job" etc etc, please don't insult my intelligence. Facile platitudes irritate me. You are a brave man, and yes I know Joel has conveyed my feelings to you but frankly this isn't good enough. Third party expressions of gratitude are third class in intent when it comes to sincere appreciation.

'Thank you Marc Rey for looking after me, and thank you for risking your own life in order to preserve mine. Trust me, it will never be forgotten.

'Secondly and God forgive my appalling lapse into brooding sentimentality, it's the champagne that's my story and I'm sticking to it.' Charlotte followed this up with a giggle that would have shamed a schoolgirl out on her first date. 'I will miss you. I will miss your impertinence, your objectionable sarcasm but most of all I will miss knowing that my back is being protected by an extremely capable and courageous man.' Charlotte raised her glass. 'To you, young Marc Rey and may the Fates be kind to you.'

Rey lifted his glass. He didn't know what to say. All this coming from a Supreme Court judge? He knew the woman had a soft, human side, he had seen it more times than he cared to remember but this? He was rather touched.

'Thank you Lady Charlotte and I will say 'Lady' whether you like it or not because that's exactly what you are.'

'Today Marc, you can call me what you like and I'll probably deserve every word. Now then back to business, there's another bottle courtesy of the Home Office to get through. That husband of mine will no doubt play hell when I get home but well, bugger him. Oops, I'm being crude again. Lovely isn't it?'

Rey laughed, what else could he do?

CHAPTER 40

Latif Khan leaned against a concrete pillar covered with graffiti. The pillar was no different from the rest of the East London housing estate where he lived and where gloom and an insidious madness raged against those who struggled to hold a life together in a back to back hell of neighbourly suspicion.

Latif was eighteen years of age. He had been left behind. The education system had given up on him, society had spat in his face. Hatred had eaten him up and spat him out. He was one of life's "A List" losers and going nowhere.

Dressed in the uniform of his age, jeans, trainers, a short leather jacket and tee-shirt, he leaned and waited. He blamed everyone around him for giving him so much expectation, telling him that he could be whatever he wanted to be. This was the new world order where those at the top gave a charitable helping hand to those at the bottom. Equality of opportunity was the new Islam. "Islam" meant submission. Well, he had submitted and it had got him nowhere.

It was all shit of course and Latif knew it.

For a moment he tugged at a wisp of beard struggling to leap out of his chin. His hairy manhood lacked consequence but his determination did not. His deep brown eyes gave nothing away, neither did his casual posture.

He was just another unemployed young Muslim, hanging around with nothing to do except think of what might have been and what he had had heard at school.

A cyclist suddenly skidded to a halt right in front of him. A baseball cap covered the cyclist's face as he pushed a plastic carrier bag into Latif's chest and raced off again. Latif stood still. The bag was heavy. He looked inside and smiled.

They had delivered.

An hour later, Latif was in Trafalgar Square. He quickly spotted what he was after. Two police officers, one female and one male. They had their backs to him.

He walked up behind them taking the gun out of the carrier bag as he did so.

Without pausing he raised the pistol and shot each of the officers in the back of the head. They were dead before they knew what was happening.

Latif briefly looked at the corpses on the ground as he shouted 'Allah Akbar! Allah Akbar!' He then put the barrel of the gun in his mouth and pulled the trigger.

Whilst Latif Kahn was making his way to Paradise, two young men walked calmly into the John Lewis department store in Cardiff, Wales' capital city.

No-one noticed them.

Within a few split seconds they had withdrawn their Kalashnikov automatic rifles from underneath their coats and started firing at will.

Anything that moved was a target.

Two hours later, sixty two people including three unarmed security personnel were dead.

The two terrorists had killed as many men, women and children as possible, before being shot dead themselves.

They had never intended to walk out of the department store alive.

CHAPTER 41

One hour and forty two minutes later, seven of the most powerful men and women in Great Britain were sitting at a table in Cabinet Office Briefing Room A (COBRA).

A response to the crisis had to be worked out and fast.

'More attacks could well be imminent, Prime Minister.' Sir Henry Davidson said without preamble.' The Security Services cannot guarantee that we are on top of this. As you aware, there is no defence to random terrorist attack, and both these attacks appear to be random. We had no warning, no intelligence. Nothing.'

'You didn't see any of this coming, Sir Henry?' The Prime Minister asked as he tried to put both anger and fear aside. This was not a time for recrimination.

'No. I'm afraid not sir. I did warn you.'

The PM turned to the head of London's Metropolitan police service.

'And you, Sir Harry?'

'Nothing, Prime Minister.'

'Where are we now, Sir Harry?'

'All leave has been cancelled and so on. I'm talking with all our Chief Constables in the rest of the country. We are getting as many officers out on the streets as possible, in order to preserve public confidence if nothing else. The reports I'm getting back are serious, Prime Minister. We must consider an explosion in social unrest and I'm not exaggerating. I am already receiving reports of mosques coming under attack, Muslims being subjected to physical violence and looting. The situation is out of control in my opinion. We must adopt some emergency measures to restore order, immediately. If

219

there is another attack, killing, then I believe we are facing wholesale rioting and possibly mass murder on our streets.'

'Thank you, Sir Harry. One question. How the hell did these young men get hold of such powerful weapons? This isn't fucking America!' Carlton couldn't help himself, for once he let his self-control slip.

'Honest answer? I don't know Prime Minister. Not right now anyway but we will find out.'

'You do that, Sir Harry.' The PM turned to Sir Robin Miller, Chief of the Defence Staff, and the professional head of British Armed Forces.

'Sir Robin. Your views, please?'

'As you know Prime Minister I leave politics to you, but if you are asking me whether the army is ready for civilian peace-keeping then yes it is. As you know, we have had contingency plans for such an operation on UK soil for quite a while. You only have to give me the word.'

'Thank you, Sir Robin.' Carlton nodded. 'I take it then, that the Security Services, the police and the armed forces are ready for any emergency action that may be required. Am I correct?'

All heads around the table nodded in unison.

'Right, do we know anything, anything at all about these terrorists?'

Sir Henry was the first to speak. 'Loners, all of them. No history of extremism. From poor backgrounds, not that well educated. Radicalised in their local mosques and schools, no doubt about it. Islam being their only hope, literally, their only way out.'

'These young extremists are getting clever. No social media or mobile phone footprints. Some of this lot were quite obviously working together. Al-Kaida, Isis? Doubtful. My people are already searching their homes but so far nothing. We know that none of them have been to Syria or received any kind of training, but then of course there is the Deep

Web, where any kind of information is possible. They knew how to fire their weapons to maximum effect. It may be that that there were others, more experienced, pulling their strings. Of the local variety. If there were, we will track them down.'

'I hope so Sir Henry, for all our sakes. What are our options?'

This time Jane Anders, head of MI 5 (the domestic counter-intelligence and security agency) spoke up.

'As head of inland security and having been fully appraised of the situation on the ground, I am compelled to counsel an immediate State of Emergency with curfews, the military to be brought in to ensure implementation. I also advise that we begin to action the contingency plan in relation to internment of Muslims.

'Prime Minister, this is no time for prevarication. Time is of the essence. We must act now before bodies start piling up in the streets.'

Carlton looked at the head of MI 5. A remarkably pretty woman, a woman who on the surface looked so demur and passive.

'Interment is a last resort, Jane.'

'Yes I know, Damien,' Anders replied using the Prime Minister's Christian name, they had been friends at university, even bed mates on the odd occasion, 'but is there any other alternative?'

The Home Secretary Jim Davies, stepped in.

'Prime Minister, we need to be extremely careful here. There is enough antagonism in the country already, between our own as it were and the Muslim minority. The Indian and black communities as we well know, have integrated quite well. Regrettably the Muslim community has not, at least not as much as we would like. I am mindful here of adding more fuel to the East-West occidental fire and in my view, internment will do just this.

'We all know that this is a vicious, crazy minority at work. This last lot do not even appear to be affiliated to any particular terrorist organisation. They are quite obviously a bunch of crazy, inadequate bastard's intent on causing as much mayhem as possible. We can all agree that this is not the work of your average law abiding Muslim citizen. There will be a backlash if we proceed along the interment line and don't forget we tried this in Northern Ireland and it didn't get us anywhere. What concerns me is the political instability that will result if we do this, not to mention what will undoubtedly be perceived as a declaration of war on Islam. Dangerous territory, and I don't need to remind everyone here how far this got us in Iraq. I say tread carefully, bring Community leaders in and try conciliation and consensus. We need them as much as they need us.'

'Bollocks!' Jane Anders interjected. 'So, as far as you're concerned Jim, its nicey nicey time. Come on Abdul, come to No 10 for a nice cup of tea and bring your fucking Kalashnikov with you. I mean really! Christ Jim, its bloody appeasement that's got us all into this mess. If we'd been brave enough in the first place to open our mouths and step on extremism instead of keeping quiet for fear of offending our mostly moderate Muslim brothers we wouldn't be in this ghastly mess would we?'

Davies kept quiet, he knew he didn't have much of an argument and the last time he had got into one with Jane fucking Anders he had been left battered and humiliated. Well, he wasn't going to give her a second crack of the whip.

Carlton looked around the table and said slowly, 'the rest of you?'

All heads nodded again in agreement. Briefly, Carlton wondered what history would make of his decision. As Jane Anders had made quite clear, this was not a time to prevaricate. He had been chosen by the people to lead and this is precisely what he must do, come hell or high water.

'Very well, a State of Emergency will be declared. On the interment question, we have a public emergency and therefore Special Powers, to hell with the European Commission of Human Rights and the liberal left; there is also the Anti-Terrorism, Crime and Security Act 2001 where foreign nationals are concerned. Pull in all Imams, Muslim community leaders etc who have even a remote hint of radical inclination in their backgrounds. Sir Henry, Jane, Commissioner, you will intern anyone and I mean anyone, whom you may consider to be a threat, regardless of whether they have done anything illegal. If they have as much as posted one radical Tweet I want them interned. Do I make myself clear?'

'Prime Minster.' Jim Davies said quietly. 'Erm . . . forgive me, but what about civil liberties?'

'Put your civil liberties case to the relatives who have just had their loved ones shot to pieces, Jim.' Carlton replied. 'The Government's first and foremost duty is to protect the citizens of this island and this is exactly what we will do, regardless of the cost to an individual's liberty.

'Gentleman and ladies you know what to do and Sir Robin, no trigger happy soldiers on the streets please, this isn't America.'

'Very well, sir. I may add that we are a trifle more disciplined than our friends across the Atlantic when it comes to shooting people.'

'I'm sure you are Sir Robin but I'll not have a repeat of Bloody Sunday. Now, get on with it.'

As the meeting was breaking up a mob of people had gathered outside an East London mosque. A white man with a cockney accent was standing on a makeshift platform screaming hatred for all Muslims and pointing at the doors to the mosque. It didn't take long for the mob to burst into the mosque and drag out the Imam.

Within minutes the holy man's twitching and battered body was sprawled across the pavement.

The crowd that had gathered wasn't made up of disgruntled students or looters looking for a fast buck.

The people who had done the murdering were normally law abiding citizens, some middle aged, some educated, some middle class.

The sleeping monster in them had been let loose.

In another part of the UK, Birmingham's Jewellery Quarter, another mob, this time made up of young Muslim men, attacked Jewish shops and Synagogues with bricks and petrol bombs. One Rabbi and a shop owner were hauled into the road and beheaded.

The country had gone mad.

CHAPTER 42

The following day, Sir Henry Davidson looked at the file on his desk. It was now or never. If his precious country was to be saved from itself he had to act and quickly. Deadly rioting and looting had broken out all over the country.

The death toll had risen to hundreds. Jews, Muslims, whites, blacks, the violence hadn't discriminated.

A state of emergency had been declared, curfews imposed and a process of internment began.

His last throw of the dice was all there in the file. Sexed up Islamic plots and political chaos. The recent outages in London and Birmingham, the chaos across the country had played right into his hands. The police and army had restored a semblance of order but this couldn't go on forever. The solution had to be political. The imagined Islamic plots in his file of more to come would merely add further panic, which is exactly what he wanted. The more fear and nationwide panic, the more amenable the people would be to a single leader and the suspension of democratic government.

The liberal, bleeding heart political left wing in the country would be annihilated once and for all. Immigration would be stopped and wholesale deportation of undesirables would begin. He had every confidence that the rest of Europe would follow suit. The peoples across the European land mass had had enough. Enough of rule by a cosy elite in Brussels, enough of the pitiful delusion of everyone, no matter what their colour, creed or religion, living together happy ever after.

This farcical and unrealistic contempt for reality hadn't worked, it never would work and the violence breaking out all over Europe confirmed the fact.

For a moment he considered the Prime Minister.

A strong leader and decisive. Sir Henry had been impressed at the way he had handled that last COBRA meeting. Carlton would be well placed to lead a national government, only this time if Sir Henry had his way, such a government would not be an accommodating mix of every political party with an axe to grind. Left and centrist politicians would be kept out. The country needed another Churchill and Sir Henry's money was on Carlton.

He opened the file one last time and removed a pre-pared press release, as expected his deputy had been compliant and so indeed had the PM. Before closing the file he read again some new intelligence that had come in regarding the three MP's intent on a socialist revival. He raised his left eyebrow for a brief moment and then closed the file.

He made a quick call on a cheap 'Pay As You Go' mobile phone he had bought that morning, put on his coat and made his way out of his office. As he passed his secretary's desk he gave her the press release.

'Dorothy, please make sure this goes out at 5pm and not a minute earlier. I want it reported on the evening news bulletins.'

'Yes sir, leave it with me.' The secretary replied easily.

'Jolly good. I will be out for the rest of the day, so I'll see you in the morning. If any media hacks want me, refer them to the Prime Minister's communications people. They know what it is all about. Goodbye.'

An hour later Sir Henry was sitting on a bench overlooking the River Thames. His mind considered recent events with a calmness that only an unforgiving pragmatist could employ. Out of adversity often came opportunity, he concluded. Not once in his secret world had he felt any doubt or apprehension. Not once had his determination to save his beloved country wavered.

Before his mind was able to ponder the morality of what he was about to do, Joel Samson sat down next to him.

'Ah Mr Samson, thank you for coming.'

'Alight Sir Henry, let's dispense with the formalities. What do you want to see me about?'

Joel knew Sir Henry Davidson, at least they had met at a number of formal 'establishment' dinners and social gatherings. Joel had never liked the man, he knew what he did and like most frontline soldiers had nothing but contempt for spookish manipulation.

Sir Henry opened his briefcase and pulled out three sheets of paper.

'Read these.' He ordered.

Joel read, his face remaining impassive.

'I see.' He said when he had finished reading. 'What do you want me to do about it? Surely this is for your department?'

'In some ways yes, Mr Samson. But in these dangerous and unpredictable times, expediency must be the order of the day.'

'I repeat, what do you want me to do about it?'

'Eliminate them.'

'Just like that?'

'Just like that Mr Samson and as soon as possible. Never mind yesterday, more like last week. Trust me, all three are a serious threat to the well-being of this country, which I don't have to tell you is in enough upheaval at the moment. Right now we have a political void and they are seeking to exploit it. A new Marxist-Socialist nirvana is their intention. They have the unions and even the police in their pockets. On top of the social unrest and general assault on the rule of law that we have in this country at the moment, we believe that devastating industrial unrest is imminent. A possible general strike is on the cards, instigated, aided and abetted by our three friends. I don't have to tell you what this would do to the country in its present state.

'Where Lady Treharne is concerned, allow me to observe that the evidence is incontrovertible, they are behind the two recent attempts on her life. Although I must point out here, that Eden appears to be acting as a sole contractor. We have no evidence to suggest that Meechan and Griffin know that he is behind the assassination attempts. This being said, as far as national security is concerned, it makes no difference. All three need to be neutralised. Permanently.'

Joel looked at the cold certainty staring at him. 'And the business with R&ZR Capital?'

'Oh, the unfortunate greyhound and close shave of your step son? That was Seloski but I assure you he has had nothing to do with the attempts on your wife's life. An American he may be, but even he is not that reckless or stupid for that matter. Apart from anything else, as you probably know, Seloski is presently in custody and has enough of his own problems to contend with.'

'And the identity of the assassin, there's nothing here?'

'Rumour and innuendo. Nothing concrete. We believe there is an expert female killer on the loose but like I say, we have no firm evidence. Security services have been aware of her for quite some time but no-one is even close to catching her or finding out exactly, who she is.'

'The botched first assassination attempt on my wife, what was that all about?' Joel pushed. 'The assassin missed deliberately, I'm sure of it. '

'I concur, Mr Samson. We can only conclude that the failure to kill was an aberration, maybe the assassin was just having a bad day. Maybe there was a moment of mercy, who knows? We believe the assassin, whoever she is, is no longer a threat, indeed it is our view that she has already left the country. Speculation granted, but nevertheless the intelligence we have on Eden confirms this.'

'Intelligence?'

'"Need to Know" I'm afraid, but I will go as far as to assure you that the surveillance around Eden is so tight that we would know within seconds if he is planning any further attempts on your wife's life.'

'So Sir Henry, you want me to casually go out and kill three politicians? What's wrong with your own people? You're pretty expert at this kind of stuff, you've had plenty of practise after all.'

'Very droll Mr Samson, but it could be messy and as I am sure you are aware your own shall I say services, are non-attributable and naturally deniable – by the way, a nice touch with Mr Seloski's index finger. May I also hazard, that knowing your personal history as I do and indeed the love you have for your wife, I would have thought that such an opportunity to balance the scales as it were, would be tantamount to irresistible.

'Am I not correct?'

'Perhaps, Sir Henry. But here's the thing, I know the world you operate in. I do your dirty work then you kill me. Loose ends and all that garbage. Let's face it that's your only option, it would be mine if I was in your position.'

'Not at all, Mr Samson. Your wife is a Supreme Court judge and you belong to a powerful family, all a bit rich for our humble security services I think?'

'You may *think* Sir Henry but I know. Can I keep this information?'

'Please do. None of it can be traced back to my department. There is nothing there that your average Red Top hack hasn't got lurking around in his hard drive. Everything is there. Addresses, private telephone numbers, sexual activity, where they go etc etc.'

'I may or may not be in touch, Sir Henry.' Joel said as he stood up.

'Do be so good as to use the number at the bottom of the last page, Mr Samson. Um . . . more private.'

'One more thing, Sir Henry.' Joel said before turning to leave.' You say that you have no firm evidence on this assassin? Neither do you have any inkling as to her identity, who she is, where she comes from?'

'Correct.'

'You are not even certain that she has left the country?'

'Correct again, Mr Samson. An educated guess is all we have.'

'And there is nothing on file?'

'Nothing that cannot be removed and certainly nothing that can ever be put into the public domain. There will be no record of this conversation anywhere either, before you ask.' Sir Henry knew exactly where all this was going but said nothing. The unknown assassin would be Samson's scape-goat and his personal anonymity insurance. The two men looked into each other's eyes for the briefest of moments. An understanding had been reached without the need for words. 'Before you go Mr Samson, perhaps I should point out that should indeed anything untoward occur where out three honourable friends are concerned, by way of tragic accident or otherwise, we will not be looking too hard into their untimely deaths.'

Sir Henry watched Joel's back disappear along the path. Human nature he thought, it was so wonderfully predictable. Samson would do the job of this he was certain.

He smiled to himself: pride and love, the ruination of us all he thought as he stood up and made his way to his Piccadilly club.

CHAPTER 43

The sound of crunching gravel always made Eden feel at ease. He had no idea why, maybe it had something to do with a Downton Abbey style homecoming? It was odd he admitted, if not somewhat perverse, but then perversity had been his way of life ever since he had been old enough to observe the rights and wrongs of the world he lived in.

He drove the Range Rover up to the front of the manor house, switched off the engine and paused for a moment. Home. He loved the place. Gravel crunching time again. The house had been in his family for generations as had the estate that went with it. Situated in the West Country, it had been built close to the Severn Estuary, the old way, by hand from local stone and timber.

He got out of the vehicle and was immediately confronted by his two twin daughters shouting 'Daddy! Daddy!' and jumping into his arms. His wife Daphne, looked on from the doorway of the house, her eyes declaring a secure if convenient love, a love that knew how to entrap with sexual passion when required and thus ensure her social status and financial well-being.

Daphne was aware that her husband sometimes wandered, men needed the improbable if not impossible fraud of piquant sexual adventure from time to time, it was just a fact of life and nothing to get upset about. George loved her, cared for her and was a good father. He always came home and this was all that mattered.

She enjoyed her diversions too, they just weren't as impossible. Both knew, both accepted the other's needs without rancour or spite.

There were occasions however, when she disagreed with her husband. The dropping of his title being one of them. She was from old, ruling stock herself and felt a certain divine right to be called 'Lady' Daphne. It went with her natural beauty and aristocratic bearing but as usual George had won the argument, at least she had given in gracefully. The line of least resistance had always been her way so why change things for the sake of a silly title? Why indeed.

Carrying his two young daughters in his arms he walked up to his wife and kissed her cheek.

'Hello darling. Have these two little monsters been behaving themselves?'

'They have George. They dare not do otherwise!' Daphne smiled.

'Good. Now then, we have two guests for dinner. Two associates of mine at the House. No need to go the whole hog my darling, they're a pretty rough pair of buggers but indulge them as you deem fit. I'll leave it to you.'

'Fine George. You must be hungry. I'll tell cook to rustle something up for you. Some game pie? There's a good few hours to go before dinner, oh and what do I wear?'

'The pie sounds good and as for dress, nothing formal. Our two guests wouldn't know a self-tie black tie if it slapped them across the face!'

'Don't be cruel, George. You're the one who is always going on about the nobility of the working class. Will they be staying the night?'

'Quite right Daphne. Shameful of me and no they won't be staying, not if I've got anything to do with it anyway. They are political associates, not friends. Now, I'm going to get out of these smelly city clothes and have a shower. We can enjoy a glass of wine together when I'm done.'

He kissed his wife on the cheek again, put down his two daughters and then disappeared inside the house.

Daphne remained standing in the doorway. If George had invited these two politician's to the house then she knew that it had to be something important. Secretive even. Daphne was no fool, in her world false impressions were everything. She was an ambitious woman and clever enough to know when to keep her mouth shut, at least where her husband was concerned. Like most men, George believed that he called the shots, he had yet to realise that she simply allowed him to call them.

Her passivity was calculated, it was all about time and place. Women had always held the power, they could manipulate and exploit better than any man, which is why Daphne had nothing but contempt for pathetic feminist outrage.

She knew where her husband was going, the top job in the United Kingdom, and she would make damned sure that he got there no matter who stood in her way or what the cost.

Later that evening, Eden, Griffin and Meechan were sitting in Eden's study. The dinner had been difficult. Had it not been for Daphne's perfect social skills, no doubt it would have ended in disaster. Eden was instinctively repelled by ill manner and intellectual ineptitude. Meechan and Griffin excelled at both. They were council estate fodder, distasteful sorts but necessary, as much as it annoyed Eden.

Some of the walls of the house were covered with some of the most valuable tapestries in the country and history rummaged around in every corner dark or bright and yet his two guests had failed to ask even one inquisitive question.

'We must move now, gentleman.' Eden said firmly. 'The circumstances are perfect. First, a vote of no confidence in the House, then uncompromising demands for a general election. The people are ripe for the picking, they are desperate for a new political order and they want stability at any cost. The government is on its knees. What is the position with the unions and the police, Michael?'

Meechan was lounging in a straight backed leather arm-chair. His feet up on what he assumed to be a coffee table from IKEA – it was in fact an extremely valuable Regency antique. He was swirling some brandy around in a large cut glass tumbler and puffing on a fat cigar. He hadn't removed the paper band around the cigar. A pleb of the first order, Eden thought unkindly as he looked at the man who hated anything to do with privilege but was the first to wallow in it when it came free of charge.

'The unions are ready, so are the police. As soon as a general strike is declared the coppers will come over to us. The final nail in the law and order coffin. As for the government, it will be destroyed and we can make our move.'

Eden looked across at Griffin.

'MP's?'

'More than enough will come over to us, we also have the minority parties in our pockets. Plaid Cymru, the Greens, the Irish and Scottish nationalist parties are with us. They all want what we want. Re-nationalisation, they are as keen to take private companies back into state ownership as we are, George. Plaid wants to make the whole of Wales Welsh speaking and impose a Welsh language Citizens Test on any-one moving there, all bollocks of course but we'll just have to humour 'em for now.'

'Well then,' Eden said, 'it's all about timing. I suggest a week tomorrow the unions declare a general strike, the police come out on their side and refuse to carry out orders, regard-less of the illegality. The army will have a tough time going up against the police, apart from anything else they just don't have the manpower. Rather than be responsible for any more bloodshed, the government will fold, we can be sure of it. This is Great Britain after all. A state of emergency is already in place, interment is creating huge unrest. It's only the rifle that is keeping the peace right now.

'Our time gentleman, has come. We finally have a real opportunity to create a fairer and more just society. We will bleed the rich dry and if they don't like it they can get out. Social justice, unhampered freedom of movement and a state controlled economy will be our banners. We will not make the mistakes of the past. The disadvantaged will be allowed to prosper and flourish. All minorities be they Muslim, Hindu, Afro-Caribbean or Sikh will be treated equally. We will be in the vanguard of a new, multi-racial super-European state.

'We will win, gentleman. We must win. Go back to London tonight and put things in motion. A week today we will have a new future, a future that doesn't ignore and spit on the weak.

'We will give the people stability. A lasting stability.'

'And hear hear to that.' Griffin grudgingly mumbled.

Meechan puffed on his cigar as he tried to control the excitement raging in his gut.

The following morning Eden was driving around the estate checking the condition of hedge rows and stone walls. Everything appeared to be in order. Eventually, he parked up alongside a woody copse. He had come here often as a child. Alone and self-contained, even then he had known that he was destined for greatness.

He had been a leader from the very first day he had been able to walk. He had led his siblings, led the other schoolboys and bent them all to his will without exception. He would do the same thing again, only this time he would lead millions of people into a new world order.

For a moment he considered his two repulsive associates. They would have to go when the time was right, when they ceased to serve any useful purpose; a mobile phone call or two would soon see to their inconvenience. Power, absolute power could not be shared and Eden knew this, his will could never be divided or delegated.

He got out of the Range Rover and walked up a slight hill in front of the copse. He paused for a moment and turned around to look at the sloping plains in front of him. It was a clear and sunny day.

He looked and absorbed. Destiny time again.

Eden didn't see the red dot that appeared in the middle of his chest, neither did he hear the bullet that forced his heart to explode into a bloody mess of mutilated human matter.

He sank slowly to his knees, then fell face down onto the ground.

Eden's destiny had arrived sooner than expected.

CHAPTER 44

'You must dissolve Parliament and suspend the democratic process, Prime Minister. There is no other way. The people are demanding strong leadership. Stability.'

'In other words Sir Henry, a dictatorship.' Carlton replied quietly.

'A benign dictatorship Prime Minister and a short lived one. As you are aware, there are political precedents. The country is facing mob rule and anarchy.'

Carlton was sitting behind his desk at No. 10 Downing Street. There were no staffers in the room taking notes, this was usually the case when any meeting with Sir Henry took place. Recent events had taken their toll. Carlton's face was drawn and pale. He was exhausted.

'But nevertheless a dictatorship in everything but name, Sir Henry. I am a democrat. What you are suggesting goes against everything I believe in. It has taken this island of ours hundreds of years to lead the way in freedom and liberty. What you are suggesting is anathema to me.'

'With respect Prime Minister, there are no other options. You must put your personal beliefs aside. The country and the people must come first, in that order.'

Carlton sighed. He was cornered and he knew it.

'You must be stronger than anybody else, sir. More resilient.' Sir Henry continued. 'The situation demands a ruthless decisiveness. This may well be unpalatable for you, but you must put personal feelings aside. This is no time for sentimentality and weakness. You must, I repeat must, act.'

Carlton looked across his desk at the refined elegance of a man who was suggesting he demolish a lifetime of belief and principle.

'Sir Henry, I will not be bullied and you would do well to recognise the fact. I fully appreciate that now is not the time for indecisiveness or pussy footing around. I will take further counsel from my advisers and Cabinet. My decision will be made by the end of the day. Now if you will excuse me, there are other matters of state to be dealt with.'

Sir Henry Davidson left the study in little doubt that Carlton would see sense before the day was out.

God help Great Britain if he didn't.

And it was still 'Great' in so many ways.

Alone and left in little doubt as to what he had to do, Carlton tried to come to terms with his own political beliefs and how he should exercise them, although in many respects he recognised that the luxury of political choice had rapidly become redundant.

Like most people, Carlton was a product of his upbringing. He hated the word 'privileged', seeing such a word as an unhealthy construct dreamed up by rowdy socialists still using wealth and learning as a battering ram for their own aims. Family wealth, Eton and Oxford had been his badges of honour and he saw absolutely no reason why he should apologise for them.

Old Etonians had been calling the shots for years and people needed to ask themselves why? Macmillan had had seven of them in his Cabinet, at least Carlton only had three. Try that he would, Carlton detested the art of shallowness that had crept into the political landscape. Policy by social media and Twitter, policy stalked by the inane and trivial.

Populism deeply offended him, as did the general stupidity and raw ignorance of voters. In spite of this, he rejected out of hand any kind of exploitation of voter malaise. The people had a right to choose their own destinies, he just wished they were more informed and sophisticated about it.

There was undoubtedly a ring of truth to Bulwer-Lytton's 'great unwashed' and Burke's 'swinish multitude', even so

Carlton accepted, without condition, the right of very man and woman to choose the government of the land.

Thus his present hidden turmoil and desperate apprehension.

CHAPTER 45

Jolyan was lazing about the Chelsea apartment trying to decide how he should handle Adina's imminent departure. He had the apartment all to himself, his mother and Joel were still down in West Sussex and Adina had gone off to the West End to buy some clothes before returning to Tel Aviv, apparently they were much cheaper here than her place of birth.

He dreaded taking her to Heathrow to see her off and saying a 'Goodbye' which right now he didn't know would be permanent or not. They had become so close, so involved in each other's love. He knew that young love could be a brittle affair and yet he had heard stories of childhood sweethearts loving until death announced its final chapter.

He felt Oxford beckoning with its new beginning and different world. He also felt a deep sadness.

Adina would not be with him. She would not be there at night and first thing in the morning. He would not be able to kiss her wet hair as she stepped out of the shower, or dry her back with fluffy white towels. Who could replace her smile, her touch? Who could replace that delicate early morning beauty that always made him reach out and lose himself in the simpler figments of reality?

Jolyan had never been the 'needy' sort and had always rejected out of hand any kind of dependency on anyone. He had been brought up to be his own man and not to compromise, and yet wasn't love the purest dependency of all and the most compromising of all compromises? Both frustrating and yet at the same time so lovely?'

He wandered around the apartment trying to find something that would take his mind off airline tickets and distant lands. It was hopeless. Adina kept battering his head. No matter which way his mind turned, no matter how hard he tried to reconcile his fears of 'goodbye and see you in another life', his thoughts came back to the same question:

What the hell was he going to do without her?

He was about to go outside for a cigarette; it was alright for his mum to smoke indoors but not him, that was Supreme Court judges for you, full of Habeas Corpus, Magna Carta and liberty but sod anyone who tried to exercise these rights!

Just as he was about to leave the apartment the entry buzzer went off. He pressed the intercom button and who should it be but Al.

'Look Jolyan, I'm sorry for my behaviour the last time we saw each other.' Al immediately said into the outside intercom. 'It was wrong of me. Can I come up to put things right?'

Jolyan paused for a moment. What with Adina about to go back to Israel he had forgotten all about his erstwhile friend. Not one to bear grudges and being one of those live and let live types, he immediately responded with a, 'of course, come on up, oh and no need to apologise Al, we all say stupid things from time to time but thanks anyway.'

By nature Jolyan was the forgiving sort and he couldn't stand bad feeling amongst friends and he still considered Al a friend in spite of his angry outburst. They had worked together and spent a lot of time in each other's company, at least until Adina had come along, so what the hell, life was too short.

A minute or so later Al was standing in the kitchen while Jolyan made them some coffee.

'How have you been Al?' Jolyan said without turning around. 'Looking forward to starting medical school shortly?'

241

'Yes, yes I am Jolyan' Al replied slowly. There was something in his voice that made Jolyan begin to turn around but this was as far as he got. Before he knew it he was lying unconscious on the kitchen floor.

A minute or two later he started to open his eyes, God his head hurt. His mouth was gagged and he couldn't move. His arms and legs were tied to the chair. As his eyes began to focus and fight off the pain he saw Al leaning against one of the work tops facing him. He was holding a small portable camcorder in his hands. Another man was standing in front of him. He was about thirty years of age, dark skinned with black stubble covering his lower face.

'Good, you've come round *kuffar*,' the man said calmly. 'We want you to know what we are going to do to you. How we are going to avenge the slaughter of our Muslim brothers. I am going to behead you . . . slowly.'

Was this some kind of fucking joke?! Was all Jolyan could think. This was crazy!

He tried to struggle but it was hopeless, all he could see around him were eyes of merciless and raw hatred. Al was looking right through him as if he didn't exist. All his doubts about his friend came rushing into his mind, even so he still couldn't believe what was happening.

Sheer terror was crushing his mind. The hours Al spent alone with his laptop. The self-containment and anger at Adina's lack of modesty. His views on women and alcohol. The lack of humour. It was all coming together in a few hideous seconds. His friend was a fucking Islamist maniac!

Before he knew it the man standing in front of him had pulled out a long bladed knife from underneath his jacket. The sort Jolyan had seen being used on the internet to behead people.

Christ, this couldn't be happening to him! It couldn't! Suddenly his bladder loosened and he pissed himself. The older man said nothing as he moved behind him. Next thing

Jolyan's hair was gripped and his head wrenched back to expose his throat.

Oh no! Oh no!

He heard Al and the man shout 'Allah Akbar! Allah Akber! Death to all infidels!'

Then some screams coming from the kitchen doorway. It was Adina.

She rushed toward him as shots rang out from behind her. Jolyan felt his face being splattered with blood and grey matter. It was all so fast, so unreal. So mad.

He saw Adina pick up the knife that had been dropped into the floor, he didn't see what she did next. Al had been mortally wounded but was still standing. He managed to look at Adina with eyes full of dreadful murder.

'You Jew bitch . . .' He managed to rasp through lips spouting blood. Adina didn't hesitate. With an ancient and instinctive will to survive and avenge the boy she loved, she dug the knife into Al's neck with all her strength and forced it across his throat cutting the carotid artery.

Adina knew how to kill, he died within seconds.

As Al was dying, a man was cutting through the bonds tying Jolyan to the chair.

'It's ok Jolyan. It's ok.' The man said gently. 'It's all over. You're safe.' Jolyan's demolished mind only just managed to recognise the man.

It was his mother's bodyguard, Marc Rey.

THE FINAL CHAPTER

Within six months of the UK's State of Emergency and martial law being imposed, it had pulled out of the European Union along with two other European countries, repealed the Human Rights Act and placed severe restrictions on immigration.

The eight million people of Scotland and Wales were given full independence. The other fifty six million Britain's had finally lost patience with the constant anti-English bashing and ingratitude. It was their taxes after all, which kept both 'countries' on their feet. The Scots and Welsh didn't have a monopoly on political passion after all. "Fuck off and good riddance!' had become the new outcry on English streets. Parliament quickly enacted new laws that made absolutely certain that if either of the new sovereign states got into trouble, financial or otherwise, they were on their own and serve them right.

There would be no Bank of England bailout, no help from their former fellow countrymen.

The noble European project was in tatters. The liberal dream of a most perfect and 'diverse' multi-cultural Utopia ruined, the cult of victimhood and unkempt social justice silenced once and for all. Europe had become a lesson in catastrophe: free trade, free movement of people and currency union garrotted and rapidly becoming yet another of Europe's "Great Mistakes."

Far left parties with an agenda of anti-austerity, anti-business and anti-capitalism were causing economic convulsions right across the continent, as the money markets took flight and withdrew their money and investments from European financial institutions.

Germans, being dictatorial in nature, were starting to growl again.

Chaos had become the new European strapline, as far right extremism, social disorder and violence raged through the streets of its cities.

The UK had managed to avoid most of the contagion. Its island status once more saving it from the ravages of fatal economic and political torment taking place across the English Channel. An out an out dictatorship had been avoided but only just. Carlton had proved himself to be the strong man of the hour and an uncompromising leader, a new 21st Century Churchill.

He presided over a National Government concocted from a hotchpot of compliant political parties, all with the same agenda:

Peace and stability at any cost.

Prime Minister Ramsay MacDonald had formed a National Government back in the early 1930's in response to the Great Depression. In his diary for March 1919, he had written, "In youth one believes in democracy; later one has to *accept* it."

Carlton had been forced to reject it. Democracy and general elections had been put on hold for the foreseeable future.

Thousands of Muslims were interned regardless of guilt or innocence, and their communities left in no doubt that if greater efforts to integrate were not made, then deportation without appeal would result. Sharia law courts were forbidden by Statute. The burka and niqab were banned in public places and a good number of mosques, schools and universities shut down.

Permanently.

It was when in Rome or else.

An extreme socialist revival never happened. The killing of George Eden had seen to that. The radical right had won.

The liberal left annihilated.

The people had spoken.

Anarchy had been avoided and law and order restored.

Carlton's centrist inclinations had been sold as a price for peace. How long this peace would last remained to be seen. The streets of the UK's major cities were silent but tensions remained. History would repeat itself, just as it always did. He knew that the situation could never last and that sooner or later there would be a backlash, radical left wing politicians were quiet for now but this was merely a hiatus and Carlton knew it.

In many respects he sympathised with them. This was not the country he wanted. He deplored extremism, be it left or right, it was deadly in all its forms. Ideology poisoned intellect and reasoned argument. It reduced men to savages. One day a balancing would come, it had to, but Carlton doubted it would be in his lifetime.

Lady Charlotte Treharne went back to the Supreme Court. What else could she do? The new political order demanded profound judicial scrutiny more than ever before. The future was grim and uncertain. She was sickened by what had happened to her precious country but she knew that she had to be in to win.

She would fight to the death to see true democracy returned and personal liberty reinvigorated – with Joel behind her anything was possible.

Seloski and Goodwinson were facing long prison terms for insider trading. Their successful prosecution was assured, however the American authorities knew that years of legal wrangling would result in none of their victims ever being compensated but then this perhaps was just a form of vicarious justice.

Why should greed be rewarded?

The authorities also knew that it was business as usual where rampant free market capitalism was concerned. Friedman and his Chicago Boys still ruled world Stock Exchanges and there was nothing they could do about it.

A month after the killing of Eden, Griffin and Meechan were lost at sea. They had gone on a fishing trip, disappeared presumed drowned.

Their bodies were never found.

Prime Minister Carlton had overruled his Home Secretary, Jim Davies in respect of Marc Rey. He was to continue protecting Lady Treharne but in a less overt way.

Alvand Asadi had died a martyr's death, everything he had wanted and longed for was now his. He had entered Paradise with open arms and a sneer at worldly irrelevance. His sharp intelligence had kept him out of the hands of the security services. He had beaten them with a radicalisation that had avoided internet footprint or too obvious an enthusiasm for extreme Iman teaching.

He had radicalised himself. Quietly and with a discretion that had avoided any comment from either his family or friends, such as they were. He had always been a good Muslim but nothing more. No-one had noticed the extreme Islamic texts hidden under his bed or the frequent visits to different Islamic bookshops across London.

Sayyid Qutb, the figurehead of the Muslim Brotherhood executed in 1966, had become Al's hero. It had been Qutb's extreme jihadist ideology that had possessed and driven the aspiring young man of medicine into a destiny of violent death. The older man who had been with him during the attack on Jolyan, had been an ignorant soldier of the Caliphate, recruited by Al from the disillusioned, human flotsam and jetsam that hung around Mosques waiting to find some purpose in life.

Jolyan and Adina continued to love each other across sea, land and exams. A bond had grown between them that turned distance into a different kind of love. A love that didn't always require immediate touch and togetherness but a love all the same.

Would it last? Only time would tell.

On the 'Glorious Twelfth' of August, Sir Henry Davidson raised one of his beloved Purdey shotguns up to the sky and waited for the rapid flight of grouse. As soon as they came into his line of fire he gave them both barrels.

In a split second his Purdey and his head exploded.

The Coroner recorded a verdict of death by misadventure, following evidence that Sir Henry's shotgun cartridges had been dangerously defective.

The assassin was never heard of again. Her identity even her sex, would remain the subject of speculation and fanciful conspiracy theory for years to come. Had she been behind all the political assassinations and disappearances? No-one would ever know.

Her reason or reasons for sparing Charlotte's life in the first instance, would also remain an enduring mystery.

Mercy? Conscience? An eye for an eye fatigue?

You the reader must decide.

Postscript:

When the Christians conquered Jerusalem in 1099 they massacred the Muslims, every man, woman and child. When Salah al-Din re-took Jerusalem in 1187 he spared his Christian victims and gave them safe passage.

The Koran is a book about peace and love, as is the New Testament.

It is human beings who kill and annihilate.

THE END

"The meteoric rise of 'Britain's Greatest Boy Soprano' back in the mid 1930's rivalled that of any X Factor overnight sensation." Daily Express.

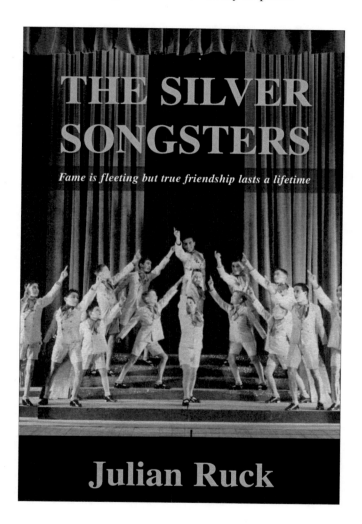

THE SILVER SONGSTERS

Fame is fleeting but true friendship lasts a lifetime

Julian Ruck

www.julianruck.co.uk

'Like all good books The Bent Brief *has brilliant observations on life . . . readers will be on the edge of their seats to find out the truth . . .*' Frost Magazine.

RUCK

The Bent Brief

www.julianruck.co.uk

Also by the same author:

THE RAGGED CLIFFS TRILOGY . . .

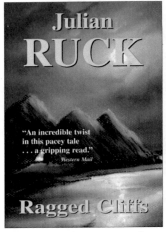

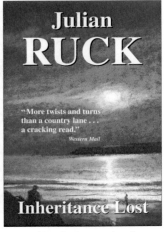

'Once you pick it up you can't put
it down . . .' Evening Post.

'A gripping read . . .'
The Bookbag.

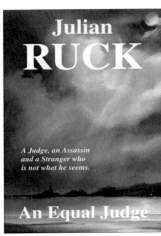

'I will be scouring the bookshelves for Julian
Ruck's name . . .' The Welsh Books Council.

www.julianruck.co.uk

ABOUT THE AUTHOR

Julian Ruck is the author of six novels to date
(see www.julianruck.co.uk)

He is a broadcaster, newspaper columnist, political
journalist/commentator and guest public speaker.

He originally trained as a lawyer in London before doing a short
stint as a law lecturer and going on to manage Legal Aid
contracts in the Not For Profit Sector.

He is also the founder and editor of the new and controversial
'Letters From Wales Uncut'

see: www.lettersfromwalesuncut.com

#LFWUncut

---

www.julianruck.co.uk